After studying art history in Glasgow, Tom Pugh invented a career as a travelling copywriter and teacher, living and working in London, Sydney and Tokyo before settling in Berlin with his wife and two children. *The Lord of Worlds* is his third novel.

THE LORD OF WORLDS

TOM PUGH

Published in October 2021 by Crux Publishing Ltd.

ISBN: 978-1-913613-07-5

Requests for permission to reproduce material from this work should be sent to:

hello@cruxpublishing.co.uk

For Frieda and Max

CONTENTS

Chapter 1

*9 March, 1569. Border lands between the Ottoman
and Persian Empires*

Covered in a scab of sand, Matthew Longstaff muttered
curses as he slid from the saddle. The horse was heavy,
hooves sinking with each laboured step. Murad began to follow
Longstaff's lead, an expression of perfect trust on the young
face. Longstaff shook his head. The boy was skinny, his pony
a better match for the conditions. Bad enough that Longstaff
had dragged him here. An orphan from the streets of Istanbul,
this wasn't Murad's natural environment any more than it was
Longstaff's.

Three days had passed since they left the great trading
road to enter this Godforsaken wasteland. For a while, silently
rehearsing the arguments in favour of this adventure, Longstaff
had kept his misgivings in check. Now, far from the comforts
of Istanbul, with the wind whistling its note of endless despair,
London's demands seemed less compelling.

Abu Risha's instructions were clear: remain on the floor of
the *wadi* – a jagged crevasse which ran through the landscape
like a scar. Longstaff rearranged the loose robe he wore over his
jerkin. Murad's pony stumbled. Still smiling, the boy coaxed
it onwards. A stranger in the Ottoman Empire, in company
Longstaff was powerless to follow the shifts in mood, prevented
by ignorance from obeying even the most basic demands of
courtesy. Murad had kept him out of trouble on the boat from
Istanbul, purchased their horses in Antioch, translated for him
at the caravanserai near Bira where the landlord's demands had
been so extortionate.

"Daylight robbery," Longstaff had called it, speaking the
lingua franca of Istanbul – a bastard form of Italian with traces

of French, Turkish, Greek, Arabic, Spanish – the only language he and Murad had in common.

The complacent landlord had pointed to watchtowers at each corner of his property. "Security costs money. You're welcome to take your chances among the bandits."

Unconsciously, Murad had imitated the man as he translated, palms open, a mock-mournful expression on his face, making Longstaff smile as he listed the horrors waiting beyond the walls. They'd seen no sign of murderers in the days since, nor of captive djinns, or sorcerers or man-eaters. Only this desolate emptiness. Longstaff shook his head, no longer inclined to smile, fretting that he should have left the boy in Bira.

"We still have enough food and water to reach the caravanserai," he said, "but only if we turn back now."

Murad looked at the saddlebags on Longstaff's horse. "We've come this far."

The sun beat down with steady fury. The *wadi* twisted left and right. The further they went, the more it resembled a killing ground. Longstaff felt a moment's nostalgia for Suffolk. It was March; the servants would have built a fire in the great stone hearth at Martlesham. He could almost hear the snap and crackle of dried oak, warming rooms which knew nothing of Islam or the pitiless demands of Ramadan.

The boy cleared his throat.

Longstaff squinted at the high ridges, unwilling to trust his own senses in this alien landscape. "What?"

"Nothing. I'm thirsty, master."

"Then drink."

Murad shook his head. "It will be dark soon."

It had been a deliberate decision to arrange this desert rendezvous during the month-long fast – to take advantage of the lethargy it induced. In Istanbul it had seemed a clever notion. Now it just seemed cruel.

"Master!"

Shouted commands wove a harsh melody through the warp of wind. Riders appeared on the ridges. A troop of six pushed their animals into a wild descent. Longstaff's hand went to the hilt of his sword. He'd been a soldier for many years; long enough to know he stood no chance against these men on their own terrain. He raised his arms as they galloped nearer, the horses kicking up great clouds of sand.

"Abu Risha," shouted Longstaff. "Abu Risha is expecting us."

The horsemen circled, naked blades flashing in the sunlight. Longstaff heard Murad's voice through the whirlwind of sand.

"Submit to their demands, Master. All with be well."

The horsemen pressed closer, dressed in sand-coloured robes and turbans. Rough hands pulled Longstaff from the saddle. His wrists were bound, a blindfold tied across his eyes. Almost with contempt, they neglected to take his sword. Robbed of his sight, smells struck Longstaff with the force of blows. Horse sweat and sunburnt leather. The desert warriors forced him up the ridge before they let him mount again. Someone jerked hard on the lead rope. The horse shied. The men were grumbling. Not in Turkish. Was it Arabic? Persian? Another language entirely? Aurélie would have known. Longstaff thought of his wife, searching for the scattered remains of a long-forgotten past to the north. She had counselled him against this journey, reminding him of Walsingham's broken promises. Queen Elizabeth's spymaster had made it sound so simple – establish a trade agreement between England and the Ottoman Empire, frustrate the interests of France and Venice.

Longstaff felt an unwelcome shiver of resentment – a small landslide of sand fell from his forehead. Without money, it was impossible to gain a foothold in the Great Turk's capital. Elizabeth refused to open her purse, insisting that the merchants of London's Muscovy Company should bear the cost – and they wouldn't pay until the sultan recognised Longstaff as England's ambassador. A position he was powerless to secure without spending vast sums on gifts and bribes.

A volley of shouted instructions interrupted his thoughts. "Murad?"

"Stay where you are. Do not attempt to remove the blindfold."

"Are you all right?"

"They have not hurt me. It is time to pray, nothing more."

Maghrib. The evening prayer. Maghrib meant sunset. Sunset meant water. Just the thought of it made Longstaff's tongue swell as the men performed their devotions. The final, plaintive call still echoing in the empty landscape as his ropes were severed, a waterskin pressed into his hands. Longstaff drank until he was dizzy for lack of air.

The temperature dropped as they pushed on. Longstaff hoped the men had thrown a blanket around Murad's skinny shoulders. He couldn't seem to talk over the sound of his own breath. The gentle creak of leather. Shrill laughter in the desert.

Jackals.

Scavengers.

Sure enough, a rising tide of sound began to lap at the darkness – a great number of people sleeping lightly, guards sharing a joke, a stringed instrument whose notes Longstaff did not recognise. Rough hands removed his blindfold. Beneath a vast sky, rows of sheepskin tents stretched into the distance, campfires winking at regular intervals.

Longstaff slid from his horse, scrutinised by half a dozen desert warriors. Hard-bitten men who roamed these borderlands between two empires, eking out a living in times of peace, growing rich when the blood flowed in earnest. Four of them raised lamps. Fuelled by the black tar which leeched from the earth in these parts, the smell was heady and acrid. A man strode into the centre of the welcoming committee.

"Abu Risha," murmured Murad.

The newcomer was lean and hard, dark eyes giving nothing away. "*As-salāmu alaykum.*"

"*Wa-alaikum us-salām,*" replied Longstaff carefully.

The bandit chieftain switched to his native tongue.

"He says your horse is ridiculous," translated Murad. "Too big, too fat. Too lazy for this country."

Abu Risha stared, as if daring Longstaff to disagree.

"The horse is tired," he replied. "So am I. Does he propose that we conduct our business now?"

The bandit smiled. His teeth were stained black. "In the morning," he said in the lingua franca, "*Insha' Allah.*"

God willing. Longstaff and Murad were taken to a tent at the camp's edge. The silent warriors made no attempt to inspect their saddlebags or weapons. Out here in the desert, they didn't even post a guard. The tent was a simple thing. Longstaff touched the outer layer of matted fleece before ducking inside. Blindly, he gathered cushions from the floor to make his bed, then lay down fully dressed – despite the grinding weight of his jerkin.

During the course of his life, Longstaff had been a merchant's apprentice, soldier, thief, and gentleman farmer. He had never expected to add 'smuggler' to that list, but he needed money to fulfil England's demands and there were vast profits to be made in these untracked wastes – for anyone willing to break the sultan's embargo on Persian silk. The sudden scarcity in Europe had pushed prices to a record high.

"You did well today," he told Murad. "Pay no attention to the tales you've heard. No harm will come to us here."

"I'm not worried."

Longstaff nodded in the darkness. Around his neck, he wore a small medallion with Aurélie's profile stamped on one side. He raised it to his lips before closing his eyes.

Chapter 2

Breakfast arrived before dawn – a dish of rice which Longstaff and Murad ate together at the entrance to their tent, waiting impatiently for sunrise and a first clear view of their surroundings. A *muezzin* sounded the call to prayer, his ghostly voice echoing far beyond the camp.

Abu Risha's men knelt on clay tablets covered with small carpets. Some wore scarlet turbans, some black, some were the colour of the desert itself. In long, neat rows, they raised and lowered their arms like barley before the wind. "What now?" asked Longstaff when their devotions came to an end.

"They have not forgotten us," replied Murad, carefully folding his own small prayer mat.

Longstaff brushed the dust from his robe. "We can't sit here like a pair of beggars."

They made a slow tour of the camp. Birds of prey perched outside nearly every tent. The horses were corralled in large pens, separated from a smaller herd of pack animals, nostrils cut to help them breathe in this inhospitable land. A group of men formed a loose circle around a pair of well-matched wrestlers. A leopard stood chained to a stake set fast in the bone-hard ground. An armed warrior, his black hair caught in a ring of bone, interrupted Longstaff's progress.

"Abu Risha will see us now," translated Murad.

The formalities came first. Abu Risha repeated the terms which Longstaff had agreed with his intermediaries in Istanbul – an eye-watering sum of money in return for a substantial quantity of silk. Longstaff nodded. The price was high for a reason. Determined to destroy their enemies in Persia, the Ottomans were enforcing a strict embargo on their most valuable export. Longstaff knew he faced torture and execution if he was caught moving the silk.

"I'm aware of the risks," he said.

Abu Risha signalled. A young warrior stepped forward. Dressed in a long *khameez* and loose *shalwar* trousers, he wore a curved scimitar at his belt and carried Longstaff's heavy saddlebags as if they were empty. A crowd began to form. The warrior emptied the bags at Longstaff's feet; fresh shirt and linens, a whetstone – several pieces of broken masonry covered in an indecipherable script.

Murad looked at Longstaff in alarm, even as he continued translating Abu Risha's words. "As you say, the details were settled in Istanbul. Half the gold now, half when you take delivery of the silk in Bursa."

Two hundred men stood around them in a loose circle. Longstaff saw the odd flash of colour – silk cuffs, a turban set with semi-precious stones – but most aped their master's dark robe. The silence was terrible. Abu Risha raised a hand. His men produced great rolls of silk, translucent in the sunshine.

"From Kashan," translated Murad. "Suleiman the Magnificent may have taken Babylonia, Mesopotamia and Media – but the Persian Shah still controls the production of silk."

"Useless," said Longstaff, "if he can't bring his wares to market."

Abu Risha ignored him. "I have kept my side of the bargain. It's time for you to keep yours."

The young warrior drew his curved sword. Longstaff spat before reaching for his own weapon. The bastard was a head taller than him and at least ten years his junior.

"What are you doing?" Murad's voice rose an octave.

Longstaff raised one hand in the universal gesture of peace. With the other, he drew his sword and threw it down in the dust. Forcing himself to remain calm, he removed his belt and robe, revealing the bulky jerkin beneath. He plucked at the laces; the garment hit the earth with a heavy thud.

"Your gold," he gestured at the jerkin.

Another of Abu Risha's men slashed at the leather with a wickedly sharp knife. Gold coins slipped from the padded lining onto the hard ground. Freed from the weight of so much gold, borne over so many days, Longstaff rose up onto his toes.

No one spoke until the count was finished. "It's all here."

Longstaff could feel Abu Risha reassessing him – shoulders muscled from years of swinging a war-sword, scars appearing at the open collar of his shirt like rivers on a map. Only slowly did he realise Murad had stopped translating. The boy was speaking on his own account.

"What are you telling him?"

Murad flushed crimson. "He wants to know if I am blind, that I did not realise you were carrying so much extra weight."

"Tell your master I took precautions to prevent you from discovering the truth."

Murad's eyes appeared to double in size.

"You knew he worked for me?" said Abu Risha.

"He was too good to be true – but there are others who might have been paying him. I hoped he worked for you."

"Because now you don't have to kill him." The bandit nodded, then snapped his fingers. The warrior fetched him Longstaff's sword from the ground. He swung it easily back and forth. The crowd had grown larger, attracted by the pile of golden coins. "I almost executed you last night," he said. "For entering my camp on such an ugly horse."

The moment of decision, thought Longstaff. The pain was coming now, after so many days of carrying the gold, creeping through his joints. He thought of Aurélie, her smile, the wrinkle between her blue eyes which he loved so well. Abu Risha took a step closer.

"I should kill you now."

"You could," agreed Longstaff, not taking his eyes from the gaunt chieftain. He could feel his life weighed in the balance. "You *might* find another buyer for your silk. Then again, you might not – once people learn how you honour your agreements."

"An agreement with an infidel." Abu Risha shrugged.

"But it's an infidel you need," said Longstaff. "Who else will buy your silk? Who else can ensure it reaches Christian markets?"

The bandit lifted Longstaff's *katzbalger* sword. "The weapon speaks in your favour," he said. "Let's see how you use it."

He threw the sword at Longstaff's feet, then nodded at his tall champion. Longstaff repressed a groan. It had been years since he'd fought a duel. The surrounding men stamped their approval, raising a ring of dust from the dry earth. Longstaff stretched his neck and shoulder muscles, forcing thoughts of Aurélie to one side. Slowly, he bent to retrieve the sword. He was parched, tongue probing bone-dry teeth for a hint of moisture. After two years in the Ottoman Empire, he knew better than to ask for water during Ramadan.

"I hope you don't expect me to kill him."

Abu Risha stared. "You object to spilling blood?"

"I came to trade, not fight." Longstaff swung the *katzbalger* in a wide arc. "None of this is necessary."

"Oh, but it is," smiled Abu Risha. "I like to know who I'm doing business with."

His champion raised the wickedly curved scimitar above his head. Two hundred men cheered. Longstaff attacked, aiming for the gut. The desert warrior turned his blade aside with ease. Longstaff struck at the head, then forced his adversary back with a series of heavy blows. The clash of steel produced another roar from the crowd. He swung again, willing his sword-arm to move with the old fluency. His adversary moved like the desert wind, head still, retreating smoothly.

Longstaff disengaged, already out of breath. The young warrior offered him no respite, teasing with feint after feint. Longstaff watched his feet, trying to anticipate each new stroke, growing gradually furious with himself. He was here to trade – ten days' journey and Aurélie left to fend for herself in Bursa. He was damned if he'd play this swordsman's game, damned if he'd have his arse handed to him by someone young enough to be his son.

Longstaff stopped retreating, his sword an extension of his arm, guided by the memory of a hundred fights, but his feet set as if in stone. He was too good to fight so badly. What would the young warrior make of him? Longstaff waited for a moment of confusion. There! The warrior's eyes rolled left, seeking guidance from his master. Longstaff burst forward, letting the scimitar slide the length of his blade, crashing one furious fist against the swordsman's jaw.

The eyes widened in surprise, then rolled so that only the whites were showing. The young man sat down hard, head raising dust a moment later.

Abu Risha took Longstaff by the shoulders, kissing him on both cheeks.

"A man after my own heart," he said. "Together, you and I will cheat the shah and sultan both, *insha' Allah*."

That night, Longstaff was given a seat beside Abu Risha at the head of a long table. Silent women, hidden behind veils, brought platters of pears, melons, quinces, oranges, pistachios, almonds – and great earthenware jugs of strong Persian wine. As in Istanbul, it seemed, the Prophet's prohibition on alcohol was honoured in the breach. The bandit chieftain proposed a toast. Longstaff had done what he could to improve his appearance – washing his hands and face in the gloomy tent, rubbing a halo of dust from his hair. The women disinterred whole sheep from nearby firepits. No one spoke for several minutes – eating and drinking in reverent silence after the day's fast.

Abu Risha signalled for Murad to begin translating. "There were Franks at the shah's court not long ago," he said. "Seeking a military alliance against the Ottomans."

Longstaff nodded warily. *Franks* was a term used to describe anyone who came from west of the Bosphorus. "I hope the shah wasn't foolish enough to listen. We're too busy fighting one another to make war on the Ottomans."

Abu Risha's curiosity was piqued. He wanted to know why the Franks fought each other. About the Hapsburgs and the Valois, about Luther and the great divide in Christendom. Longstaff was impressed. If he'd been as inquisitive since arriving in Istanbul, God knows what he might have learned by now. He raised a hand, forestalling the next question.

"When do we leave for Bursa?"

"You leave in the morning," replied Abu Risha, with heavy emphasis on the first word. "Murad will accompany you as far as Antioch. We will meet again on the first day of *Bairam*. The celebrations will mask our arrival outside Bursa."

Bairam; the festival which marked the end of Ramadan. Eight days.

"I would prefer to travel with you," said Longstaff.

Abu Risha looked past him, into the great darkness surrounding them on all sides. He spoke like a lover. "There's nothing for you out there. Not enough water to drown a man, nor wood to burn him, nor earth to bury him – and still a thousand ways to die."

Longstaff wanted to object. He was interrupted by the rumble of kettle drums. Abu Risha raised his cup in yet another toast. Dancers appeared to a great chorus of whistles. A blur of arms and legs in the half light, teasing the wine in Longstaff's veins. Abu Risha hauled him to his feet. "Come."

The music faded quickly, trapped among the tents, swallowed by the enormous sky, then replaced by the soft whickering of horses. Abu Risha called for torches. The animals came at the sound of his voice, a dozen of them gathering in the pool of smoky light.

"A good horse should be proud," he said, separating one of the animals from its companions. "This is Khamseen."

"She's beautiful," acknowledged Longstaff.

"I know that," said Abu Risha. "Tell me why."

Another test. Longstaff tried to focus on the animal in front of him. "The eyes are soft and clear, ears straight as spears." He reached forwards, cupping the horse's cheek in one hand. "Small teeth, narrow shoulders tapering to a broad, flat back. She's a fine animal."

"She's yours," said Abu Risha. "A gift to save you time and trouble. Eight days to reach Bursa; you won't manage it on the pig which brought you here."

Longstaff knew he should refuse. He knew he should insist on accompanying Abu Risha overland to Bursa. He had fought for his life once already today and there was still so much to do if he truly hoped to establish an embassy in Istanbul – and still so many enemies waiting with their knives sharpened for his first mistake.

Chapter 3

13 March, 1569. Istanbul

The patient flinched whenever his foreign physician approached.

"I have to set the break," explained Gaetan Durant in broken Turkish. "I can't do it without touching you."

The man – a wealthy merchant with thick grey hair and rolls of affluence on his hips – spoke across Durant, addressing the younger man at his side.

"He says," reported Khalid in the *lingua franca*, "that foreign devils can't be trusted not to make mistakes."

Durant smiled. He would have to introduce the merchant to Longstaff; the two of them were made for each other. It had become a mantra with the Englishman: *Never forget we're strangers. One mistake – they'll run us out of Istanbul faster than you can swing a sword.*

Durant missed his friend – off with Aurélie somewhere in the south – but not the constant worrying.

"Tell him I've been setting bones since before you were born."

It was nearly true. In his mid-twenties – the age Khalid was now – Durant had studied medicine at the University of Montpellier, but left before sitting for his physician's cap. It wasn't until arriving in Istanbul – after years of living as a sawbones and a thief, with his daughter now safely settled in France – that he'd rekindled the embers of that earlier ambition, pestering Ben Chabib until the renowned physician agreed to accept him as a student.

He waited while Khalid persuaded the fat merchant to accept a foul-smelling tea made from dried cannabis leaves.

Soon afterwards, the merchant slipped gently into a dreamless stupor. Khalid stepped aside, careful not to block Durant's light.

"Show me."

Despite the open windows, it was hot in the *maristan*. Out of respect for his colleagues, Durant hadn't eaten since *sahur*. He could ignore his hunger easily enough but found the constant thirst a torment. He paused to wipe his forehead while Khalid applied pressure to the patient's torso. The merchant was a man of influence in the neighbourhood; a favourable report would do wonders for Durant's reputation. He took hold of the leg, pulled, twisted, then pushed in a single smooth motion. Bone scraped against bone. The patient barely stirred.

"Not bad for a barbarian," he said with satisfaction.

Khalid didn't reply. Durant turned to find Ben Chabib himself looking over his shoulder at the plump merchant. "He sustained the break falling from his horse?"

Not waiting for a reply, the senior physician leaned close, nostrils flaring slightly as he inhaled. In his late fifties, still lean with an oddly unlined face, there were times when Ben Chabib reminded Durant of a cloistered monk.

He didn't seem so unworldly now. What had Durant missed? He lifted the sheet. The patient had relieved himself.

"Should we be concerned?" asked Ben Chabib.

"I don't think so."

"No?" The physician studied him. "The patient's urine has a marked sourness. The fact he released so little when you set his leg could suggest an active illness – perhaps a wasting sickness – drying his vital fluids from within."

Durant took a moment to steady himself. Ben Chabib was one of the world's foremost diagnosticians. Worse still, Durant was aware that his limited Turkish made him sound like a child, unable to hedge his opinions in flights of clever qualifications.

"The patient doesn't appear to have lost weight," he said. "The burst capillaries in his nose suggest a drinker – which would explain both the odour and his evident dehydration."

Ben Chabib smiled. "Then I suggest you prescribe a diet of fruit and water – at least until the break heals."

He moved on to the next bed. Durant stretched, joints popping along the length of his back. Nervous energy. He'd been working too hard. Months of making up medicines, performing amputations, dressing wounds, removing piles.

"Enough for today," said Khalid.

Durant gestured at the merchant. "I should be here when he wakes."

"He'll be in foul mood. Give him some time to appreciate your work first."

They left the *maristan* together. The winter shutters had been removed from the windows a few days earlier, the scent of disease less pervasive than it would have been in London or Paris – though strong enough that both men drew a deep breath when they reached the exit. Most of their peers lived in tiny cells adjoining the *maristan,* but Durant was too old, too attached to his comforts, and Khalid was already married, the father of two young children. Both were glad of the chance to leave each day, to escape the smell of illness and the cries of pain for a few hours. They ducked through a small garden where musicians played to soothe the sick, past the two-storey *medrese* and the grey-domed mosque. The grounds of the complex were crowded with imams, doorkeepers, lesson readers.

"It was a trap," said Durant. "Ben Chabib wanted me to diagnose our fat friend with a wasting sickness!"

"He was teasing you," replied Khalid. "It means he likes you."

Durant shook his head. Pure chance had brought him to Istanbul. Two years ago, he'd helped Longstaff and Aurélie prevent an alliance of Catholic powers from making war on England. Instead of celebrating their achievement, Walsingham – the English queen's ambitious intelligencer – had barred them from returning home. It had been too dangerous to remain in France. Aurélie was wanted by the Inquisition in Italy and

Spain, and Tzar Ivan of Russia still had men scouring central Europe for any sign of Longstaff. So Walsingham had sent them east to Istanbul.

To his own astonishment, Durant had found new peace of mind in this city between two worlds – and did not want to run again. "You don't think Ben Chabib is tiring of me? People were upset when he agreed to take me on."

Khalid laughed. "They're jealous."

"They have names for us."

"I know. The cross, the carpet, and the candelabra – may Allah forgive me."

"Astaghfirullah," murmured Durant. *May God forgive me.*

Khalid laughed, a sound of genuine pleasure echoed by the afternoon call to prayer. "Why not come with me today?"

"Me?" Durant shook his head. "I'd make a poor Mohammedan."

"We're not Christians," corrected Khalid. "We don't submit to the Prophet, only to Allah Himself."

"You'd better not keep Him waiting then." Durant stood quietly while his friend ran up the steps, retreating into shadow until the *muezzin* fell silent. Even Rome – especially Rome! – couldn't rival Istanbul for piety. During Ramadan, the city's vast population seemed to form a single religious order.

Durant resisted an urge to return to the hospital's well-stocked library. Longstaff had left him holding the fort; a mountain of correspondence had accumulated over the last few weeks. He bent his steps in the direction of home, picturing himself at the Englishman's desk. This time, he promised himself. No more excuses. He would open the embroidered pouches in which the Turks sent their letters – the sealed envelopes from Walsingham in London – and come to grips with the impossibly vague nature of Longstaff's ambitions.

Just thinking about it made him hungry. The covered stalls at the food market were quiet. Tame kites picked at scraps between the cobblestones. Durant thought of the cookshops of Paris, jugs of cheap wine, rushes thick with filth and spittle. And the noise – voices roaring in argument and laughter. The markets of Istanbul were a bed of whispers by comparison. He bought a pair of aubergines. The vendor served him with sleepy patience. Durant had cooked for Longstaff and Aurélie before they left for Bursa, his interest in food developing in parallel with his renewed devotion to medicine. Both disciplines required intellect, both were driven by the senses. The house would be empty when he got home. No distractions from Longstaff's correspondence and no one to cook for. He would slice the aubergines and fry them slowly in butter. A simple meal for a lonely bachelor. Would Khalid have reached home by now? Durant felt certain he could picture his young friend's family – the wife shy and pretty, the children lively and confident. But the rooms remained a mystery. It wasn't something that worried Longstaff or Aurélie – they hardly seemed to notice how small their world had become in this enormous city – but Durant's patients were Turkish. How could he treat them when he knew so little of how they lived?

The few women he passed in the streets were indistinguishable from ghosts, gliding silently in their shapeless robes. Durant wondered how he must appear to them – what little they could see of him through their gauzy veils – a stranger in parts of the city where Christians rarely ventured. Experience had marked his features with a cynical cast. The lopsided grin sat oddly as he pressed deeper into the warren of streets, aubergines swinging carelessly at his side, battling the temptation to run a hand through his dark hair. A walker by nature, his heart began to beat more swiftly. Each day, he swore he would avoid this neighbourhood, each day its Judas trees and poplars drew him back. Wisteria trailed from rooftop to rooftop. A group of men walked past with flowers in their turbans. The streets grew narrow, upper storeys almost touching overhead. How many eyes watched him pass, hidden behind the latticed windows? Istanbul – a city of glimpses; that's how it had been with the woman in the window. Several weeks ago, he'd glimpsed her by chance with her shoulder against the frame, eyes closed, face tilted towards the winter sun. He still remembered her intake of breath when she'd seen him below – the ghost of a smile before she closed the shutters.

The street she lived on was out of his way; half a dozen homes leading to half a dozen more. Durant returned nearly every day, as if his feet had a mind of their own. He tried not to think of whether she would be waiting today, whether he would see her silhouette in the window. Was he placing her in danger? There were no ground-floor workshops in this part of the city. Ottoman bureaucracy dwarfed anything comparable in Europe. Turkish men could have as many as four wives.

The shutters opened a fraction. He saw her high brow, a hint of dark hair beneath the linen headscarf. She smiled at him, though her eyes seemed filled with sadness. Something fell from the window, blown off course by a breath of wind before it struck the cobblestones. Durant felt clumsy. How often had Longstaff complimented him on his talent for the dramatic? He stooped to gather a daffodil in his palm. Three small white flowers lay nearby. It couldn't be coincidence. She was gone by the time he straightened. Slipping the flowers into his sleeve with the skill of a card-sharp, he forced himself to walk on.

He knew the meaning of a daffodil in the secret language of love. *"What would you risk for me?"*

From their high minarets, the city's *muezzins* began the evening call to prayer. Durant waited impatiently at the water's edge. It took an age for the *bostanci* oarsmen to make their devotions, slake the day's thirst with great drafts of water, opening a cool passage for the food which followed. Full night had fallen by the time they were willing to ply their trade again. From his seat in the crowded *caique*, Durant looked back at the hills of 'Stanboul – at slender minarets glowing in the light of a thousand candles, the great dome of Hagia Sophia rising like a second sun. Gently, he held the three white flowers in one hand. He had studied medicine for long enough to know them. Ipomoea, called moon flowers because they bloomed at night, their fragile petals closing at the sun's caress. Three flowers. Three nights. *What would you risk for me?* Durant hardly dared believe it; his mystery woman – the woman in the window. Was she proposing that they meet? Was there any other way to interpret her message?

Chapter 4

Working by the light of a flickering torch, in a chamber no one had entered for more than a thousand years, Aurélie unearthed another of the thin, clay tablets. She traced the delicate surface with her fingertips, wondering what secrets lay hidden in the strange, wedge-shaped lettering.

A dead language, still tantalisingly present on ancient monuments throughout the region. Most people – when they thought of it at all – dismissed it as a basic numbering system. Aurélie wiped the sweat from her forehead, hands covered in the dust of ages. Thousands of tablets. Once upon a time, they must have been stacked side by side on shelves in this chamber. Discovered a few months earlier, when a young shepherd boy fell through sand and space to land on the marble floor, the locals believed it was a place of magic, where jinns appeared in light and flame.

Moving heaven and earth, Aurélie had come to see for herself.

She raised the burning torch above her head, waiting patiently as light filled the corners of the chamber. How had this space looked a thousand years ago? Who had served here? What laws and sciences did they know? Given the number of tablets Aurélie had found, this chamber could have been a library.

The noise of fighting reached her from outside. Aurélie climbed the rope ladder with a matchlock musket slung over one shoulder. The men were gathered in an angry knot below. She remained on higher ground, shouting at her foreman to report.

Korkut had a wonderfully smooth face for a man his age, a thick white beard and dark eyes beneath the turban. Aurélie might have been paying the men, but they worked for Korkut. And he worked for the *Sanjak Bey* in Bursa – who had agreed to humour her as a favour to his friends in Istanbul. None of them wanted her here. Any one of them might kill her at any moment. Korkut gestured at a shapeless hill of stone.

"Who did it?" she demanded in the *lingua franca*.

Korkut stood aside. Two of his lieutenants held the vandal. Aurélie knew his face, though she'd never learned his name. Small revenge for his steady refusal to look her in the eye. She could feel his contempt as she knelt beside the ruined statue.

"Was it in good condition?"

"Perfect," replied Korkut. "The figure of an armed soldier."

Aurélie's sadness must have shown in her expression. The vandal spat a volley of furious abuse. Some of the men muttered their agreement.

"I would rather not translate his words," said Korkut.

"I caught his meaning well enough."

One by one, she stared at the men. Was this the moment? Would they finally look at her – slip Korkut's leash and murder her for being both a woman and an infidel?

The clay tablets were not the issue – they'd been taught to revere the written word. Graven images, raised in homage to a false God, were a different matter.

The silence stretched into the empty desert. Aurélie held her breath, musket at her waist. Not today, it seemed.

"Pay him," she ordered at last. "Send him on his way."

The men faded from view, points of reluctant movement around her work – a long trench, eight feet deep, extending to the top of the next rise as she attempted to trace the outlines of this ancient complex – six connecting rooms so far, the third of which had yielded the precious clay tablets in such extraordinary quantities. She yearned to slip back down the rope ladder, return to her work of unearthing and cataloguing

– but it wasn't safe to leave the men when they were in this mood. The sun was already low on the horizon, illuminating the city of Bursa two miles to the west. Aurélie had promised Longstaff she would never make the journey after dark.

As always, her foreman escorted her to the city gates.

"Until tomorrow, Korkut."

"Insha' Allah."

Aurélie had taken lodgings in the tiny Christian quarter, with an English family who lived at the corner of Christ's Church Street. A groom came to take her horse. "The family are still out, ma'am."

The tiresome merchant. His wife and daughter locked in their endless dance of visits. Standing at the stable door, Aurélie realised she was shaking slightly. She calmed herself by staring at the clay tablets inside, stacked against one wall.

A maid hovered inside the front door, her normally capable fingers clumsy as she unlaced Aurélie's cloak.

"What is it?"

The maid blinked in fright. "A visitor for you, ma'am."

"In my room?"

"He said he was expected."

Longstaff! At last.

Aurélie paused at the top of the stairs. What if it wasn't? There were men in the city who objected to her work. Others who saw her as easy prey. She drew a dagger from the folds of her shapeless robe. Weight balanced on the balls of her feet, braced for attack.

Her husband lay asleep on the bed. She did not wake him immediately, taking a moment to match the travel-stained reality with the picture she carried in her mind's eye. Smiling, she hit him with a pillow.

"You might at least have undressed before getting into bed."

Longstaff blinked under the sudden assault, grinning as his wife came into focus. "Nice to see you, too."

"Are you trying to get yourself killed?" She returned the dagger to her robe.

"Never." He pulled her onto the bed. "I've enemies enough – they need no help from me."

He held her close, breathing her in; the smell of sun-warmed sand. Briefly, unexpectedly, he thought of the first time he'd seen her, fair hair cut short, held captive by a priest convinced her learning must be a form of demonic possession. The same undaunted determination shone in her face now, along with a deeper faith in her own strength. She placed her hands on either side of his head. "I didn't expect you so soon."

"A good horse and a following wind." He winked at her. "How have you been getting on without me?"

"Come and see."

"Now?" He tried to kiss her.

"It's the middle of the day."

"Nearly dusk."

"All the more reason to hurry."

Reluctantly, he followed her past the bashful servant into the courtyard. It took a moment for his eyes to adjust to the gloomy stable. A series of thin, clay tablets were stacked in neat rows on beds of straw.

"What am I looking at?"

"The pages of a book."

"Very practical," he said, enjoying the excitement in her voice.

She chose to take his words at face value. "When this outpost of the Babylonian Empire was overrun, no one would have bothered with a few pieces of clay. Parchment can be scraped clean and reused. Soldiers love papyrus for starting fires and cleaning their weapons. But these? Smash them and all you get is a handful of dust." She touched the wedge-shaped markings with her fingertips. "The soldiers would have looted the gold and silver before setting their fires. The buildings themselves were transformed into kilns, baking the tablets into their most durable form."

Longstaff stared at the strange, angular marks. "Can you decipher it?"

Aurélie uncovered a slab of marble, roughly the size of a headstone. "A trilingual inscription," she said. "These two sections are written in Elamite and Akkadian. There are people in Istanbul who can read them. If I'm right – if it's the same information recorded in three different languages – then I should be able to start breaking the wedge-shaped writing down into its constituent parts. Do you understand?"

Longstaff smiled. "The more time I spend in this country, the less I seem to understand."

"You still haven't told me how it went in the south."

Longstaff replied with a shrug. He had borrowed heavily to purchase the silk – a debt which felt heavier than the gold he'd carried from Istanbul. "We're committed now."

She put her hand on his forearm. "The *Sanjak Bey* has promised to send word as soon as there's news of the Bark Roe."

Longstaff nodded. If Abu Risha's silk was intended to provide him with the funds he needed to live in a manner appropriate to an ambassador, the Bark Roe – a merchantman out of Portsmouth – carried a princely gift for the sultan, one designed to secure him official recognition in Istanbul.

Aurélie led him to a different stall. No clay tablets this time, but crates stacked as high as the wooden roof, their contents hidden beneath hessian sackcloth.

"For the sultan," she said. "Ten thousand tulip bulbs."

Longstaff blinked. *Ten thousand?* "How much have you spent, Aurélie?"

"When the silk reaches London, we'll have more than enough to cover the expense."

"*If,*" he corrected her, his voice rising. "*If* the silk arrives in London."

"If it doesn't," she replied evenly, "we're ruined anyway."

Longstaff forced himself to take a deep breath. It didn't help that she was right. "I'm giving him one of the mechanical wonders of the world..."

"To set in a garden of his favourite flowers," she completed his sentence. "We're committed now, remember?"

He felt nauseous. The silk was due to arrive in Bursa in two days' time – assuming Abu Risha kept his word. "We have to finalise the details of the handover."

Aurélie's landlord and his wife stepped into the courtyard, drawing a pale young lady in their wake.

"Mr and Mrs Tarlowe and their daughter Elizabeth," said Aurélie.

"Named for our queen, of course," said the merchant.

"Of course," murmured Longstaff. The Tarlowes pressed him to stay for dinner. Longstaff felt Aurélie kick him when he attempted to beg off. The food was welcome – a dish of barley porridge washed down with Soghdian wine – but the conversation was nothing more than a litany of complaints: business, this city, the climate, the locals and their religion.

Were these the sort of people Walsingham had in mind when he demanded a network of informers in the region? *Men who can facilitate commercial opportunities, provide military intelligence about Ottoman activities, and agitate against the Spanish.* Longstaff felt uncomfortable in their company. A year from now, he promised himself, they would no longer be his problem.

A burst of noise reached them through the windows. The evening call to prayer. Mr Tarlowe threw down his knife in disgust. Longstaff rose to his feet soon afterwards, bidding their hosts good evening.

"Aurélie and I have business in town," he explained. "Unfortunately, it can't wait."

"We lock the doors at midnight."

Elizabeth fetched Aurélie her cloak and a light veil.

"My God," said Longstaff when they finally reached the street outside.

"There's no harm in them."

"Why do they eat so early? To thumb their noses at the Turks?"

"To save on candles. Their business has been crippled by the Ottoman embargo on silk. The money for my lodging is all that's keeping them afloat."

The streets were light with suppressed excitement. *Eid al-Fitr* was close – three days of feasting to mark the end of Ramadan. Longstaff lowered his head as they passed a pair of armed janissary soldiers. The wooden houses grew shabbier near the docks. A group of stevedores played backgammon within spitting distance of the sea.

"The Golden Bass," announced Aurélie.

A wooden fish hung suspended from two thin chains, flakes of yellow paint curling from head to tail.

"You're sure?" asked Longstaff.

"If you want Padron Lettero, this is where we'll find him."

The door stood crooked on its hinges. Longstaff kicked it open, pushing into a fog of smoke and silence. Only two tables were occupied, two men huddled in a corner and a bigger group near the centre of the room. No sign of Lettero. Longstaff raised an eyebrow.

"He'll be here," said Aurélie. She chose a table against the far wall, where the thick-bodied landlord brought them wine. "You still haven't told me about your journey."

The drink burned a brutal passage from Longstaff's mouth to his belly. "You were right about Murad." He handed her a piece of paper from his jerkin. "In the caravanserai where I stayed, there were scraps of paper carefully wedged in the cracks. I thought you might know what they were."

"It's Arabic," she replied. "I have no idea what it says. There's a story in Islam about the Day of Judgement. On their way into heaven the faithful have to cross red-hot irons, barefoot except for whatever bits of paper they save while they're alive."

The tavern door swung open. Longstaff looked up. A fiddler entered, playing a mournful seaman's song. The men in the tavern joined in with the chorus. One of them stood. Longstaff watched him approach, a sinking feeling in the pit of his stomach. The man was good-looking after a fashion, his eyes hard and flat as he performed an extravagant bow.

"Would the lady care to dance?"

"No," said Longstaff. "She would not."

The sailor straightened, eyeing Longstaff with a smile. It was a toss-up whether he was more interested in dancing or fighting. He had a mind for both, probably.

"She can answer for herself, I'm sure." He reached for Aurélie's hand.

Longstaff stood. His chair fell with a crash, loud enough to interrupt the fiddler's song. The sailor reached for his knife.

The door opened a second time. Padron Lettero strolled into the candlelight, his weathered face black with scorch marks, forearms covered in tattoos beneath the sleeveless jerkin. "Fuck off, Jack," he waved the sailor away.

"Signor Lettero," acknowledged Longstaff, still on his feet. The man was dangerous, captain of an armed pinnace – smuggling only the most respectable of his trades.

"Signor Longstaff, I assume your trip into the interior was a success?"

"I wouldn't be here otherwise. The cargo will arrive in two days' time."

Lettero nodded his approval before taking a seat. "The locals will be celebrating *Bairam*."

"As planned," agreed Longstaff, righting his own chair without taking his eyes off the pirate.

"And my money?"

"Half when you collect the silk, half when I get word the merchandise has reached Malta. You know what to do when you get there?"

The pirate nodded. "I'll keep my end of the bargain."

Longstaff let the silence gather. The pirate had more to gain by keeping his word than breaking it. At Aurélie's urging, Longstaff had been careful to suggest that this would be the first of many such consignments.

"How long before you reach Malta?"

"Depends on the wind. Depends on who we meet on our way. The lanes are growing busy again. A ship out of England touched at Crete not long ago. She'll be the first of many."

Longstaff kept his expression carefully neutral. "What ship?"

"Called the Bark Roe, out of Portsmouth."

"When will she reach Istanbul?"

Lettero smiled. Not a reassuring expression on his scorched face. "You've an interest in the boat?"

The sailors had started calling for him. Acknowledging them with a tip of his head, Lettero rose to his feet. "You know where," he said. "I trust you'll have the gold ready."

"The Bark Roe," repeated Longstaff. "How long before she docks in Istanbul?"

"They'll want to take on water, let the men stretch their legs. Two days. Three at the outside." Lettero shrugged. "I wouldn't linger if I were you. The boys have been drinking since noon."

The pirate went to join his companions. Longstaff's mind was racing. He had to meet Abu Risha and pass the silk on to Lettero. At the same time, he had to reach Istanbul ahead of the Bark Roe. The ship was bringing his gift for the sultan – a mechanical wonder from England, as well as the young engineer responsible for its construction. Everyone knew of the sultan's weakness for Western curiosities – including Longstaff's enemies. He could just imagine what the ambassadors of France and Venice would do if he weren't there to protect his investment.

"You have to go," said Aurélie quietly.

"I have to stay," he replied, casting an uneasy eye in Jack's direction.

"I can manage Abu Risha and Lettero." She placed her hand on his. "This is good news, Matthew."

"They're dangerous men."

"It's business. For all their posturing, they know they can't do this without you." She looked him in the eye. "I have to stay here anyway, to catalogue the last of the tablets and arrange the shipping. Remember the promise you made me?"

He would have smiled, had they been anywhere else. "You need my trust, not my protection."

She winked at him. "I've managed this long, haven't I?"

Chapter 5

The sun was high when Durant slipped quietly into the kitchen, as if afraid Elif and Hamid would judge him for neglecting his duties at the hospital. The two servants were in their fifties but seemed older. Durant assumed they were a couple – they arrived together each morning and left together in the evening. He also assumed Elif would clip him round the ear if he were bold enough to ask. Neither appeared to find it odd that he was still at home, nor that he was dressed in new *shalwar* trousers and his finest silk *khameez*. Elif brought him breakfast without comment – a kind of sour milk which she had taught him to mix with water and breadcrumbs. A cup of coffee appeared a moment later. Durant relaxed. He even sat back with a sigh of contentment. This was his favourite room in the house. A generous space with wide doors leading into the courtyard. His shifts were covered. Ben Chabib had given him permission to take the day off – his first since starting at the *maristan* more than a year ago. Elif had no way of knowing that. Durant resisted the temptation to tell her. Hamid shuffled past in felt slippers, taking kitchen scraps to the compost heap outside, muttering a brief apology to the djinn who lived there. Three days had passed since the woman in the window had thrown the daffodil and moon flowers down from her window. Three days during which Durant had done nothing but worry. They had always communicated without words, eyes meeting for a second as he strolled past her home. Durant stood so abruptly he upset the table. Elif rolled her eyes, still thumbing the beads of her rosary. Durant bade her an elaborate farewell before striding across the courtyard. The winding streets of Galata lay before him, sloping steeply to the docks where a *caique* stood ready at the quay, waiting to ferry him across the Golden Horn.

The men who sent the light craft skimming towards 'Stanboul were unaware of the band which seemed to tighten around Durant's chest with each long pull of the oars. Women in this city were murdered for adultery. He'd seen their bloated bodies in the hospital mortuary, dragged from the same waters he crossed so lightly now. He searched for omens as he walked the city's longest street, no better than his patients at the *maristan,* caught helplessly in the hands of fate. Two halves of a rosebud lay in the gutter. Women moved as if through a parallel city, shrouded in their cloaks and veils. Should he turn back now? Tread his meandering path through life, lost in the healing and culinary arts.

The buildings here were ramshackle lean-tos, thrown up by recent arrivals from the countryside. The Turkish quarters of 'Stanboul were growing crowded, in contrast to the Greek and Jewish neighbourhoods. Durant pressed himself against the wall to avoid the swinging haunches of an oncoming packhorse. He caught a first hint of the flower market, a lighter scent, playing through the coarser smells of sweat and refuse, building into a heady, riotous bouquet. The sight of it was overwhelming after the dark and crooked streets. Durant knew herbs, knew their properties and uses. Flowers had always struck him as whimsical in comparison. The sight that met him now, every shade of every colour in the bright, spring sunshine, such an assault on his senses that he grew fearful. She was putting her life in his hands. Stall after stall covered every inch of the enormous square, rows of permanent shops along two sides and every approach guarded by children selling nosegays. He handed a few *aspres* to the nearest child, sticking faded narcissi in his collar as he moved among the stalls. Jasmine, irises, roses, lilies, carnations, hyacinths. Women seemed to move more freely here, dressed in bright veils, calling noisily to acquaintances.

Durant clasped his hands behind his back, strolled the narrow walkways with eyes half closed. It was cool after his long walk through the city; the vendors kept their wares well-watered. How would he recognise her? How did women recognise one another – by the patterns woven into lace and velvet? Was she playing a game, an idle second or third wife searching for excitement? Women in Istanbul were so often invisible. Durant wasn't allowed to treat them at the *maristan*. Was that why the sight of her framed in the window had ignited such a fire? He felt sick, as if he'd betrayed her already. Just by thinking that any other woman might have had the same effect.

A figure brushed past, making slight contact. Durant caught the scent of lavender, saw the flash of twisted gold at her wrists. He followed at a distance, marvelling at how lightly she moved, careful not to match his step to hers, falling back then drawing near. She paused to admire a bright display of daffodils. Durant glimpsed a narrow strip of henna running from the knuckle of her middle finger to the top of her wrist. The covered stalls were separated from one another by thin partitions, with small stock rooms at the back. The woman – his woman from the window – stopped before a display of white carnations: *innocence*. Durant paused at the shop next door, hoping to hear her voice through the partition.

"The call to prayer will begin shortly," the vendor interrupted him. "Please forgive the discourtesy, but I must perform my ablutions."

"Of course."

The man shut himself inside his stock room. A concealed panel opened in the partition beside Durant. She let the veil fall to one side. He wanted to lose himself in every detail. Strong and handsome, she was just as he remembered from the window, eyes the colour of mahogany with fine lines at the corners. No longer in the first flush of youth, which came as a relief – until he saw her fear and felt it as an accusation.

"Why do you haunt the street outside my window?" She spoke the *lingua franca*. Her voice was low, the anger unmistakable. "Why do you jeopardise my safety and upset my peace of mind?"

Durant attempted to smile. "I meant no harm. I'm sorry." He had no idea what she was thinking. "Tell me what to do."

"Never come to my home again." The silence grew. Durant waited with a growing sense of despair. He understood so little of how this city worked. She took a deep breath.

"We don't have long. When the stallholder returns, buy a dozen flowers at whatever price he asks. Return here in a week if you want to see me again. He'll have instructions."

Durant grinned, unable to hide his joy. "My name is Gaetan."

Muezzins began the call to prayer from the heights of their slender minarets.

"Leila." She closed the panel. The vendor reappeared, already unrolling a prayer mat and falling to his knees.

Chapter 6

The horse was tireless, cantering past isolated villages which reared like ships on the horizon, past peasants forced by barren soil to massage their fledgling crops by hand. Longstaff worked himself into a fury as he rode. Promising to treat Aurélie as an equal in their marriage was one thing. Something else again to have her dealing with pirates and smugglers on his behalf. He was still muttering as he clattered aboard the day's last ferry at Altinova, crossing Izmit Bay in near darkness and watering the uncomplaining horse at a caravanserai on the far side.

Of course she'd manage the transfer of silk. Aurélie was one of the most capable people he'd ever met. But what if she didn't? What if those two bastards caught wind of one another – decided to cut Longstaff from the deal and keep Aurélie for themselves? He fell asleep remembering the touch of her fingers on his forehead, where she'd laughingly attempted to erase the worry lines. He was bathed in sweat when he woke, fingers reaching for his sword – still arguing with himself hours later when the scent of brine reached him on the breeze.

Despite himself, a smile took hold of Longstaff's weathered features. Istanbul. Refuge of the world, city of a million souls. Soon, he told himself, the sultan would acknowledge him as England's ambassador to the Ottoman court. He allowed himself to imagine it – a trade agreement between England and the Ottoman Empire, and finally some stability for Aurélie and Durant.

He and the horse were able to rest for the final leg of their journey, leaving the hard work to a team of oarsmen. 'Stanboul slipped by on the left, a skyline of domes and minarets rising from a sea of red-tiled roofs. It was a longer journey to Galata, the

European enclave on the far side of the Golden Horn. *Caiques* skimmed the surface swift as the gulls overhead. Longstaff shaded his eyes against the sun's glare, waiting impatiently as the Imperial Dockyards came into view.

Only one European ship lay at anchor, a swift carrack from the *Arsenale* at Venice. Longstaff threw an arm around Khamseen, standing patiently beside him on the deck of the wide-bottomed boat. The horse would dine on the finest oats that evening, sleep on a bed of fresh hay for as long as she remained in Longstaff's possession. Thanks to her, he'd beaten the Bark Roe home.

Home.

There was a time Longstaff would have bridled at the word, jealous to hear it applied to any place but Martlesham in Suffolk. He looked at the houses arranged in jagged rows on Galata's hill. The boat was close enough now that he could pick out individual warehouses along the commercial docks – including his own, empty since he'd signed the lease a year ago. He'd chafed at the expense, but Francesco insisted it was necessary – for the look of the thing, claimed the *dragoman*. Longstaff thought of Aurélie's tablets, the tulip bulbs, the Yorkshireman's mechanical marvel on its way from Crete. The warehouse wouldn't lie empty much longer. Two years of non-stop work coming to fruition. Longstaff had little patience for the life of a diplomat. As soon as the trade agreement was signed, he would ask Walsingham to send a replacement and retire on the proceeds of his silk. God willing, he and Aurélie would start a family – the subject had become an awkward one recently, but there was no reason to think it wouldn't happen.

The oarsmen brought their boat to a gentle stop. Khamseen's hooves struck the cobblestones with a satisfying ring. The taverns of Galata were filled with merchants, porters, sailors in search of work or pleasure. With *Eid al-Fitr* only hours away the atmosphere of barely suppressed excitement was tangible, even here in Christian Galata. Longstaff led his horse up through the maze of streets, broken every few hundred yards by a square, each with its own small church. He was breathing hard by the time he knocked at the familiar wooden door.

"Durant!" Longstaff caught his friend in a rough embrace.

"Welcome home." The Frenchman sounded hoarse.

"Are you sick?"

"Hungover. Where's Aurélie?"

"Still in Bursa. Hamid?"

"He and Elif left a few minutes ago. Nothing for them to do with just me here." He stood aside. Longstaff led Khamseen to an empty stall in the courtyard.

"Do we have oats?"

"Oats?"

"For the horse."

"Bugger the horse. Tell me what happened. Did you get the silk? Why is Aurélie still in Bursa?"

Longstaff smiled. "I'd give my right arm for a cup of coffee."

Durant had become a connoisseur since arriving in the city, assembling an impressive collection of grinders, sieves, scales and cups. The smell soon drifted into the courtyard. Khamseen looked happy enough with her new quarters.

"The Bark Roe has been sighted," said Longstaff, standing in the open doorway. "Aurélie needs more time to complete her work."

"She's found something then."

Longstaff described the towering stacks of clay tablets. "I know you're hungry for news, but I've been travelling since dawn."

Durant pressed a cup of coffee into his hand. "I'll make us something to eat."

Longstaff found a mountain of post waiting for him in his study on the upper floor. There were six letters from London – a seven-week journey via the Republic of Venice. Longstaff drew a deep breath, hoping the smell of ink and beeswax would calm him. He hadn't expected Durant to follow his own daily round – greasing palms, keeping track of the latest diplomatic gossip – but at least he could have opened the damned post.

Taking down his copy of Castiglione's *Book of the Courtier*, Longstaff began deciphering Walsingham's most recent letter. What would it be this time, he wondered, coffee cooling at his elbow – trading privileges for English merchants in the Ottoman Empire? A network of spies? Perhaps another request that the sultan's fleet engage Spanish shipping in the Levant.

Walsingham was no fool, but his image of the East had been formed by traveller's tales. The London playhouses swarmed with deceitful Turks, their false moustaches and wickedly curved daggers apparently more convincing than Longstaff's own descriptions of Istanbul – and little wonder; it would take a truly gifted writer to capture the strangeness of this place. An absolute monarchy without an aristocracy, an Empire governed by slaves, a system powered by *jihad* and uniquely tolerant of religious minorities.

There was also a fortune to be made here. A single vessel with a cargo of silks might deliver a hundred thousand pounds on an investment of less than half as much. Walsingham remained unconvinced – and so Longstaff had been forced to take matters into his own hands.

London, Jan 27, 1569

Longstaff,

Once more, I am the bearer of unhappy tidings. Elizabeth won't loosen her purse-strings until the merchants of the Muscovy Company agree to match her pound for pound. The merchants maintain they are already over-extended in Russia and Persia. Despite my best efforts, both parties remain immovable. A simultaneous attempt to generate enthusiasm for a popular subscription has proven equally ill-fated. Meanwhile, the papist monarchs of Europe remain relentless in their efforts to prohibit English goods from reaching continental markets. Our exports in cloth have fallen to catastrophic levels. I fear widespread

penury and unrest will follow unless you succeed in agreeing
Capitulations with the Ottoman sultan.

I beg you, remind him that Elizabeth, as Mistress of
the English Faith, will never unite against him with the
other princes of Europe. On the contrary, he should count
her a steadfast instrument for disturbing and thwarting such
alliances...

Longstaff threw the letter down in disgust. *Remind the sultan?*
Two years in Istanbul and he still hadn't laid eyes on the man!
The Yorkshireman's device was his last throw of the dice – a royal
gift to secure an audience with the Lord of Worlds – purchased
with the last of his own money. As for the rest – the silk, the
tulips, Aurélie's researches, and Durant's medical training – he
continued slipping further and further into debt.

"Are you coming?" shouted the Frenchman from the foot
of the stairs.

The dining room was deserted. Durant had laid a table for
two in the kitchen. Longstaff took his place beside the stove.
This early in the year, the evenings were still cool enough that
he was grateful for the warmth. "Who did you cook for while
we were away?"

"I didn't. You've no idea how much I missed it." Durant
pressed Longstaff to try an aubergine fritter. "Ramadan has half
killed me."

With perfect timing, a cannonade of fireworks reached
them through the open window. Across the Golden Horn,
the feast of *Eid al-Fitr* was just beginning. Trying the food,
Longstaff closed his eyes in helpless admiration. The Frenchman
could be an infuriating companion, but he was undeniably a
superb cook.

"What news from Francesco?"

"In truth, it's been some time since I saw him last."

Longstaff stopped eating.

"He implied that I was neglecting your affairs," continued
Durant awkwardly. "We may have had a small falling out."

Longstaff thought of the unopened letters on his desk. Francesco de Testa was his translator and guide through the maze of Ottoman diplomacy. A *dragoman* whose family had been in Istanbul for generations, the only member of his profession willing to represent Longstaff's interests in the city. The others – who plied their trade on behalf of France, Spain, Venice or Poland – had refused for fear of angering their existing clients.

Durant wrinkled his nose. "The women at the market assured me this was a calming dish. Perhaps I added too much salt."

"You think it's funny? I know you have obligations at the hospital, but it's my work which keeps us here. I could have died in the south. You can't even bring yourself to open a letter!"

A shout reached them from the courtyard. Grateful for the distraction, Durant hurried to the door. "Speak of the Devil," he muttered.

Francesco was out of breath. "The Bark Roe," he panted, frantically cleaning his eyeglasses. "You have to come, Signor Durant." He blinked owlishly when Longstaff appeared.

"You're back?"

"An hour ago."

"Thank God. There's not a moment to lose."

Longstaff hadn't washed or changed and now there was no more time. From the top of the hill, he saw a flash of ghostly white canvas against the looming Fortress of Seven Towers. The steep gradient forced his tired legs into a shambling run. More fireworks illuminated the Bark Roe, gliding serenely across the inky waters of the Horn. Longstaff cut diagonally towards the Imperial Docks, where foreign vessels were obliged to make port.

"We still have time," said Francesco. "Catch your breath." At twenty-seven, the *dragoman's* high forehead already carried worry lines, half-hidden beneath a blush of fair hair.

The Imperial Dockyards were a city within a city, stretching for one and a half miles along the coast with space to launch whole fleets of ships – and lodge an army of oar-slaves. Escorted by four long *caiques,* the merchantman approached under a single sail. Longstaff saw sailors standing at the rails as he forced his way through the gathering crowd, then the ship's name on the bow, picked out in gold: *Bark Roe*.

"Why are there so many people here?"

"They've spent hours staring at the fireworks in 'Stanboul," said Francesco. "They're restless."

The ship swung gently across the last few yards of water. The final scrap of canvas was whipped from the foremast. To cheers from the crowd, ropes flew back and forth between the sailors and the stevedores on the wall. Longstaff stared at a group of men on the quay, beyond a line of *Bostanci* soldiers positioned to keep the rubberneckers at a distance. Admiralty officials waiting to board and inspect the ship. Stevedore gangmasters. Merchants with an interest in the Roe's cargo of English kerseys. They wouldn't be able to collect their goods tonight – not until the customs duty had been paid in full – but Longstaff could understand their reasons for coming. He couldn't say the same for the rest; a senior counsellor from the *Magnifica Communita di Pera*, a delegate from Florence, the Podesta of Genoa, both the Venetian and French ambassadors – a tight knot of Galata's most notable figures, all smiling as if the Bark Roe had come at their express command.

"They know," said Longstaff. "How in God's name..."

"Relax," said Francesco, pushing his eyeglasses onto the bridge of his nose. "It's a compliment. They've begun to take you seriously."

They reached the front of the crowd. Francesco began talking to the soldiers. Longstaff cursed under his breath when he saw the Venetian ambassador detach himself from the group of notables. Sleek and fat, like a well-fed seal, he approached with a broad smile on his face.

"I was wondering when we'd see you here."

"Raimondi." Longstaff nodded. The ambassador wore rings on seven of his fleshy fingers. Precious stones glittered in the moonlight as he waved the soldiers aside. Longstaff set a course for the ship, looking for Master Gale, the young engineer who'd designed his gift for the sultan – who had come from England to reassemble it here. Raimondi took his elbow, steering him back towards the waiting group of dignitaries. Longstaff nodded impatiently at the representatives of Florence and Genoa, bowed to the Greek Patriarch, a robust looking man in his forties who took great pleasure in playing the European nations against each other. The French ambassador – tall and cadaverous, a man of numerous forenames and ancient lineage – continued his policy of pretending that Longstaff didn't exist.

"Don't mind the chevalier," said Raimondi, taking Longstaff by the arm. "He'll change his tune once your position in the city has been formalised."

Longstaff grunted. He was no good at these games, the feints and bluffs that keep an adversary off balance. A short man with huge forearms barrelled into the group – the captain of the Bark Roe.

"Matthew Longstaff?"

"This is the man you're looking for," said Raimondi, pushing him forward.

Longstaff was aware of the sudden silence around him. The captain thrust a thick sheaf of papers into his hands.

"Where's Master Gale?"

"Guts turned to liquid as we passed by Sicily." The captain shook his head. "The papers are for you. His machine, as well."

"I can take it now?"

"It's a gift, isn't it? The *pasha's* already given his say-so."

Behind him, a team of stevedores manhandled half a dozen crates along the gangplank. The wood had rotted clean through in places. In the torchlight, Longstaff caught a glimpse of mouldy hay and discoloured brass tubing. Pipes tumbled to the stone quay with a tuneless crash. The French ambassador erupted in a loud whinny of amusement.

"Where did you store it," thundered Durant. "In the damned bilges?"

The captain ignored him. "For what it's worth, Master Gale was a fine young man. All you need to know is in these papers, he told me. For putting his contraption back together."

Longstaff stared at the rows and rows of incomprehensible symbols. He ached to bloody the chevalier's smug face. If anything, Raimondi's expression of sympathy was worse. Longstaff pinched the soft flesh on the inside of his forearm, willing himself to relax, to think like a diplomat.

"Chin up," said the Venetian ambassador. "Your queen will weather the loss, I'm sure. In time, you'll think of some new way to secure the sultan's favour. Perhaps something a little less elaborate." He rubbed his jewelled thumb against two fat fingers.

Longstaff didn't tell him that Elizabeth had refused to contribute a single penny. The chevalier and the Greek patriarch broke into sudden laughter. Raimondi twisted his rings, as if embarrassed by their lack of consideration. The representatives of Florence and Genoa strolled closer. Given the chance, they'd soon start digging their fingers among the bruised and battered workings.

Longstaff drew Francesco to one side, speaking in an urgent whisper. "We can't let them use this as an excuse to cancel my audience with the sultan."

Francesco gestured hopelessly at the tangle of pipes and tubes. Longstaff took him by the shoulder. "Visit your contacts," he said. "Make it clear we have more to offer."

"English kerseys?"

Longstaff smiled, turning slightly so the ambassadors could see his face. Even in distant Bursa, Aurélie continued to act as his guardian angel. "In a few days' time," he whispered, "ten thousand tulip bulbs will arrive in Istanbul. They were meant to accompany Master Gale's gift – now they'll have to take its place."

Francesco's eyes lit up. "What variety?"

Longstaff forced himself to keep smiling. "How the devil should I know that?"

He ordered the stevedores back to their feet. He'd been a soldier and knew the trick of making men jump. Within seconds they were shouldering the damaged crates, forming up in two neat lines on the quay.

"And lift your heads," he snapped in the *lingua franca* of Istanbul. "You've a gift for the sultan in those damned boxes!"

Chapter 7

Aurélie was exhausted by the time she finally reached Istanbul. Abu Risha and Padron Lettero had behaved like perfect gentlemen, but the whole business had been nerve-wracking, even more so than cataloguing and crating over a thousand fragile clay tablets. Then she'd lost days finding suitable gifts for the local *Sanjak Bey* and the Tarlowes, packing the tulips, paying Korkut and his men, and arranging protection for the site.

The pinnace which brought her north from Bursa didn't attract the attention of a European merchantman. There were no crowds waiting at the Imperial Docks, only an ill-tempered customs officer and a gang of stevedores lying sprawled in the shade, as if the whole city were still recovering from the excesses of *Eid al-Fitr*. The warm sun on her back, Aurélie leapt down onto the quay. The roofs of Galata had worn a thin coat of snow on the day she'd left for Bursa. She couldn't imagine it now, greeted by the scent of saffron and agarwood. The customs officer raised an eyebrow when he saw so many worthless slabs of clay. She calmed his suspicions with a healthy bribe, patiently explaining that the tulip bulbs were a gift for the sultan. She resisted the impulse to send a boy for Longstaff. Digging her heels in, he would have called it, but she knew he would have managed alone had their positions been reversed.

She was ill-tempered by the time the stevedores finally settled the first load on their backs. The leering customs officer insisted on accompanying them along the docks – past boats jostling at their moorings, sailors squandering their wages on jars of *boza,* street vendors and seagulls fighting their endless battles – until they came to Longstaff's small warehouse at the far end. Aurélie pushed through the double doors, already anticipating her husband's praise for having dealt so adroitly with the smuggler and the pirate. She found him behind his desk, contemplating an unholy mess of ruined metal on the warehouse floor. His face broke into a smile at the sight of her.

"Did you bring the tulips?"

"Is that any way to greet your wife?"

He looked awful, pale and gaunt in *shalwar* trousers and a long, collarless shirt. She gestured at the train of stevedores behind her, then knelt beside the heap of broken pipes, running her fingertips along the rough, discoloured edges of ships designed to sail on automated waves, dancing figurines, planets that should have aped the movements of the heavens. A thousand separate pieces scattered in an order stripped of meaning.

"What happened?"

"The Yorkshireman died at sea, God rest his soul."

"Your audience with the sultan is in three days' time."

"Perhaps." Longstaff shrugged. "There's been no word from the palace since the Bark Roe landed."

A stevedore cleared his throat. Aurélie looked round. Had the warehouse always been so gloomy? The only light came from a small window set high in the wall. Papers covered Longstaff's desk. Chains swung from the great beams above, the floor covered in sackcloth and sawdust. While the customs officer kept a running tally, she had the men stack their crates along the walls, then return to the landing quay for the next load.

"Can't we repair it?" she asked.

Longstaff gestured helplessly. "I've been working non-stop. It's not just the damage. Master Gale disassembled his machine before setting sail, packing each component separately. I can't make head or tail of his notes."

A stranger appeared in the doorway, of a similar age and build to Longstaff. Dark eyes studied the warehouse from between a pale turban and thick, salt and pepper beard.

"I've been sent to look at your contraption," he said in perfect Italian.

"*Contraption!*" snapped Longstaff. "The very word Raimondi used."

The stranger shrugged. "My instructions come from the sultan."

Aurélie stood aside. His words might mean everything or nothing – in theory, every act within the ever-expanding borders of the Ottoman Empire took place at the sultan's command. She studied the stranger as he knelt beside the maze of metal parts. There were traces of stone dust in his hair and on his clothes. She had the impression he could make more sense of the machine in a single glance than Longstaff had managed in days. He took his time, apparently unaffected by the gathering silence. Not a talker, then, but his movements were eloquent as he lifted and weighed each individual component in his hands.

Longstaff remained silent. He was standing directly above the hidden trapdoor, she realised, as if hoping it would open and swallow him whole. Aurélie took his hand. "It's a good sign," she whispered. Exhausted from the journey, she could have killed for a hot bath and a glass of wine.

Without asking, the stranger began flipping through the notes on Longstaff's desk, lips moving slightly as he read. He took a pen and ink holder from his sash, making a note of something on the back of his hand.

"What?" demanded Longstaff.

The stranger smiled, revealing strong, white teeth. He was an attractive man, Aurélie realised.

"In his notes, your Master Gale describes this machine as a 'chronometer'. From the Greek for time." He was already striding towards the door. "A better word than 'contraption', perhaps?"

"What..."

"Someone will be in touch."

*

The barber used a razor to scrape Durant's hairline. The Frenchman's skin tingled beneath a libation of spirits. He closed his eyes, enjoying the sensation. Khalid sat beside him in the next chair, wrapped in white cloths while the barber's boy applied a sweet-smelling lather.

Had he slept? It seemed that no time had passed and suddenly Khalid was pulling him to his feet. Durant did not check his appearance in the mirror, certain his reflection would tell him nothing except that he was too old for romantic adventures. He barely had time to press a coin into the barber's hands before they were in the street, following the smell of coffee spiced with aniseed.

"This was an excellent idea of yours," said Khalid.

Durant grinned. It had been his suggestion to cut their afternoon classes on religious doctrine. Khalid had agreed at once – much against expectation – and now sat glowing with excitement among the paraphernalia of ceramic cups and brass pots. They were the only customers. Durant ordered two cups of coffee from the shopkeeper. Quietly, he asked whether they also sold *boza*.

"Circassian or Albanian?"

"Albanian."

Khalid raised an eyebrow. "At this time of day?"

"Your imams have no great love for coffee, either."

"How right you are," agreed Khalid happily.

"They claim it addles the mind and rots the stomach."

"There are no imams here. Too busy spying on medical students, making sure they put their duty to Allah ahead of their duty to their patients."

So that was it, thought Durant – the reason Khalid had agreed to come on this adventure. Conscientious *and* pious, his friend was torn between the conflicting demands of reason and revelation.

"Khalid?"

"Yes?"

The shopkeeper returned with their coffee and a large, earthenware mug for Durant. He took a long draft, closing his eyes in pleasure. Albanian *boza* was a more than acceptable substitute for beer, especially when it was iced with snow from nearby Mount Bakir.

"What do you know about flowers?"

"Their medical properties?"

"In a manner of speaking." Durant felt the blood rush to his face. "I was thinking more of their symbolic properties."

Slowly, a broad smile spread across Khalid's handsome face. "Who is she, my friend?"

Durant's blush grew deeper. He only knew her first name – and felt reluctant to share even that much information.

"You act as if you've never been in love before."

"Am I in love now?" Durant thought of his wife, the lonely years which had rolled by since her death. "I hardly know. It's been so long since I felt this way."

Khalid sipped his coffee. "I don't know how it is in your country. In Istanbul, the language of love is generally silent; flowers are among its most eloquent dialects. A rose might stand for love, but there are further layers of meaning. Violets stand for truth but removing the head of one becomes a statement of devotion: *I would submit my neck to the bowstring without a murmur.*" He looked at Durant. "And so on."

Durant raised an eyebrow. "I had no idea you were such a skilled practitioner in love."

Khalid laughed. "You have a rendezvous with her today?"

"I do."

"And you're sitting here with me?" He rose to his feet, turning towards Mecca and thanking Allah for their coffee. "Get on with you now. I'll expect a full report tomorrow!"

Durant's route took him past the city's most notorious Dervish *tekke*. A lamp burned sweet oil in a niche outside, coloured rags had been tied to the window grating. The smell of incense reached him, along with the sound of chanting, tempting him in – to hide his excitement in their fervent song. The sort of reckless behaviour of which Longstaff would certainly disapprove. Durant kept walking across the rowdy Hippodrome, fast enough that his breathing became laboured. The previous days had crawled by. Seeing her in the window, he'd feared he was building a fantasy which no flesh and blood woman could ever match. But the spell hadn't broken at the flower market. There was no trace of winter left in the air. She wanted to see him again. *Why?*

Angry and shy. Fearful and brave. He skirted the gardens behind the *Rustem Pacha* mosque. Pollen drifted in the warm air. The mosque's white stones shone warm and luminous in the sunshine. Durant hurried onwards, past a group of children, slim again without their heavy winter garments. He was getting closer – only a few short streets away according to the directions he'd been given. It wasn't only for Leila's sake that he moved carefully. Longstaff would be ruined by any scandal. What was the proverb Khalid liked so much? *The world is a cucumber; one day it's in your hand, the next it's up your arse.*

The *hammam* was huge. Durant walked past the main entrance, past a grocer's shop, a herbs and notions shop, then left into a side street. He knocked three times on a door at the far end. A veiled woman let him in without a word. Durant barely had time to register the wood-panelled corridor before she ushered him into an interior chamber.

The door closed behind him. Durant heard a key in the lock. Inside, on a low table, he saw plates of black caviar and grilled pistachio nuts. He felt a moment's strange panic, worrying he hadn't brought sufficient money. Where was she? Who was she? In his mind's eye, Leila had become a silent house, doors and windows closed, in which a single light burned like a beacon of hope. She was waiting for him in shadow, perched awkwardly on the edge of a divan. Durant took his place beside her. She met his eyes. Slowly, he reached forward to unhook the veil. She wore a blush of make-up on her cheeks. Strong and handsome, just as he remembered. She broke eye contact, stepping away from him, returning with a cup of amber-scented coffee. Durant didn't know how to put her at ease.

"This room is extraordinary."

He couldn't ask how she'd found it; she might take offence. There was a painting on the far wall, beneath a ceiling crowned with red and blue arabesques. A young man's face, ghostly white against a background of green leaves, spying on a woman who swam naked in a woodland lake. Every detail picked out in glorious moonlight. "Who are they?"

"Hüsrev and Shirin. It's a famous story."

Durant looked closer. "The man casts no shadow. Is he a creature from the spirit world?"

She looked at him strangely. "Allah has no need of light to see us."

He saw her smile. "Are you teasing me?"

She shook her head, dark hair falling across one cheek. "I knew a painter once, in the place where I grew up. He drew after the European fashion. Such wild faces. Such attention to detail, as if the sitter were the most important person in the world."

"What happened to him?"

"Domenikos? I don't know. I was still half a child when they took me from Crete. He'd recently been apprenticed as a painter of icons." She looked down. "His master had no idea what to do with him."

"You loved him?"

"Life had other ideas."

"You were brought here as a slave?"

"Until my master made me his wife." She seemed to forget her earlier modestly, staring directly at Durant with something like defiance. "His third wife, but still free."

"Barely allowed to leave the house."

"I'm here, aren't I? Tell me why?"

Durant ached to touch her. He had a sudden, unwelcome memory of his first wife as he nursed her through the last stages of plague. Bathed in sweat, body arched in pain, her eyes had always remained gentle – determined on his behalf. She had known him – and loved him – like no one before or since. Not even Longstaff or Aurélie.

"What do you want to know?"

"Who are you?"

"A doctor." He thought of the letter he'd slipped inside his tunic for luck, from his daughter, Laure. She wrote beautifully, a sure sign she was happy in France. He'd wanted her near today, hoping her influence might stop him doing something stupid.

"I grew up in a fine, stone house in the south of France," he said. "My daughter is mistress there now." He took out the letter and began to read.

Do you remember the stretch of plain with the wave of vines rolling up the hills? The dried riverbed crossed by an ancient bridge. Further away, the shattered rocks running along the floor of a valley. A local farmer called it the Valley of Memories, though he couldn't say why. Soon, wildflower will appear in the meadows again, the sun will turn our muddy roads into strips of dazzling white dust...

Durant looked up, thinking of those hills and valleys. Above his head, ostrich eggs hung from the ceiling to keep insects away. He felt Leila's small hand come to rest in his own open palm. She spoke softly, telling him more about her childhood on Crete. Somewhere in the vast *hammam*, Durant could hear music. A tar player, the higher notes of a zarb.

"You're nervous."

"Aren't you?"

"Terrified."

He leaned forward to kiss her. She raised a hand. "I could be killed... You understand? This has to be our secret." She faltered. "My life hasn't been easy."

"We've all done things we regret."

"You're a doctor."

"I thought I could make a difference once, find a cure for the plague and write my name in history. It cost me my daughter's love." Durant had never admitted as much before, not even to himself. "Now I just do what I can," he said. "One patient at a time. If I keep at it, perhaps I'll earn a measure of happiness."

"My father was a fisherman," she replied. "The man I loved was an artist. I thought we'd live quietly – on his passion and my fish." She lowered her eyes. "I haven't been mistreated in Istanbul. Not compared to others. But it's been lonely."

"I want to be something good in your life," said Durant. "Not a cause for fear. Or shame."

She drew a deep breath, reaching out to touch his face with an expression of wonder.

"I'm not ashamed." She unhooked her robe, letting it fall to her feet. He looked at her, at her ankles, her hips, her shoulders. It was like standing too close to a painting; he couldn't see her, couldn't move. He desired her and desired not to desire her. Was it love, that threatened to make him his own worst enemy?

He took a strangled breath. "I want to be something good in your life," he repeated.

She closed her eyes. "I believe you."

Chapter 8

Aurélie had managed to catch up on sleep. She'd enjoyed a hot bath and more than one glass of wine. The pleasure of having Longstaff hang on her every word still eluded her.

He'd wanted the details of course – confirmation that the handover had gone smoothly, that Lettero had sailed from Bursa with the local janissaries either bribed or none the wiser – but he'd hardly encouraged her make a tale of it, filled with moonlit assignations and acts of derring-do. He'd been distracted, an ear cocked for a knock at the door. The palace still hadn't confirmed whether his audience would go ahead. She could hear him now, pacing in the courtyard outside the empty stable she'd appropriated as her workroom. Gold for silk, flowers for favours. She knew how frustrating he found these games. Silently, she closed the window and returned to tracing the wedge-shaped markings onto paper. The first few hundred tablets were stacked against the wall behind her. How many people would recognise this as a treasure hunt, she wondered? How many agree that this was a treasure worth hunting? So far, she'd only rescued a single word from the trilingual inscription: *Marduk*. The name of Babylon's storm god. Aurélie continued tracing, half-humming the words of a poorly remembered psalm while she worked. *By the rivers of Babylon, there we sat down, also we wept as we remembered Zion. / On the willows, in the midst thereof, we hung up our lyres, / For there our captors demanded a song: "Sing us from the song of Zion." / How can we sing the song of God in a strange land?*

The sound of bells made her sit up straight. Such an everyday part of life in Europe and so alien here in Istanbul. The Ottomans were tolerant rulers, but nothing in Istanbul was permitted to compete with the Muslim call to prayer – except on Easter Sunday.

The heavy bells which had once swung in the church towers of Galata had long since been recast as cannon. The noise Aurélie heard now was made by priests and choir boys, swinging handbells and cowbells with wild abandon. She stood, rolling her shoulders to work out the kinks. As the bells faded, she heard the thump of a steel-tipped arrow strike its straw target. Longstaff, practising with his Turkish bow – a sound with which she had become wearyingly familiar. One moment he was full of confidence, certain the sultan wouldn't refuse his gift because the Turkish word for tulip – *lale* – contained the name of God. The next moment, seized by a sense of hopelessness, he would take up his bow. Aurélie flinched as another quarrel struck the target with a heavy thud.

Did it even matter if he met Walsingham's demands? What difference would it make if he became England's first ambassador to the Ottoman Empire? The three of them were happy in this house. She couldn't imagine Longstaff surrounded by French footmen, Arab grooms, Turkish guards, Russian housemaids, Italian stewards. Even now, he could hardly bring himself to mingle with the city's diplomatic community.

The sound of splintering wood propelled her into the courtyard, where a still-quivering arrow had buried itself in the stable wall. Longstaff stared at the ox-horn bow in disgust.

"Boys half my age can hit a thaler at thirty feet," he muttered. "I don't know how they do it."

"The same reason you can swing a war-sword like it's made of tin. They're trained to it from birth."

"I'll match them yet."

"Not today. I need an escort. It's Easter Sunday, Matthew." She was already tying a scarf over her golden hair. "Time to enjoy ourselves."

"I don't know."

"How will you charm the sultan if you've forgotten how to smile?"

For a moment, she thought he might refuse. He slipped the bone rings from his thumb and tossed them aside with the bow. "I should change."

"You're fine as you are." Aurélie liked him in the simple *shalwar* and *khameez*. Most Europeans in the city ended up shunning pleats and jewels, if only from a desire to avoid the mockery of their hosts. She saw no reason to make an exception just because it was Easter.

The streets around Galata's famous tower swarmed with people. Greeks, Armenians, Poles, Italians. A scattering of Muscovy merchants come to trade in amber and furs. Turks, who'd recovered sufficiently from the celebrations to mark the end of their own Lenten period. Children ran back and forth in their Sunday best, gorging themselves on slices of fried bread and marzipan. Aurélie put her arm through Longstaff's, smiling at a stray memory.

"What?"

"The party the chevalier threw to mark the beginning of Lent."

"We weren't invited."

"Thank God. People nearly died of boredom."

"The French ambassador is a fool."

"Sometimes I think he might be the wisest man in Galata." Longstaff looked at her in amazement.

"Whatever mistakes he makes," she said, "he never dwells on them. I imagine he sleeps like a baby."

"Forgive me if I'm reluctant to take the man as a role model…" His voice was stiff, eyes sliding away from hers.

"Why is it so important what Walsingham thinks? He does nothing to support your efforts…"

"You think I care about Walsingham?"

She had to lengthen her stride to keep pace with him. "I didn't mean to upset you. No doubt my obsession with a long-forgotten civilisation is just as incomprehensible."

Longstaff came to an abrupt stop. "Walsingham isn't the only person who writes from England. Nicholas Bacon writes. The steward at Martlesham writes. They all say the same thing – English exports have collapsed. I don't care about Walsingham; he'll be fine whatever happens – people like him always are. But small-holders, shepherds, shearers, provincial merchants? They'll starve if we can't find new markets for them here."

"Finally," she exclaimed.

"What?"

"You don't think it would have helped to tell me that earlier?"

A sheepish grin spread slowly across his rumpled features. "I'm not sure I knew it until just now."

Aurélie squeezed his hand. Durant found them a moment later, standing together near an enormous marzipan sculpture of Christ draped across his mother's lap.

"Not the most tasteful representation I've ever seen."

He steered them further into the square, where tables had been set up in front of the *Palazzo del Commune*. Aurélie found herself wedged between the two men. Like a conjurer, Durant produced cutlery and a bottle of good Cretan wine before serving them from the communal pot. Tuscan bean stew. People shook hands with their neighbours. Tears appeared in Aurélie's eyes. She hadn't realised she was so hungry – or still so attached to the foods of her youth. The pots were scraped clean within minutes. The wine kept flowing. When a group of musicians began to play, she dragged her husband onto the makeshift dancefloor. He moved awkwardly at first, growing steadily more graceful as the music worked its magic.

In his arms, close enough that she could feel his heartbeat, Aurélie willed him to let go – of Walsingham's endless demands, the fate of his chronometer, the consignment of silk on its perilous journey to England. It was late when she finally led him to the edge of the giddy crowd, planning to take him home and continue their dance in private.

Francesco appeared in their path, blinking furiously behind his eyeglasses. "Your audience has been confirmed!"

Longstaff gripped the *dragoman's* arm. "You're sure?"

"I've been looking for you everywhere. The sultan's advisors met this morning."

Aurélie fixed the smile on her face as Longstaff turned to her. She was happy for him, proud of him. "Congratulations, Matthew. You've done it, despite all the obstacles."

A look of panic gripped her husband's face. "Ten thousand tulip bulbs," he said. "It's Easter Sunday. How in God's name am I going to get them wrapped?"

The following thirty-six hours passed in a blur. Longstaff was everywhere at once, sourcing ribbon, repackaging the tulips, boning up on the intricacies of Ottoman court etiquette. Now, with only hours remaining before he was due to arrive at the palace, Francesco insisted he stop.

"You have to look your best," he said, pushing Longstaff into a chair and personally applying lather to his jaw. "Anything less will be seen as an insult.

Longstaff couldn't sit still. "I should be at the warehouse."

"We've been over this," said Aurélie. "Durant is there."

Along with a troop of stevedores, dressed in spotless white tunics at Longstaff's expense, ready to load the tulips onto *caiques* for their trip across the Golden Horn.

"That's meant to reassure me?" Longstaff scowled at Francesco, sitting back in the chair with obvious reluctance. "Tell me again. There was a meeting at the *divan...*"

Francesco took up the razor. "By convention, the sultan's advisors behave as if he's present at their deliberations, hidden behind a curtained niche. In practice, they assume he's in the harem or drinking with his friends. We've been paying one of the military judges to lobby on your behalf; he raised the subject of your tulips, recommending that you be given permission to present them in person."

He began to work on Longstaff's eyebrows. "The grand vizier rejected the suggestion out of hand. That should have been the end of the matter – our judge won't risk a break with Mehmed Sokollu over a few gold coins – except that on this occasion the sultan *was* on the other side of the curtain. Selim spoke in your favour. He even mentioned you by name."

Longstaff closed his eyes while Aurélie wrapped him in a pale blue robe. Not the colour he would have chosen but apparently one of three the Ottomans associated with good fortune. The others were orange and violet. The robe was plain, at least, but he didn't understand why it had to be so long.

"I'm dead if it comes to a fight," he muttered.

"Your enemies will be wearing embroidered kaftans."

The image made Longstaff smile – Raimondi and the chevalier dressed as walking tapestries.

"These people don't fight with their fists." Aurélie rapped her fingers against the side of his head. "You have to make them wonder what's going on in here."

"How?"

"By keeping your mouth shut." Francesco coloured slightly; he rarely expressed himself so frankly. "A thousand people will be watching you, waiting for any opportunity to laugh at your ignorance. Don't speak in the sultan's presence. Remember, this isn't an audience. Selim has agreed to receive you at the same time as he pays his janissaries their wages. That's all. Fall to your knees when the chamberlain announces you and keep your eyes on the floor."

Longstaff made a sour face.

"They've all done it," added Francesco. "The patriarch, Raimondi, even the bloody chevalier."

He kept talking, the words filling Longstaff's head like a swarm of insects. A list of warring institutions. Francesco ticked them off on his fingers. "The inner service, the outer service, the ulema, the janissaries." Half of them made up of members of the Turkish aristocracy, half of them men of the gathering, the *devsirme* – Christians taken from their homes in the Balkans as children, stripped of all ties except loyalty to the sultan in a deliberate policy of divide and rule.

"You've told me this before," said Longstaff. "My head's fit to burst."

"Your head is bare." Aurélie took a step forward, crowning him with a round hat made from black felt. "Perfect."

Longstaff took her hand. "I'm sorry you can't be there."

"Not your fault."

She came as far as the docks. Durant was already herding the stevedores and their cargo of gaudy boxes onto a string of waiting *caiques*. Longstaff stood in the lead boat, staring blindly ahead on the crossing to 'Stanboul. Francesco had arranged for horses on the far side. Longstaff tried not to think of the expense – the high-stepping animals, new tunics for the stevedores – the kind of extravagant theatre which always set his teeth on edge. Pedestrians stepped smartly out of the way. Pedlars offered *boza,* strips of fried mackerel, sweet pastries. They swarmed around the palace gates alongside taverners, tailors, brothel-keepers. In a few short hours, five thousand janissary soldiers would come pouring into the great square with their pockets full of gold.

Longstaff used his horse to force a passage through the crowd. The guards at Coldfountain Gate stood aside at a word from Francesco. The racket set up by the pedlars faded as they passed beneath the thick walls. Longstaff and his companions dismounted in silence on the far side. Grooms appeared to take their mounts. Servants relieved the stevedores of their boxes and sent them back the way they'd come. Animals moved freely across the lawns – gazelles, peacocks, turtles, ostriches, antelopes – among people dressed in robes of every cut and colour. From the hill above Galata, the Imperial Palace resembled a series of pavilions sweeping down towards the Golden Horn. From within, the buildings seemed less well-matched. A man waddled towards them in a kaftan of brocaded silk, cut straight from collar to hem, flared at the waist, decorated with leaves picked out in golden thread. It took Longstaff a moment to recognise Raimondi Maltrapillo – and then only by the man's unctuous smile.

"You look extraordinary."

"A gift from the sultan."

The Venetian ambassador spread his arms, turning once in place before taking Longstaff's arm and leading him towards the distant Gate of Salutation.

"It's your first time," he said. "I hope you'll allow me to act as your guide."

Durant and Francesco fell into step alongside Raimondi's own more substantial entourage. Deliberately, the Venetian ambassador took them past a series of rotting heads, with marble columns where the bodies should have been – men who'd fallen foul of the sultan or his grand vizier in recent weeks. Women were thrown into the Bosphorus without ceremony. Raimondi insisted they stop.

Longstaff felt sick. Stuffed with straw, the mouths of the executed men shifted just enough to conjure images of the maggots at work inside.

"The stuffing reflects their rank," noted Raimondi with ghoulish satisfaction. "Cotton for viziers, straw for lesser officials. We play a game for high stakes, my friend. This is what happens when we lose."

He walked on without a backward glance. "We have to present a united front," he continued. "All the Christian nations. However much we might admire our hosts."

They reached the entrance to the Gate of Salutation. Raimondi released Longstaff's arm, idly twisting the rings on his fingers. "Not everyone could have navigated the waters of this city so adroitly," he said. "Enjoy your day. Don't forget to lead with your right foot when they present you."

What united front? What was he talking about? Longstaff shook his head in frustration. A few short years ago he'd been one of the most feared soldiers in Europe, laying siege to fortified cities, standing his ground at the bloody heart of battlefields. He looked at Francesco.

"Lead with my right foot? You didn't tell me."

"I did. He's trying to rattle you."

"Perhaps he was simply trying to help," snapped Longstaff.

"Being nervous is one thing," retorted Francesco, blinking rapidly behind his glasses. "Being stupid quite another."

"I only meant..."

The *dragoman* cut him off. "Raimondi isn't like you," he said. "He won't look for solutions that benefit all sides. He wants to win – for him, that means someone has to lose."

Chapter 9

The Gate of Salutation was a hundred strides deep, finally opening into a second courtyard so big it might have swallowed the world. Longstaff came to an involuntary stop, mouth open in wonder as he stared at rank upon rank of silent soldiers in their famous feather-topped hoods. Five thousand men, so still that Longstaff could hear the gentle play of water in the fountains. Francesco pulled him towards an arched colonnade. Raimondi and the French ambassador were already there, along with the Podesta of Genoa, the legate of the King of Poland, and dozens more.

Longstaff ignored them, staring instead at the sultan's elite fighting corps. The bastards might have been made from stone. The silence grew deeper still when Mehmed Sokollu appeared, walking the serried ranks to a covered platform before the Gate of Felicity. The grand vizier was a product of the *devsirme*. A slave, in other words, despite his wealth and power, taken in childhood from his home in Bosnia. And yet he stood before them at ease, barrel-chest thrust forward, alert features nestled comfortably in his beard.

"Don't be fooled," whispered Francesco. "There's a hole where his heart should be."

The *dragoman* didn't have a good word for anyone today, it seemed. Longstaff only half-listened. It would take a lifetime to make sense of this place, he thought, where a peasant became master by becoming a slave. The janissaries were slaves. The sultan's mother had been a slave. The fountains in the courtyard grew louder – heralds of crisis or climax – waters rising in a high plume to mark the sultan's appearance. The soldiers lowered their heads, feathered hoods rippling like a field of corn. Astride a midnight-black stallion, the sultan was dressed in dazzling white from the tip of his boots to the top of his jewelled turban. An endless stream of servants poured from the shadowed gateway behind him, moving in perfect formation until a plate of rice had been set before each soldier. Five thousand men ate in silence. Longstaff had never seen a display of such naked power. The servants reappeared, replacing the empty plates with bags of coin. Selim raised one fist before turning his horse, disappearing back through the Gate of Felicity.

Marching four abreast, without hesitation or misstep, the soldiers left the courtyard via the Gate of Salutation, heading into Istanbul to spend their wages on the finest food and women the city could offer. The parade ground became a garden again, servants set tables beneath an awning of vines. The city's dignitaries struck up conversation in a babel of languages.

"Selim will keep us waiting." Francesco helped himself to a glass of wine. "Tell me how you feel about him."

"About the sultan? I've never met the man."

"You admire and respect him," corrected the *dragoman*. "You sympathise with him."

Longstaff scowled. *Sympathise? With the Lord of Worlds?*

"Remember the rules of Ottoman succession," said Francesco. "When a male heir reaches adulthood, he's sent away to serve as governor somewhere in the empire. When the sultan dies, it becomes a race – the throne going to whichever of his adult sons reach the city first. The rest are put to death."

Longstaff shuddered. "And Selim was first."

"He was neither the oldest nor the favourite son," murmured Francesco. "Suleiman sent him a thousand leagues from the city. If he's sultan today, it's because his mother conspired to murder his half-brothers."

Pages of the privy chamber appeared at the entrance to the Gate of Felicity. "It's time," said the *dragoman*.

At ease in their fine kaftans, the ambassadors of Venice and France proceeded Longstaff into the sultan's presence. The throne room glittered like the inside of a jewel box.

Selim reclined on a bed of cushions surrounded by servants and courtiers. He'd changed since leaving the courtyard, into a kaftan of yellow silk trimmed with black sable, replacing the ostrich plumes in his white turban with a golden rosette. He appeared less regal at close quarters, soft and pampered beneath the fine robes, his cheeks rosy with the heat. Thanks to Francesco's careful tuition, Longstaff could identify the various factions around him – chamberlains in scarlet, the ulema in purple, viziers in green. The head chamberlain began to read, his statement couched in such rarefied Ottoman Turkish it sounded almost like music.

"Lower your eyes," hissed Francesco.

Longstaff recognised the word for infidel – *gawur*. Two servants appeared on either side of him. He stumbled forward – right foot first – then dropped to his knees, the sultan's slippered feet only inches from his head. He hadn't expected to be so close; the arrogance of it took his breath away.

"The sultan welcomes you to his court..."

Francesco had crawled forward to provide a running translation. "He acknowledges the existence of England and thanks you for the tulip bulbs. They will be planted in the palace gardens. He hopes you will return to see them when they flower."

A second invitation! Longstaff knew better than to open his mouth. The chamberlain concluded by saying how much his master regretted that he couldn't see the English machine. Longstaff was ready to shuffle backwards. The grand vizier stepped forward to interrupt proceedings.

"Why shouldn't his majesty see it?"

Francesco translated Mehmed Sokollu's question in a breathless whisper.

"His Majesty was given to understand," replied the chamberlain, "that it was damaged beyond repair."

"On the contrary, I've heard the damage only appears extensive because the machine was disassembled for its voyage."

Forehead hovering a wrinkle's distance above the carpet, confused by the note of satisfaction in the grand vizier's deep voice, there was nothing Longstaff could do. A wizened man in purple stepped forward – the grand mufti, head of the Ulema.

"These vile mechanicals are a blasphemy. The Franks do not seek to praise God's creation. Driven by hubris, they compete with Him. Nor do they mean to honour us by these gifts, but only to reduce us to their own pathetic state."

"Surely, you're not suggesting we should fear them," countered Mehmed Sokollu – as if offended on the sultan's behalf.

The chamberlain raised his voice. "Is the machine beyond repair or not? The Englishman may speak."

Even without the collective intake of breath, Longstaff knew that his audience had strayed from time-honoured protocol. How many times had he been told not to open his mouth? The silence grew. He felt a sharp prod in the small of his back.

"Your majesty," he said without looking up. "The man who created the chronometer died at sea."

"And his papers?" persisted the chamberlain.

"I have them..." Longstaff grew flustered. "The chronometer has come from England at great expense. There's nothing I'd like more than to see it restored to its former glory, but..."

"I would so love to see it working," interrupted the sultan. Shocked by the sound of Selim's soft voice, several seconds passed before anyone drew breath.

"You are the Lord of Worlds," purred Mehmed Sokollu. "Your word is law. I imagine the Englishman had planned a performance in the palace gardens – with the tulips as a natural backdrop to the mechanical arts of his country?"

"That's right," stammered Longstaff.

"The tulips will bloom within the next three weeks, by my calculations. Of course, we'll have to consult the head gardener and the imperial astrologer before settling on the exact date."

Longstaff turned his head slightly as Francesco translated, eyes wide with panic.

"Don't move," hissed the *dragoman*. "The chamberlain is consulting with Selim."

A page stepped forward, holding a beautifully embroidered silk bag – a kaftan for the English visitor.

"Peki," murmured the sultan, one of the few Turkish words Longstaff knew. *It is well.* Selim's long sleeve swam into view. Longstaff pressed his lips to the soft silk. The head chamberlain cleared his throat. Francesco began translating again.

"The Frankish machine will be presented on a date to be decided by the imperial astrologer in consultation with our head gardener. The slave Hector will assist the Englishman in his labours."

"Is that necessary?" interrupted Mehmed Sokollu.

"Repairs to the machine will be carried out in the palace grounds," continued the chamberlain. "Within a pavilion erected for the purpose."

The audience was at an end. Longstaff shuffled backwards with his head still lowered, pursued by the hum of excited conversation. He realised he was covered in sweat, muscles trembling as if he'd been in battle. "What in God's name just happened?"

"Keep your voice down." Francesco spoke without moving his lips. "Keep walking. Smile!"

They emerged, blinking, into bright sunshine. Durant came striding towards them across the lawn, a smile on his narrow face.

"Three weeks?" said Longstaff. "How in God's name am I meant to repair the chronometer in three weeks?"

It wasn't possible. He felt numb, exhausted by the exchange he'd just witnessed.

"It's good news," said Francesco. "The sultan wants you to win." He raised a hand to welcome Durant. "Congratulate your friend. He'll have an opportunity to present his chronometer to the sultan after all!"

"What do you mean he wants me to win?" demanded Longstaff. "Why?"

The *dragoman* had perfected the art of ventriloquism. "Selim is beginning to resent the constraints imposed by his over-mighty grand vizier. I suspect he wants to promote someone new – someone without connections to the old regime."

"Me?"

"Assuming you succeed."

"And if I fail?" Longstaff remembered the note of satisfaction he'd heard in Mehmed Sokollu's voice. The grand vizier had spoken against him at the *divan*. What game was he playing in all this?

"People are watching," said Francesco, smiling broadly at his client. "As the sultan himself would no doubt say, the future rests in God's hands alone."

"*Insha' Allah,*" muttered Longstaff with a weary shake of his head.

Chapter 10

Aurélie was late. Scattering sand over the ink, she thrust her papers into a bag and hurried towards the docks – remembering at the last moment to fix a veil over her face. She resented the convention less and less, finding power in the ability to see and not be seen in return. She found space in the bow of a swift *caique*. One day, women will walk these streets without fear, she thought, watching the approaching domes and minarets of 'Stanboul. Always the optimist, Longstaff would have said, putting no limits on what people could achieve if they rose from their knees and took responsibility for their lives. Aurélie doubted there was a God. If He did exist, she certainly didn't subscribe to the notion that He was cruel. Didn't humanity already have the tools it needed to free itself from want, disease, envy, and war? What more did people want?

Makarios lived in an imposing brick and stone villa in the ancient district of Phanar. Servants led Aurélie through the house to a gently sloping garden where a dozen men chatted among the trees, wearing togas which wouldn't have looked out of place in ancient Rome. Removing her veil, Aurélie smiled at them without stopping. Her mouth fell open in wonder when she reached the far end of the garden. Makarios had erected a wooden pavilion on the tideless waters of the Golden Horn – a stage bordered on either side by a pair of marble busts.

He appeared beside her a moment later. In his mid-sixties, the once powerful body slowly slipping earthwards, he took her hands with obvious pleasure. "Do you recognise them?"

"Plato and Hypatia." Aurélie felt a sudden surge of gratitude. Makarios, at least, was willing to accept that a woman could make a meaningful contribution to the life of the mind. "I hope you haven't built this just for me?"

"Did you think I'd make you stand on a box?" He grinned at her. "Nervous?"

"I am now."

"Come and have a drink."

"I should go over my notes."

"Perfect is the enemy of the good," he announced grandly. "And would almost certainly be wasted on this audience."

Determined to keep a clear head, Aurélie accepted a glass of deliciously cold rosehip juice. Makarios and his friends, whose families had all been prominent before Istanbul fell to the Ottomans, liked to style themselves as gentleman-philosophers – the heirs to Plato and Aristotle. Without their help, Aurélie's trip to Bursa would have been impossible. They had provided introductions, recommendations, access to their libraries, and guarantees of good conduct. In return, she had promised them a full report on her discoveries.

"How's your husband?"

Aurélie blinked in surprise. "Why do you ask?"

"Partly to distract you. Partly because his pig-headed determination is beginning to make an impression."

"What have you heard?"

"Everything. You know what a gossip I am beneath this polished exterior."

His eyes widened at the appearance of a new guest. "This is an unexpected honour."

The newcomer was younger than his host, dressed in a silk tunic cut to show off his figure. Three was something attractive about him, decided Aurélie – despite the tedious regularity of his features. He looked worldly – a man of affairs – energised rather than wearied by his responsibilities.

"Aurélie," said Makarios, his smile less than convincing, "allow me to introduce Joseph Nasi."

She knew the name, of course, along with everyone else in Istanbul. A Jewish merchant and close confidant of the sultan's, whose family had been forced to leave Spain a hundred years earlier. Successive generations had been hounded from city to city – Lisbon, Antwerp, Venice, Ferrara – accepting constraints on their liberty each time, moving on again when these descended into outright persecution. Nasi had risen high since arriving in Istanbul. Aurélie felt an unexpected swell of affection for her adopted home – a Muslim city where both she and Nasi could pray and live as they chose. There was another reason she felt well-disposed towards him, however. In addition to his many other interests, Joseph Nasi was her husband's principal and confidential creditor in Istanbul.

"I'm flattered," she said. "That such a prominent individual should come to hear me speak."

Nasi smiled, as if he knew exactly how much weight to give her compliment. "Not at all prominent, I fear. Just a humble man of action."

"With an interest in natural philosophy?"

"Qualities we should hardly regard as exclusive. Without reference to action, thought becomes absurd." Pointedly, he looked around the garden. "Don't you agree?"

Makarios cleared his throat. "Shall we?"

He led her to the stage. Aurélie stared down at her audience. Looking for a friendly face, her eye landed on Nasi. The merchant smiled, as if indicating it was time to begin. She removed one of the precious clay tablets from her bag.

"You've seen these marks before," she said. "On old monuments in the city, on ruins near your homes in the countryside. They look strange to our eyes, almost as if birds had walked across wet clay, so much so that it's tempting to dismiss them as little more than a simple numbering system." Aurélie paused, waiting until she was sure she had their attention. "The tablet I have in my hands now is one of eighteen hundred numbered pages, divided into sections that can only be understood as paragraphs and chapters."

She was honest with them, admitting she couldn't read the strange, wedge-shaped script. "But alongside these tablets," she continued. "In a chamber no one had entered in more than a thousand years, I also found a piece of marble, tall as a man stands, on which a single inscription is carved in three different languages. The first two have already yielded their mysteries." Slowly, she recited the haunting lines:

He split her in two, like a fish for drying,

Half of her he set up and made as a cover like heaven.

He stretched out the hide and assigned watchmen,

And ordered them not to let the waters escape.

The lines made perfect sense to Aurélie – as an account of how the world was made from a female body split in two, an upper sphere of water that formed the sky and a lower sphere out of which the earth emerged.

"The tri-lingual inscription is the key," she said. "It will open the story locked in these eighteen hundred consecutive tablets. And not just any story. From hints and clues, culled from a dozen different sources, I believe I can already tell you its name – *Enuma Elish.*"

She took a deep breath, speaking more quickly now. "An alternative account of the origins of humanity, with unmistakable echoes of our own – a mysterious garden, a magical tree, a talking snake – but a kinder story, which doesn't demand the same impossible contortions in logic or ethics..."

"Contortions?"

Tightly wound anger made the word sting. Looking up to see who'd interrupted, Aurélie registered the shock on every face. Rows of men staring at her with hard, accusing eyes. To some extent, she'd planned it this way.

"How else would you describe the sudden shift from perfect innocence to absolute wickedness?" she asked. "Or God's prohibition on the one piece of knowledge which would make it possible to obey His law? Or the terrible punishment handed out for such a relatively insignificant crime – inflicted on all humanity and for all time?"

An old man rose to his feet. "Makarios," he demanded. "What is this?"

Suddenly, there was uproar. They were intelligent men. Was that why they attacked her so aggressively? Their commitment to the truth was clouded, the flame of inquiry having burned low long before the Ottomans arrived. More interested in talk than action, too wealthy to want genuine change. She should have presented her evidence first – now it seemed she'd never get the chance. Makarios joined her on stage. Aurélie saw the look of entreaty in his eyes.

"You may have been too hasty," he prompted.

She nodded, hating herself for it. This was a social club, a way of asserting intellectual superiority over the Ottomans. God forbid it should demand anything from them in return. Not courage, not curiosity, certainly not an open mind. "Of course," she said. "It's only conjecture at this stage."

Makarios began to clap, persisting until his friends joined in – to rescue her and bury her. The noise died quickly, the men drifting into conversation as if that brief flurry of applause had erased all memory of her words. Makarios herded them away, listing the delicacies which waited in another part of the garden, until only Nasi remained.

"You must have known how they'd react."

Aurélie sat down beside Hypatia's bust. "I wanted to make them think. They didn't give me a chance."

"You mean there was more?"

"The *Enuma Elish* is proof that Adam and Eve weren't the first man and woman. Only the founders of a sect born long after the world was already filled with people."

Nasi shook his head in mock wonder.

"It's not a hypothesis that would have troubled Plato or Aristotle," persisted Aurélie.

"Two men who lived before Christ."

"Before God sent his only son to prohibit us from believing what we see."

Laughter danced in his eyes. "You wanted to tell them their magical trees were just an imitation of someone's else magical trees?"

She scowled. "It's your story, too, isn't it?"

"It's our story *first*. To the best of my knowledge, we've never claimed it should be taken literally."

She looked at him. "I know so little of what your people believe."

He shrugged. "Judaism, Christianity, Islam; they're no different from any other idea – subject to the forces of history, continually changing in form and nature. There isn't an organisation in the world that can survive without a little flexibility, a fact which religions conceal behind grand claims about the immutability of human nature. We won't become free until we learn to believe the opposite – that we can become anything we want. Isn't that what you're really hoping to prove?"

Aurélie looked at him in wonder. She'd never thought of it in those terms before and yet he was right; that was her dream exactly.

"My regards to your husband, by the way." Preparing to take his leave, Nasi handed her a single golden coin. "Would you give him this for me."

"You owe him money?" She heard the confusion in her own voice.

Nasi laughed. "Merely a token of my esteem. A Venetian ducat – for his collection."

Chapter 11

The streets of Istanbul overflowed with life. Durant yearned to stroll with Leila through the markets, studying her face in the sun's warm light. He wanted to hire a *caique* and visit the surrounding valleys with her, picnic in meadows strewn with wildflower. But these were hopeless dreams, he knew. At least for the present, their meetings could only take place at the *hammam*, on the divan beneath the painting of Hüsrev and Shirin, in the round pool of heated water in a corner of the secret chamber. Among the silk cushions and rosewood bowls.

The room was elegant, but it wasn't theirs. Making her smile, hearing her laugh, quickly became Durant's consuming passion during the hours they spent together. For her benefit, his life became a poem, an epic from the age of heroes – deliberately undermined by a seam of dark self-mockery. He embellished half-remembered escapades from his childhood, adventures from his youth. Best of all, she loved the tales from his years as a reluctant thief. The man in black. The near misses. He wasn't like Longstaff, a human punchbag absorbing punishment until his enemies exhausted themselves. Instead, he'd been a shadow, operating by sleight of hand and speed of thought. A blank canvas for the preoccupations of his adversaries.

"I was always good at it," he said without false modesty, trying to help her know him. "It's a question of meeting expectations. People looked at me and saw what they needed to see – a servant going about his business, a gambler with a reckless streak, a merchant down on his luck."

He assumed a wry grin. "Stealing was easy. Holding onto the proceeds not so much."

She didn't smile. Durant sipped his wine, attempting to hide his disappointment. "What is it?"

"We have more in common than you realise." A flash of frustration crossed her face. "I was just fifteen when the corsairs took me from Crete. A slave – with skills and qualities my owners sought to exploit. Do you think I've been locked in a cupboard for the last twenty years?"

"I'm sorry." Durant swallowed. "I didn't want to pry."

"Or didn't want to know."

Durant reached out to touch her face. "I want to know everything about you."

She began hesitantly, as if worried about how he would react. He heard a growing note of pride in her voice however – the justified pride of a master-craftsman. "Istanbul is a city of secrets," she said. "There are men who devote their entire lives to ferreting them out."

"You were a spy?"

"There was a time in my life when I was whatever I needed to be. A maidservant, knuckles raw from scrubbing floors, careful to let my mistress think I spoke no language but Greek. A wealthy lady of delicate health, jealous of her physician's time. A dancer."

"You can dance?"

She laughed when she saw the expression on his face. "When I have to. The same way I can hold my tongue, seem more stupid than I am, remember what I'm told, ask questions without appearing to, identify liars..."

"How?" interrupted Durant. She had worried unnecessarily. He was fascinated by this new side of her – the source of her strength, which he already found so irresistible.

"Liars laugh too often and too easily – and keep their fingernails trimmed to the wick." She shrugged. "Everyone lies. Wait a day, find new ways to rephrase old questions – you'll nearly always hear a different story."

She laughed when Durant looked down at his own uneven fingernails, a sound like music. Like happiness. How could he have known she would turn out to be so capable, so courageous?

It seemed ridiculous that they were hiding here, jumping at shadows, with the world outside just waiting for them.

"Run away with me." He said it without thinking.

"I don't want to hide anymore," she replied. "I don't want to live in fear. You asked me what happiness looks like. It's never having to pretend again."

*

Longstaff gave his name to the guards at Coldfountain Gate. A servant appeared within seconds, leading him through the first courtyard with its seemingly permanent queue of petitioners, surrounded by the reassuring bustle of people at work in the granaries, workshops and stables. A bundle of the Yorkshireman's papers tucked beneath one arm, there was a spring in Longstaff's step as he strode across the gardens, past a group of deer gathered in the shade of tall cypress trees. Years ago, men had hailed him as a Lord of War. He'd tried living as a thief since then, as a gentleman farmer in Suffolk. Could he finally do some good as a diplomat at the Ottoman court?

Peacocks added an extra touch of colour. Longstaff remembered the wonderland created by Catherine de Medici at the Palais de Justice in Paris. Ponies painted with black and white stripes, dwarfs and giants strolling side by side among huge birds, highland cattle with their shaggy coats woven into plaits and finished with colourful ribbons. The winding path led to an artificial rise topped by a small pavilion. Longstaff wrinkled his nose; the paint was fresh. Wood shavings littered the grass outside. He entered a room cluttered with all the parts and pieces of his chronometer.

A man knelt beside a funnel cast in bronze – the same man who had visited Longstaff's warehouse several days earlier, wearing the same pale turban and sash. He was well-known in the city, according to Francesco, a mechanical genius responsible for the creation of new war engines and navigational instruments.

"I've brought more drawings," said Longstaff, lifting his bundle of papers. "Some early sketches I kept at the house."

Hector cleaned his hands on a scrap of cloth. "I already have everything I need," he replied in fluent Italian. Longstaff heard the note of dismissal. He took a moment to calm himself, then seized the mechanic's arm. Their eyes met. A long moment of silence before Hector winced.

"If you think you can repair the chronometer without me, you're welcome to try." He pulled free of Longstaff's grip.

"Do you have any idea what's at stake?..."

"I have no doubt your queen expects a good return on her investment."

Longstaff couldn't tell him that Elizabeth had refused to contribute a single penny. Instead, he studied the components spread out across the floor. He'd attempted something similar at the warehouse, but there was order here. A pattern he couldn't quite grasp, almost an image of beauty.

"A man named Gale designed it," he said. "He's dead now, weighted with cannon shot at the bottom of the sea – and I'm responsible for realising his dream."

Hector shrugged. He nodded at a tangle of thin copper pipes. "They need to be cleaned and oiled."

Longstaff rolled up his sleeves. Hector returned to the funnel without another word. Gradually, the silence grew companionable as the hours passed. Longstaff even enjoyed his task – it was so much simpler to unravel pipes than motives. In any sensible world, the Ottomans should have welcomed him with open arms. They had a hundred thousand soldiers to keep warm through the winter, and England an abundance of wool. And yet here he was, drowning in debt, a rag-cloth in one hand, a growing line of shiny pipes at his elbow. Francesco kept telling him to stop thinking so logically. Everyone was compromised, according to the *dragoman,* owing favours in a hundred different directions.

Palace officials peered through the windows from time to time, but no one disturbed them until a servant arrived with food. Longstaff helped himself to a flask of good, strong *boza,* raising an eyebrow when Hector joined him.

"Isn't it forbidden?"

"I wasn't born a Muslim. I'm Greek, from Parga in the Ionian Sea. Pirates raided when I was ten."

The mechanic's voice remained steady. Longstaff thought he saw the dark eyes sharpen with pain.

"I also lost my family when I was young. My father was executed for heresy."

Hector stared at him. Whatever he saw in Longstaff's crumpled blue eyes, his voice was warmer when he spoke again. "In Istanbul, anyone competent is a slave. The Ottomans like it that way – keeps us humble however high we rise."

Longstaff looked around the room while he ate. The walls and workbenches were covered in tools and instruments – hammers, chisels, jag-toothed saws. Rods and staffs for measuring the stars. "You're an astronomer, as well?"

Hector grinned, teeth flashing in the salt and pepper beard. "Show me a mechanic who isn't. The earth's a cog in a clockwork universe. Suleiman understood. For more than thirty years, he employed a hundred astronomers to chart every shift in the night sky."

"What was he looking for?"

"Longitude."

Longstaff blinked. Finding latitude at sea was straightforward, he knew, but longitude? There was no secret in the world pursued with greater enthusiasm. King Philip of Spain had offered a king's ransom to whoever solved the problem, the Estates General of Holland a prize of 30,000 florins. A soldier by training, Longstaff disliked ships, but he wasn't a fool. The Ottomans occupied the point where East met

West. If they could solve the mystery of longitude, they would have the world at their mercy.

"One hundred astronomers, working on the problem for thirty years," continued Hector. "All gone now, dismissed within six months of Suleiman's death, their observations gathering dust in Selim's treasury. The present generation isn't interested in building on the achievements of their predecessors. They only want to forget."

Longstaff smiled. He recognised the expression on Hector's face. The mechanic reminded him of Aurélie, another devotee of learning – of progress through reason rather than revelation.

"Can you repair the chronometer?"

"In the next three weeks? Probably. Not that it matters. Selim wouldn't know the difference if we hid inside and pulled the levers ourselves."

Longstaff felt his stomach heave. "Everyone knows how much he loves these machines."

Hector burst out laughing. "Do you even know how the Ottomans reckon time? From sunset to sunset, dividing the day into twelve hours that vary in length depending on the time of year. Even if I do get your chronometer working, it won't give the right time more than twice a year!" He shook his head. "If Selim loves these machines, it's for their bells and whistles. They help him believe the Franks are a race of children who spend their days playing with toys."

A toy? Longstaff had risked his life and honour for a toy?

"And the grand vizier hates them for the same reason," continued Hector. "He worries that if you Franks keep playing with your clever clocks and weapons – without fear of God or dishonour – then there's no limit to what you might achieve. The secret of longitude, for example."

Longitude again? "What do you mean?"

"A chronometer able to keep accurate time at sea would solve the riddle in a heartbeat."

"I thought you said they'd given up."

"They have – this isn't a dream for the grand vizier; it's a nightmare. He likes things the way they are."

Longstaff looked at the numerous parts spread across the floor. "And?" he asked, new reverence in his voice. "Could it work at sea?"

Hector roared with laughter. "Ships move, for God's sake. How would you shield the moving parts from changes in temperature and humidity? You'd need to use materials that don't rust or warp or need oiling and cleaning." Briefly, his eyes took on a faraway look. "I suppose it might be possible to combine different materials so that one contracts when the other expands." He shook his head. "Not our problem, thank God. We have more than enough to worry about already."

He looked at Longstaff, head cocked to one side. "Even if I do repair the chronometer, it won't get you what you want. You've made too many enemies for that."

Longstaff finished the last of the *boza,* wiping his mouth with the back of his hand. "What makes you say that?"

"The English pilgrims locked in the Fortress of Seven Towers," said Hector. "The ones you still know nothing about."

Chapter 12

Longstaff slowed fractionally as the forbidding gates came into view. Thieves were imprisoned behind the high walls, traitors tortured and heretics executed. Some were never heard of again, the doors to their cells bricked up and the men inside forgotten – but getting in was easy. The jailers looked delighted when Longstaff explained his business – which meant it was true. And they'd all known. The chevalier, Raimondi, and the rest. Not one of them had lifted a finger for the poor souls locked inside – not even to tell Longstaff they existed.

A jailer led him down a spiral staircase. Longstaff had no official position in the city, none of the resources of an embassy. Terrified he could do nothing more than bring false hope, he felt his skin flinch from the sweating walls and lowering ceilings. They were in the belly of the fortress now, cells to left and right, mould shining on the cracked ceiling. The jailer fumbled with his keys before a squat wooden door. Relieving the man of his torch, Longstaff stepped past him into a cavernous cell. The prisoners drew back from the light, squinting at him from between their fingers. Men and women kept together, filthy, hollow-cheeked, their clothes reduced to rags – but not yet beaten. The sleeping pallets were lined up neatly on one side of the cell, as far as possible from the buckets of shit. There were no torches, only a tiny window where the wall met the ceiling, precious little food or water – none of the luxuries wealthier inmates acquired so effortlessly. A woman with matted grey hair fell to her knees, breaking the silence with a prayer of thanks. Then they were all talking at once, shuffling nearer across the stone floor.

"One at a time," shouted Longstaff, "I can't hear myself think."

A slight young man stepped forward, dressed in the tattered remnants of a priest's robe. He gestured at his companions to be still.

"My name is Thomas Fitch. Who are you?"

"Matthew Longstaff. I've only just found out about you."

The woman approached on her knees, her eyes huge in the dim light. "Have you come to free us?"

"Free us," echoed another figure, further back in the shadows.

Longstaff didn't know what to say. There was no power he could wield on behalf of these poor unfortunates. "Who are you?" he asked. "Where have you come from?"

A tale of mistaken identity and ill-fortune emerged. On their way to the Holy Land, these pilgrims had been taken captive in Tripoli – as retribution for the actions of English privateers. Longstaff groaned. Only a few years earlier, his countrymen had invented a document called the Letter of Mark, which pretended to give merchants the right to recoup any losses at sea. If they claimed to have been attacked by Spanish pirates, then any ship of that nation was fair game. If the pirates had spoken French, then *their* countrymen could be made responsible, and so it went on. There was nothing to stop a merchant from selling his Letter of Mark – and no shortage of captains willing to turn pirate beneath the thin veneer of respectability which it provided.

"We have passports purchased in the Republic of Venice," continued the priest. Other voices clamoured for attention, telling stories to prove their innocence – of the churches they'd visited on Zante, Crete, and Cyprus. Of a journey characterised by sickness, bad food and spoiled beer – as if this motley collection of men and women could be anything other than what they claimed. Longstaff cut them off.

"Have you written to the Venetian ambassador?"

"As soon as we arrived. We've had no reply."

The priest continued, sentences short and to the point as he described their journey north, driven along the dusty roads like a string of horses. "We were told, unless we can pay a ransom – we'll be sold as slaves."

A second man stepped forward, face puce with ill-suppressed rage, still carrying a paunch despite his recent deprivations. "The infidels know we're innocent." He threw up his hands. "We should never have come. My brother warned me. These people care nothing for the truth. Rapacious, Godless bastards."

Longstaff stepped close, raising his voice so everyone could hear. "And what of the privateers who raid these shores? Are the men and women they took any less innocent?"

"You take their side!"

"You haven't been sold yet. More than can be said for the wretches abducted by our countrymen." Longstaff looked at the fat man in his faded finery. "Will anyone pay a ransom for you? The jailers are only keeping you in the hope you might have wealthy friends at home."

"Rapacious," replied the man, "I told you..."

"The masters of any English jail would do the same," interrupted Longstaff. "You've been through a lot. I understand your anger, but it doesn't help our cause." He looked at them expectantly. The brief flame of optimism, ignited by his arrival, had been swiftly extinguished. Men and women fell back on their filthy straw mats. Even the fat man retreated. The priest raised his hand.

"This isn't a schoolroom," said Longstaff. "Speak, if you have something to say."

"I've made a list of our names, professions, our connections at home. I thought it might be useful."

Thank God for sensible men. "You said your name was Fitch?"

The priest nodded. A man from the west of England, judging by his accent. Longstaff scanned the list of twenty-three names. Seventeen men and six women. Four had been marked with an asterisk. Fitch indicated the symbol with a surprisingly clean finger. "These men are able to raise a few pounds. We've undertaken to remain united in adversity, to pool our wealth and insist none accept freedom until we can leave here together."

Longstaff looked round the fetid cell. If it came to it, he doubted any of these men or women would keep to such an agreement. In the meantime, they needed better quarters, fresh water, more plentiful rations. All of which would cost money he didn't have. The Italians in Galata kept a mutual fund for cases like this, but Longstaff doubted they would cough up for English heretics.

"I'm not a wealthy man," he said, "I don't have any official position in Istanbul, but I'll speak to the guards. I'll do what I can to lighten your misfortunes."

Thomas Fitch lowered his head. "We will pray for your success."

*

Aurélie left her husband sleeping, slipping from the room on stocking'd feet. He'd come home late the previous evening, at the end of another long day at the palace. A sudden rush of love made her smile. He'd never been afraid of hard work. Now, in addition to all his other cares, he had to fret about the fate of two dozen unfortunates locked in the Fortress of Seven Towers.

She grabbed a piece of bread as she passed through the kitchen – on her way to one of the finest *hammams* in the city at the invitation of one of its most celebrated women.

Longstaff and Durant, much as she loved them, were both men. Makarios and his friends were men. The prospect of female companionship propelled her across the Golden Horn and on through the streets of 'Stanbul. She didn't stop until she reached the steps of the *hammam* – a beautiful building, cast in the same grey marble as the city's mosques. She slipped through the doors. A beautiful young woman waited to receive her in the dark lobby.

"Aurélie Longstaff?"

Her name sounded unfamiliar in the woman's musical accent. Aurélie nodded, "I'm expected."

The woman handed her a pair of raised wooden shoes inlaid with mother-of-pearl. Aurélie removed her sandals. Clattering against the marble tiles, struggling to keep up with her guide, she hurried into a huge, steam-filled room. In here, away from their menfolk, women had shed their shapeless robes and veils. A couple sat holding hands, staring deep into one another's eyes. A group of older women ate together, talking with such animation that Aurélie felt a sudden ache of loneliness. She looked away in embarrassment, nearly colliding with a raised pool.

"My mistress will join you shortly," said her guide.

"What am I supposed to do?"

"Whatever pleases you."

Hesitantly, Aurélie stepped out of the clogs. She handed the woman her tunic before entering the water, suddenly conscious of the hair on her legs and beneath her arms. *Whatever pleases you.* As if these rituals were as common as eating or drinking. The sensation was glorious. Aurélie could feel the tension of the past few weeks receding – tension she'd hardly been aware of until now. The young woman touched her lightly on the shoulder.

"My mistress will see you now."

She wrapped Aurélie in the folds of a thick towel, then led her to a private room. A woman lay on one of two beds, perhaps ten years older than Aurélie, wearing nothing but a thin linen shift.

"Hubbi Hatun," announced the maid.

"The famous poet," said Aurélie in halting Turkish. "I was honoured to receive your invitation."

Hubbi Hatun smiled at her without rising. She was a widow, Aurélie knew. Rumoured to be one of the sultan's most trusted advisors.

"I see my reputation proceeds me," she replied in the *lingua franca*, her voice smooth and measured, with just enough gravel to suggest she'd known her share of disappointment.

"Your poems are astonishing. I've been reading them with the help of a dictionary."

Hubbi Hatun smiled. "I'm flattered. Perhaps you could be my first translator."

"I wouldn't know where to start."

"With care and attention. Although I understand that in the west you prize originality above precision."

"Your own work is startlingly original," said Aurélie.

"To your eyes, perhaps. Only God creates."

"That's what you believe?"

Hubbi Hatun grinned at her. "Of course not!" She clapped her hands. The maid appeared at once, leading two masseuses into the room.

"We can talk later." The poet pointed at the free bed. Aurélie yielded to the powerful hands, seeking knots along the length of her back with alarming speed. Long after the women had finished, she remained where she was, lying with her head to one side, contemplating the poet's even features.

Hubbi Hatun opened her eyes. "Better?"

"My bones feel like jelly." She smiled. "What am I doing here?"

"Satisfying my curiosity. Frankish women are not expected to remove their hair?"

"Some pluck their eyebrows and the hair from their foreheads."

The poet sighed. Aurélie looked at her again, wondering what it had cost her to make a place for herself at the Ottoman court. What had she gained? Hubbi Hatun was beautiful, but there was nothing soft or accommodating in her appearance.

Aurélie felt a sudden, unsettling sense of how lucky she'd been to find Longstaff. She remembered the first time he'd taken her in his arms, on a moonlit night in the Bay of Naples. When people praised his courage, they usually meant little more than his skill with a sword. Only she knew what it had cost him to give her so much freedom – so much of his strength that it left him weak. Aurélie's life hadn't been easy, but she'd always been loved – sufficiently that she'd never grown to expect the worst of people as a matter of course.

"People say the sultan comes to you for advice," she said. "Am I only satisfying your curiosity – or his as well?"

"Women such as you and I are rare." The poet raised herself on one elbow. Something in her tone forced Aurélie to concentrate. She knew the signs by now. After nearly two years of peace, she felt her life taking on the hard contours of danger again, as if another period of crisis were approaching, a gathering storm of events to batter her fragile dreams.

"The sultan thinks your husband is among the more principled men in this city," added Hubbi Hatun.

"Is that a cause for celebration or alarm?"

"Selim is a better man that people believe."

"Of course," said Aurélie. "I didn't mean…"

"You can speak freely," the poet reassured her. "There are no spies here."

"And no men."

Hubbi Hatun smiled. "Selim may not be perfect, but he has the interests of his people at heart." She hesitated. "Trust is a rare commodity. The Frankish powers battle one another constantly, except when it comes to supplying the Ottoman Empire with munitions. Even in this respect, there is little trust among them – which is why they pay the grand vizier not to undermine their fragile unity."

Aurélie was struggling to keep up. "The grand vizier is working for the European ambassadors?"

"Mehmed Sokollu believes it would be a waste of money to invest in modern weaponry. If the Frankish ambassadors are willing to pay him to advocate for a position he already supports, he sees no reason to refuse their gold." Hubbi Hatun shifted on the bed. "The point is that Selim disagrees."

"He wants to buy munitions?"

"Discreetly. Tin, lead, some technical advice. From a nation which may not feel bound by the Catholic consensus."

"England."

Hubbi Hatun inclined her head in silent confirmation. Aurélie sat up, automatically folding her arms across her chest.

"Why approach me? I'm not English."

"Your life is forfeit if you return to the country of your birth."

Aurélie narrowed her eyes, beginning to enjoy the game. "They'll have forgotten all about me by now. Why not approach Matthew directly?"

"The sultan believes there are strong, moral arguments in favour of the arrangement. Unlike his father, he is a prudent man, able to recognise the natural boundaries of his Empire. To invade Europe would upset the delicate balance of powers on which our present prosperity depends. Selim's only concern is that people beyond the borders of his empire don't mistake his wisdom for weakness."

Aurélie stared at the poet. Even if what she said were true, it was no guarantee Selim wouldn't be succeeded by a more belligerent ruler. She stopped herself, suddenly aware of how cleverly she'd been manipulated. There were arguments against supplying the Ottomans with munitions and there were arguments in favour. Aurélie knew from Longstaff how desperately England needed to find new markets for its wares. More important than the arguments themselves, however, was the identity of the person who made them.

"You want me to convince him?"

The poet's eyes sparkled. "This is how he gets what he wants – official recognition of his status and a trade agreement which will make him the toast of London."

Aurélie burst out laughing. "That's the last thing he'd want."

Hubbi Hatun smiled. Aurélie had just proved her point. No one knew Longstaff like she did. No one stood a better chance of persuading him to break the Christian embargo on the sale of arms to the Ottomans – assuming that's what she wanted.

"This particular aspect of the trade between the two nations will remain confidential," added the poet. "Elizabeth will be able to deny it – just as she currently denies any connection to her pirates in the Mediterranean."

"It sounds as if you've thought of everything."

"The sultan is prepared to be generous." Hubbi Hatun reached up to pull a silken cord. Her attendants returned immediately, bearing what looked like instruments of torture. The poet groaned as she lay back on her bed. Aurélie looked at the beautifully smooth legs, the carefully shaped eyebrows. "I thought they'd finished."

"Finished? When they can still amuse themselves with my ears, my nostrils, the fine hairs on my forearms? Go home, my friend. Talk to your husband. Come back when you have something to tell me."

Aurélie walked the streets of 'Stanboul in a daze. All of Longstaff's hard work, reduced to a clandestine arms deal. She had no idea how she would tell him – only that she would have to choose her moment carefully.

Chapter 13

It was Friday. A day of prayer according to the city's Muslim residents, but not for Longstaff. He ground his teeth as he left the main thoroughfare, reaching the house via a non-descript side street. A servant met him in the foyer, leading him up a flight of stairs and along several twisting corridors before finally ushering him into a large salon on the upper floor. Raimondi and the chevalier were there, along with representatives from Florence, Genoa, Poland. None of them noticed him arrive, too busy craning their necks for a view of the sultan's procession outside.

He watched them for a moment, the thought of asking them for help almost more than he could bear. They would refuse – of course they would refuse. They would laugh in his face. And yet his conscience kept demanding he do everything possible for the pilgrims languishing in the Fortress of Seven Towers.

Longstaff very nearly turned tail; he could go to the palace, seek a measure of satisfaction in the simple tasks which Hector gave him, watch the great chronometer gradually assume its true proportions. He heard the sultan's macebearers shouting in the street outside. Muttering a curse, he edged closer to the diplomats jockeying for position on the balcony. Soldiers marched in eerie silence through the street below – swords at their girdles, guns on their backs – escorting Selim to Friday prayers at the *Eyüp Sultan* mosque. It was hot in the salon, too many sweating men pressed together behind the latticework. The chevalier stood at the centre of the scrum, dressed for the occasion in a silver-trimmed pink suit with buttons fashioned from Brazilian topaz.

A low hum of excitement rose from the assembled men. The Venetian ambassador appeared at Longstaff's elbow. "The elephant," he explained.

Longstaff caught a glimpse of the huge creature shuffling past. The sultan himself came next. The long feathers worn by the men of his personal guard made it seem as if he floated on a bed of clouds.

"Note the pattern on his kaftan," said Raimondi. "He's comparing himself to the sacred tree of Islam. Each leaf is said to bear the name of a living person. When angels fly, the wind from their wings sends some spiralling down. Some faster, some slower – bearing tidings of death."

The chevalier straightened. "I swear," he announced, "that man's turban grows taller by the week!"

Dutifully, the men around him laughed.

A fine one to talk, thought Longstaff. The chevalier appeared shocked to see him. The look he gave Raimondi would have withered a less robust man. The Venetian turned to Longstaff with a smile. "As a former military man, I wonder if you could help us settle an argument?"

"If I can," replied Longstaff – he was here for the pilgrims, not his own satisfaction.

"The chevalier has convinced himself the Turks are ripe for plucking. Do you agree?"

The French ambassador's cheeks turned an angry shade of purple. Longstaff would happily have throttled Raimondi just then. The pilgrims had sent this man letters, begging him to intercede on their behalf. He hadn't even bothered to reply – now he was using him to bait the French ambassador. Longstaff took a deep breath. They were all watching him. Not only the ambassadors, but merchants from a dozen Italian cities. He couldn't refuse the Venetian's poisoned chalice.

"His excellency the chevalier is right on one point. After so many decades of military success, there is reason to believe the Ottomans are growing complacent. A more prudent government would invest in modern defensive batteries – along the Bosphorus, for example."

"But..." pressed Raimondi.

Longstaff bit his lip. "But it's difficult to see how a Christian army could come within a month's march of Istanbul. When it comes to campaigning in the field, the Ottomans still have two major advantages."

"Which are?"

Longstaff looked at the chevalier, fiddling with his buttons. The Frenchman could trace his line back nearly a thousand years. For him, war was a matter of honour – not logistics.

"Rice and camels," said Longstaff. "The Ottomans have an almost unlimited quantity of both."

The chevalier burst out laughing, a high sound, full of whinnying pleasure. Hand on hip, he turned to look at Raimondi. "Your friend thinks we'd lose because of rice and camels?"

He was still laughing as he headed for a table piled high with food and drink.

Raimondi peered at Longstaff. "Are you offended? I can't tell you from your expression."

"The man's a fool."

"I imagine you were the same in battle," continued Raimondi. "Never breaking sweat even in the heat of a fight."

Was it sarcasm? Longstaff didn't recognise himself in the description. Raimondi clapped him on the shoulder. "But you do look troubled, my friend."

"Innocent pilgrims are being held in the Fortress of Seven Towers," blurted Longstaff. It took great self-control not to mention the Venetian passports, or that the pilgrims had already applied to Raimondi for assistance. Instead, he talked about them as individuals: the woman with the matted grey hair, the fat man in faded tunic and torn hose. The young priest whose good sense had so impressed him.

"They were condemned by grief and anger in Tripoli, then again by indifference here. The jailers don't care whether they're innocent or guilty. They only want to know who's going to meet the cost of their incarceration and ransom."

"But, my dear fellow," replied Raimondi, "what do you think I can do for these poor unfortunates?"

There was plenty Raimondi could do; he had money, influence at court. It was an open secret that he and the French ambassador possessed secret ratlines for getting people out of the city – usually countrymen of their own, captured by slavers and condemned to the galleys.

"I've done what I can," said Longstaff. "They're growing weaker. Left in that pit, it won't be long before they start dying."

The chevalier cut in. Longstaff hadn't heard him approach. "Done what you can? You've hardly started. You haven't even appealed to the grand vizier."

Longstaff forced himself to smile. "Mehmed Sokollu dislikes me. If I appeal to him, there's a risk I'll make matters worse."

"So the rest of us are expected to exhaust our limited influence – for the sake of two dozen heretics?"

The chevalier's smile said it all. These men had already made up their minds.

"It seems to me," added Raimondi, "that the real culprits are those damned pirates raiding the Syrian coast. Have you any idea of who they might be?"

"Does it matter," said Longstaff. "The pilgrims are innocent."

"English privateers," suggested the chevalier. "Operating under one of their cursed Letters of Mark."

Longstaff couldn't deny it.

"It's greed, pure and simple" continued the Frenchman with obvious pleasure. "Without breeding – or the steadying influence of the true faith – there's nothing they won't stoop to. You only have to look at this one now..."

Longstaff felt a hand on his arm. "It's true," said Raimondi. "You look ready to kill."

"Rumours have reached us of your exploits in Europe," said the chevalier. "They say you slew so many in battle, your men called you the Lord of War."

Longstaff could have wrung the man's scrawny neck. "I'm trying to help innocent men and women."

"Yes, but you don't make it easy for us, do you? Charging in here, veins bulging in that ridiculous neck of yours."

Longstaff couldn't stand it any longer. He turned on his heel, walking as awkwardly as any of the clockwork figures on his chronometer. The chevalier broke into another whinny of laughter. A servant waited in the corridor outside, looking pointedly at Longstaff's clenched right hand. *Raimondi.* This was how the Venetian worked – winks and nudges and notes slipped from one hand to another. Opening his fist, Longstaff stared at the scrap of paper he'd been given. F*ollow the servant.*

Trailing him warily down the twisting corridors, Longstaff was shown to a small, interior room – a single, latticed window overlooking the grand staircase. He watched a well-known Genoan merchant descend the stairs, passing close enough that Longstaff could hear him breathe.

Was this where Raimondi came to spy on his rivals? One by one, the great and the good of Galata began to trickle down the stairs. The door opened a few minutes later and Raimondi slipped inside.

"The pilgrims wrote to you," said Longstaff. "Begging for help."

"There may be honour among soldiers, my friend. Never among diplomats."

"Letting innocent people die, just to punish me..."

Raimondi raised a finger to his lips. The French ambassador swept down the staircase, the members of his entourage hurrying in his wake.

"Not so loud." The Venetian's own voice never rose above a whisper. He placed a hand on Longstaff's forearm. "We could help one another, you and I. Hasn't Walsingham made that clear?" He smiled, apparently amused by the expression on Longstaff's face. "Between them, the Spanish and French have banned English merchants from the ports and trading towns of Europe. They hope to starve your countrymen into obedience. Venice does not approve."

Longstaff frowned. For centuries, Venice had been the greatest power in the Mediterranean, but the watery city-state had suffered in recent years. The Ottomans had curbed their influence in the Aegean. Worse still, the Portuguese had forged new trade routes from east to west around the Cape of Good Hope, breaking the serene republic's monopoly on silks and spices.

"England and Portugal are allies," said Longstaff.

"No one's asking you to go to war," replied Raimondi. "I'm talking about trade. You need to find new markets for English wool. I'm saying I can make it happen – for the right price. I'll even throw in the pilgrims, though they clearly broke the terms of their agreement."

"How so?"

Raimondi smiled. "Istanbul is not on their itinerary of travel."

"They were brought here in chains, Raimondi!"

The fat ambassador spread his hands complacently. Longstaff felt suddenly exhausted. "What price?"

"A ten percent commission on English trade with Istanbul."

Longstaff felt his mouth fall open. He shook his head.

"Then Mehmed Sokollu will block any possibility of a trade agreement. Your countrymen will starve – both here and on your island."

Longstaff felt nauseous. "The grand vizier isn't a fool. If Spain destroys England, Elizabeth won't be able to support the Low Countries – at a stroke, he'll have helped unify Christendom."

"You have to stop thinking so rationally, my friend. Everyone is compromised, remember? For all his power, the grand vizier lives in fear."

Longstaff shrugged. "Who among us doesn't?"

Raimondi threw up his hands in mock exasperation. "Mehmed Sokollu wouldn't last a day if he thought like that. Nor would I for that matter. If you want to succeed here, you have to behave as if you're the sum total of England's might – as rich as all the gold in its treasury, as dangerous as its combined armies. The grand vizier isn't a man; he's an institution, an army of scribes, a web of informants. He *is* the empire – for exactly as long as he can keep shoring up his own power."

The Venetian ambassador took a step closer. "And he *will* block your efforts, Longstaff, until you agree to my proposal."

He spoke so lightly, so condescendingly. Suddenly desperate to escape, feeling his temper slip its leash, Longstaff produced a golden coin from his purse – the same one Joseph Nasi had sent him by way of Aurélie. He rolled the coin across his knuckles, then held it up between thumb and forefinger.

"What's this," laughed Raimondi, "trying to buy me off already?"

"One of yours," replied Longstaff. He pushed his chest out, forcing Raimondi to take a step back. He knew he would curse himself later, as his own worst enemy – but there had to be a limit to what he would endure. "Note the Lion of Venice stamped on the surface," he said, "along with a promise that it's pure, twenty-two carat gold." He clenched his first around the coin. "Not even close. I wouldn't be surprised if it floated."

For all his vaunted diplomatic skill, Raimondi's eyes filled with sharp fury. "One coin? It could have come from anywhere."

Longstaff forced the Venetian's fingers open, pressing the coin into his sweating palm. "Keep it," he said, playing a hunch. "I have plenty more."

The expression on Raimondi's face confirmed his guess. Longstaff felt a savage rush of joy, akin to the thrill of victory in battle. This was the moment, he knew, when he might force Raimondi to help England reach a trade agreement with the Ottomans *and* take responsibility for the pilgrims.

"I don't want anything from you," he said instead, his voice heavy with contempt. "But if the grand vizier lifts so much as a finger to prevent a trade agreement, I'll expose you in every home and trading-house in Istanbul."

"You're making a mistake," hissed Raimondi.

Longstaff left without another word.

Chapter 14

In Paris, Durant had heard men say that love could only blossom in the space of time between meeting someone and becoming intimate. He'd heard desire described as a weight, dragging men towards the satisfaction of their animal needs. Alternatively, love was wisdom. It was paralysis, its victim suspended between desire and reverence, trapped by the terrible certainty that victory was the surest route to disappointment.

Months had passed between Durant's first fleeting glimpse of Leila and the moment they'd been alone together for the first time. Durant knew himself well enough that he'd half-expected the spell to break – and yet he felt neither paralysed nor disappointed. On the contrary, he felt new-born, a shout of joy permanently on his lips, heart thumping, alive to every sight and smell, excitement leaking into all he touched. Pickled cucumbers with honey, parsley with pomegranate, cauliflower with green olives. Longstaff and Aurélie had complimented him on his recent creations, but still – he knew he needed to curb his wilder inclinations.

The giddiness of love, doubled by gratitude that he could feel this way again. A precious gift, a secret to keep if he wanted to go on seeing her – lie as he lay now, head resting in her lap beneath the painting of Hüsrev and Shirin. A flesh and blood woman. Competent, brave, with an earthy sense of humour in which melancholy flowered as easily as laughter. She was both an open book and a mystery. Every minute of every day, he held her life in his hands. She told him everything and nothing. Never before had he found happiness nestled so completely in single moments.

They'd bathed together; her skin was warm and soft from the water. The silk sleeve of her dressing gown caressed his shoulder. Durant stirred, prompted by desire.

"Don't you have to leave?" she said.

"I never want to leave again."

She rolled her eyes. Durant laughed. She was right. She was always right. He and Khalid had been invited to eat with their master at his home.

"When can I see you again?"

"In a week. Sooner if I can manage it. I'll leave word with the flower seller."

"Tell me how you'll fill the time until our next meeting."

Her long hair tickled his face. "My days are all the same. I'd rather hear about your world."

He told her about his work, his patients and their complaints. In two years, if he worked hard, he would finally qualify as a physician – an ambition first conceived twenty years earlier in the wake of his wife's death from plague.

What would he do then? Go on living in Istanbul with Longstaff and Aurélie? It rankled occasionally, the way they took his solitude for granted, assuming he would stay with them when they moved further up the hill. Longstaff had already suggested he make exploratory visits to tailors and horse-brokers – to order clothes and animals fit for an ambassador. As if his own duties at the hospital were little more than a hobby.

"What is it?" asked Leila. She looked alarmed by his sudden silence.

"Nothing," he reassured her with a smile. "If there's one man I should know better than to resent, it's Matthew Longstaff."

"Your friend?"

Durant chuckled. "The way circumstances have conspired against him. I've never met a man less suited to diplomatic work. He's at the palace nearly every day, trying to fix the machine with his new friend." He looked up at her. "I don't want you to have to go on living with your husband."

Her hands grew still. "He has two other wives," she said. "I probably won't even see him before next week."

"We don't have to stay here," said Durant. "We could leave…"

Even as she continued stroking his forehead, he felt her withdraw. "What would I do in France, Gaetan? How would your daughter react if you returned with a Greek slave in tow?"

Durant thought of his homeland, the noise of Bordeaux, the thunder of tumbrils, carts and coaches, the crash of hammers. He remembered pleasures – a plate of braised pork washed down with a glass of local wine.

"We could go anywhere," he said. "Find an empty island in the Cyclades. Imagine it; one of those little harbour towns, hills behind, a shelf of coloured fishing boats bobbing in the water."

"A dream," she said.

"Is that all it is? All it can be?"

She framed his face in her two hands, looking deep into his eyes. "Promise me you won't do anything stupid," she said. "If you care for my safety, you'll follow my instructions in everything."

He grinned up at her. "What do you think I'm going to do, beat down your door and carry you off by force?"

"It's not funny."

"I know." He reached forward, taking a single violet from the bouquet of flowers, neatly separating the flower from its stem.

"For my sake, you would submit your neck to the bowstring," translated Leila. "You're learning."

In the distance, they heard the call to prayer: *I praise the perfection of God. The perfection of God, the desired, the existing, the single, the supreme. The perfection of God, of Him who taketh unto himself no male or female partner, nor any like Him…*

Time was passing. Durant was expected in the Jewish quarter in less than an hour. Leila kissed him on the lips before pushing him gently to his feet. She began to dress. Durant watched her disappear beneath layers of clothing – damask petticoats, an embroidered dress. She wore a bouquet of glass stones in her hair, arranged to look like flowers. He shrugged into his own trousers and *kameez*. Leila's dress vanished beneath a *ferace,* her hair beneath a white muslin headscarf.

"Ready," she said.

Durant left first, slipping through an anonymous door into the deserted alleyway. In a hurry, preoccupied with his thoughts, he didn't realise that he was being followed through the crowded streets. Khalid was waiting for him at a coffee shop in the Grand Bazaar – a vast stone building on the summit of a hill between the Golden Horn and the Sea of Marmara, a maze of arcades with traders shouting their wares beneath vaults decorated in blue arabesques – salted fish, aniseed, ginger, cinnamon, a riot of sights and smells. Then, at last, the familiar courtyard. Khalid waving to him from a table.

"You're late."

"Couldn't be helped."

"I hope she's worth it."

"No idea what you're talking about."

"Come on," smiled Khalid. "Or we'll be treating bedsores for a month."

There were no ghettoes in Istanbul, no gates that closed on the city's Jewish population each night, but it remained a straightforward task to recognise the boundaries of the Jewish quarter. Turbans gave way to caps, unveiled women sold food and drink from the stalls they passed. Durant looked at Khalid; his young friend gave no sign of discomfort at this relative lack of modesty. Ben Chabib's house was made of stone, like others in the quarter, the modest facade offering no hint of his eminence. Both men stepped back in surprise when he opened the door in person.

"You're late!"

"My fault," said Durant.

Ben Chabib waved them inside. "Your loss," he said. "The garden's in shadow now. The light was extraordinary a few minutes ago." He led them into the dining room, where they startled a woman lighting candles on an ornate candelabra, her hips broad with age, dark hair streaked grey.

"My wife, Rebecca," said Ben Chabib with obvious pride. "The years have been kinder to her than they have to me."

Durant took her hand. "An honour to meet you, madam."

She gave him a mock curtsey. "Welcome to our home."

Durant looked at Khalid. The young doctor needed a moment to accustom himself to Rebecca's presence. Seeing a pile of books balanced precariously at one end of the sideboard, Durant stooped to inspect the titles.

"I remember you saying it was bad for the digestion to read at table."

"What's good for the mind is good for the body," smiled Ben Chabib.

Durant's eye stopped at a large, leather-bound book. Ibn Sīnā's *The Book of Healing*. "A previous teacher of mine owned a copy of this book," he said. "I read it soon after I lost my finger. I was plagued by phantom pain; it was the eeriest sensation. Ibn Sīnā showed me how it could be overcome." Durant touched the book's spine with the blunt end of his missing finger.

"What did Ibn Sīnā suggest?" Khalid pronounced the name with reverence. Had Ben Chabib left the book there deliberately to help his young pupil feel at home? Somehow, it was easier to ignore their differences at the hospital, where the groans and tears of their patients obscured the demands of cross, carpet and candelabra.

"It's a trick performed with mirrors," said Durant, taking his seat at the round table. "Although I didn't have one at the time. I bent over a bucket of water instead – left hand behind my back, concentrating on the reflection of my right hand. I moved my fingers, one by one, from thumb to pinkie, first with my right hand and then with my left, never taking my eyes from the reflection." He shrugged. "It may sound ridiculous, but it worked."

"You haven't told us how you lost your finger," said Khalid.

For a moment, Durant was tempted to recount the tale as an anecdote. *Would you believe I did it myself?* He shook his head. "Forgive me. It's not a period of my life I like to remember."

A servant appeared in the doorway with a heavy tray. Behind her, Durant glimpsed a man in white, bent over a selection of steaming pots. "From our conversations, I thought you did your own cooking."

"It's the eating I enjoy, not the labour." Ben Chabib took a piece of bread from the basket in front of him. "Blessed art Thou," he said. "O Lord our God, King of the Universe, who brings forth bread from the earth." He turned to Khalid. "Do you wish your own blessing?"

Khalid sang a musical prayer. Both men looked at Durant. "Amen," he said, reaching forward to help himself. The food was exquisite. Black caviar served on miniature pancakes with a generous helping of yoghurt.

"We thought of moving the table outside," said Ben Chabib.

"We were worried you would be cold," said Rebecca.

"There *is* still a chill in the air after dark," said Durant.

"The garden is so beautiful at this time of year," added Ben Chabib. "An uncluttered home to remind us of our nomadic roots." He smiled. "And a garden to offer a hint of what awaits."

Khalid nodded enthusiastically. "In my faith, also, we imagine the afterlife as a garden."

"We tend to picture a city on a hill," said Durant dryly. "God knows why."

"Istanbul is a city on many hills," said Ben Chabib, "and a city of many gardens."

"Probably why the food is so good," said Durant. He saw Rebecca touch her husband's hand as the next course arrived, a gesture full of unconscious affection. Barring disasters, this might be a picture of Longstaff and Aurélie in the future. Rebecca stood to offer Durant a second helping. Idly, he wondered how Ben Chabib might have described his two students to her. Steady Khalid, already married with children but still not sure of himself or his place in the world. And Durant, older than the other students, a hollow man inclined to take risks with his diagnoses. He thought of Leila, slowly filling the empty spaces inside – then realised his dinner companions were staring.

"The smile on your face," said Khalid.

"Not something we often see at the hospital."

Durant blinked. "You're teasing me." A blush rose in his pale cheeks, kept in place with wine as the talk flowed easily, back and forth across the table. A servant entered with a tray of sweet pastries. Rebecca rose to her feet, hiding a smile behind one hand.

"If you'll excuse me," she said. "I have to be up early in the morning."

"Why don't we finish our evening in the garden?" said Ben Chabib, producing a clay pipe. "Rebecca dislikes the smell."

Khalid cleaned his hands in a bowl of fresh water, then turned towards Mecca to thank Allah and his host for the food. The garden lay shrouded in darkness. It was a clear night; the sky above glittered with stars – like lights on land with a milky river rushing past. The same servant refreshed their drinks – water sweetened with honey for Khalid, more wine for Durant and their host.

"You're a lucky man," said Durant, making himself comfortable on the bench, "to have such a loving and accomplished wife."

Ben Chabib did not disagree. He exhaled a puff of smoke, somehow suggesting that he and Rebecca enjoyed the same comfortable relationship when it was just the two of them alone.

"I hope Tülin and I are still as happy after so many years together," said Khalid.

"Medicine is a sacred calling." Ben Chabib spun the wine in his glass, watching as if the secrets of the future might reveal themselves in the dark liquid. "A happy marriage has always seemed an indispensable part of doing it well."

It was hard to be certain in the darkness. Durant felt sure that both men were staring at him.

"I was married," he said. "My wife died."

"My condolences."

"I was still a young man when it happened." He tried to make the calculation. The date of his wife's death was engraved in his heart, but it was a long time since he'd reckoned the number of years.

"You never thought of remarrying?" asked Khalid.

Durant was relieved when Ben Chabib answered for him.

"It takes time to recover from a great loss. Some tragedies are so heavy that life never fully recovers its sweetness. That doesn't mean it has to go on being a source of misery." The physician smiled. "Recently, I've had the feeling you may have reached the same conclusion."

Durant stiffened. "I hadn't realised I was so transparent."

"You're not. Quite the opposite, but I've spent a lifetime scrutinising people." Ben Chabib chuckled. "Let me know if I can be of service. My position at the hospital gives me some influence. I'd be happy to speak to the woman's family on your behalf."

"You're very kind." Durant lowered his head, both to show his gratitude and to hide his embarrassment. Leila's only family was her husband. "As a young man, I didn't love sensibly. My father came within an ace of disowning me – but I've never regretted my decision, despite all that subsequently happened."

"And now?"

He shrugged. "I'm no different to most men, it seems – fated to keep on repeating the same mistake."

Khalid frowned in confusion. "Is it a question of conversion? Embracing Allah is a simple process. I can…"

"You're both very kind." Durant spoke more sharply than he'd intended, hoping to bring the conversation to an end. He should never have opened his mouth.

"She's married?" asked Ben Chabib quietly.

Khalid looked astonished, as if the idea had never crossed his mind. "But then, how can you love her? And, loving her, how can you agree to see her. You're risking her life."

Durant shook his head. He was an even worse man than Khalid realised. Even now, in the long, cold stretches of the night, it wasn't her safety he worried about. He knew the risks she was running, but not why. Could she really love him? Or could it have been any man walking past her window – as long as he offered the chance of escape?

"There must be some way she can leave her husband."

"We are not in Europe now!"

"She's his third wife," said Durant. "Her husband controls her without providing anything resembling a life in return. They have no children…"

"She is another man's wife." Khalid's voice grew louder. "I don't want to hear any more."

"If a man can have multiple wives, why shouldn't a woman take a second husband?"

Khalid raised a hand as if defending himself. Seeing marks of genuine anger on his friend's face, Durant took his leave soon afterwards. Khalid shook his hand after the European fashion but would not meet his eye. Durant knew he'd handled the situation badly, tempted into foolishness by the chance to talk about her, give voice to the swarm of thoughts which consumed his waking hours.

And yet he hadn't said a word about the joy he felt whenever she was near – or the doubts which continued to torment him.

Chapter 15

Fists hammered at the street door, startling Longstaff from sleep. He hadn't meant to drop off, staring at the letters piled on his desk. Demands from Walsingham and begging letters from the pilgrims. He'd grown used to Walsingham, but the letters from the fortress were still a relatively new form of torture – the same wretched phrases over and over again, gnawing at the foundations of his compassion.

Cradling his head on his forearms for just a moment, he'd seen golden coins dance in the darkness – the lion of Venice, Raimondi's pinched eyes and heavy jowls. Men drawing swords. These days, he fought more often in his dreams than in reality, defending himself against phantoms, a cornered animal, enemies pounding at the door to reach him.

He lifted his head. *What in God's name...* Longstaff stumbled down the stairs, pausing in the courtyard to splash his face with water. Cowering beneath the small grill in the outer door, Hamid made way with an expression of terrified relief. Longstaff saw a detachment of four janissary soldiers in full uniform.

"Matthew Longstaff? You're wanted at the palace."

At least it wasn't the Fortress of Seven Towers. Longstaff remained at the grill. "What's happened?" he asked in Turkish.

He knew the question was pointless. Janissaries did not indulge in speculation. Leaving them in the street, he dragged a clean tunic over his head, fastened a short cloak around his shoulders, then gave Hamid his *dragoman's* address.

"Francesco di Testa." He repeated the name twice. "You have to find him. Tell him to find me at the Imperial Palace."

The janissaries moved fast. Two ahead and two behind. A *caique* waited for them at the docks. As hard as the oarsmen rowed, Longstaff still had time to check his reflection in the water and empty his bladder from the back of the boat. God alone knew when he'd next have the chance. He noticed activity in the Imperial Boatyards. Men running back and forth, thick as flies in the rigging of the sultan's ships.

It was the fifth of May, he remembered. Tomorrow was the Ottoman Feast of Hizir – when the sultan's Kaptan Pasha would take his fleet into the Aegean on their annual tour of the islands. For the inhabitants of Istanbul, it marked the beginning of summer. The waters around them were already choked with pleasure craft – holidaymakers with picnic hampers travelling into the countryside. Longstaff counted backwards. Padron Lettero had sailed for Malta at the end of March. Still too soon to hope that his consignment of silk had reached England. Where was it now? At the bottom of the Mediterranean? In the hands of a corsair? Making its slow and steady way along the coast of Portugal?

Concentrate. As the janissaries marched him through the streets of 'Stanboul, Longstaff made an effort to walk with his head up, treating the soldiers as if they were an honour guard. Had his first attempt at smuggling been discovered? The men they passed in the outer courtyard of the palace did not appear to regard him with hostility.

The soldiers didn't break stride until they reached Hector's small pavilion. Longstaff shouldered his way through the press of people inside – palace functionaries mostly, all wringing their hands. The mechanic sat on the floor, staring stupidly at a pile of torn and twisted metal.

"What happened?"

"Your clock." He looked up at Longstaff. "Cowardly pissing vandals."

The chronometer. Not again. It wasn't possible. Longstaff turned on the mob of uniformed functionaries. "Who did this?"

An elderly man cleared his throat. "Janissaries are searching the palace. If the culprit is still here, he will be found."

Longstaff noted the gold headdress; an item of clothing worn by the sultan's most senior treasurer. Of course, he thought. This mess was his responsibility.

"It happened during the night," said Hector. "Someone set about it with a hammer. The guards were slow to react."

"I thought you slept here?"

"I have a life, Longstaff."

A young page ran into the pavilion, skidding to a halt in front of the treasurer. "The sultan wants you."

The treasurer turned pale.

"Hector and the Englishman, as well," added the boy.

The sanded pathways were crowded with servants devoted to the sultan's comfort: turban folders, coffee makers, messengers, door keepers. Could one of them be the saboteur? Longstaff thought of Raimondi Maltrapillo. Could he have bribed a palace servant to attack the clock? The sultan and his grand vizier were waiting in a pavilion built out over the Golden Horn. Still too angry to feel nervous, Longstaff dropped to his knees.

The portly monarch paced with the controlled fury of a caged tiger. The treasurer shuffled forward. "We have men searching the palace," he repeated. "If the culprits are still here, they will be found."

Selim stared at him, visibly struggling to hold his temper. "You owe the Englishman an apology."

In Francesco's absence, Hector took over the role of translator. Longstaff felt a sudden chill, aware of how much power was assembled around him. The treasurer cleared his throat.

"I've already explained what happened."

"I didn't ask you to explain."

"Your majesty," interrupted Longstaff. "Might I be permitted to ask a question. How badly is the clock damaged?"

The sultan gestured for his mechanic to answer. Hector had to perform as his own translator now, speaking first in Ottoman Turkish, then in the *lingua franca*.

"If I were allowed to work in peace," he said. "Somewhere free from distraction, I believe we can keep to the agreed date."

It was less than ten days away. Longstaff thought of the ruined clock. It didn't seem possible. The grand vizier spoke for the first time, a thoughtful expression on his hawk-like face. "They must have been watching," he said. "Waiting for you to leave the machine unguarded."

"I make the same overnight trip each week," replied Hector. "We have to ensure the saboteur can't finish what he started."

"He wouldn't dare," said the treasurer, then visibly quailed beneath his master's scornful expression.

"I'll surround the pavilion with a hundred janissaries," he said.

The grand vizier rolled his eyes. "Didn't you hear the mechanic? He needs peace and quiet, not a company of soldiers breathing down his neck."

"Perhaps the treasury?" suggested Hector mildly.

"What about the treasury?"

"It's secure. I wouldn't be disturbed. We can't allow the saboteur to win," he added, lowering his eyes.

Longstaff stared. He'd been in the city long enough to understand that this was an extraordinary request. After the harem, there was no more private space in the Empire. The sultan seemed momentarily struck dumb. The grand vizier steepled his fingers.

"Out of the question," snapped the treasurer.

"I'll be the judge of that," said Selim.

"It's unprecedented."

"What do you call an attack on my possessions? On my dignity?" The sultan took a step nearer his treasurer. "Within the precincts of the Imperial Palace?"

"Of course, there's no question of coming and going as I please," said Hector. "I no longer need the Englishman's help. Only the chronometer itself, my tools – sufficient food and drink for the next ten days."

"You're offering to remain locked inside for all that time?" asked the grand vizier.

Hector lowered his eyes. "The sultan's dignity is at stake."

Mehmed Sokollu cocked his head to one side. Longstaff wondered what calculations passed through his formidable mind before he turned to Selim.

"I see no obvious objection. The man himself is one of your treasures, after all." *As am I.* The words were left unsaid. "The final decision is yours, your majesty."

The sultan chewed his lip. For all his wounded pride, it was clear the idea made him uncomfortable – and yet the clock had been a gift. What was it Hector had said? Selim loved the Frankish novelties for their bells and whistles, as a child loves his toys. He stared at his elderly treasurer with obvious distaste. "Your most trusted aide will be sealed inside along with him. Neither man will touch any object not immediately relevant to his task – on pain of death. Both will be searched on their release and a full inventory made of the treasury contents." He turned to Longstaff. "This attack was directed against you, too," he said. "You may ask a boon of me."

The offer was unexpected. Longstaff's mind raced. Should he ask for the negotiations to begin at once, to have his position in Istanbul recognised? But those rewards would be his when Hector made the chronometer perform its magic.

"Your majesty," he said. "Twenty-four English pilgrims are currently imprisoned in the Fortress of Seven Towers, charged with a crime they did not commit. If it pleases you to grant me a favour, I ask that you set them at liberty, so that they may complete their pilgrimage or return home as they please."

Selim did not hesitate. "See that it's done." He waved in the direction of his grand vizier, then swept out of the pavilion. Mehmed Sokollu whistled softly.

"What a foolish, absurd suggestion." The treasurer was furious. "What in God's name were you thinking?"

"My lord," Hector spread his hands. "I didn't think…"

"That much is painfully obvious." The treasurer glanced at the grand vizier, clearly reluctant to continue lecturing the mechanic in front of his colleague. "Gather your things," he snapped. "Meet me at the treasury in an hour."

In the event, it took more than three to transport all the various sections of the chronometer, as well as Hector's few personal affects. Already thinking ahead, the mechanic made detailed drawings for a reinforced wagon to transport the finished clock.

"Are you sure about this?" asked Longstaff, walking alongside his friend as they trailed the servants through the gardens.

Hector laughed. "You want to talk me out of it?"

Longstaff shook his head. "But at least ask them to let you out at night. You'll go mad in there."

"Surrounded by the world's most precious treasures? For a few days, my friend, I'll be the richest man in the world."

Longstaff shook his head in exasperation. He'd heard rumours of the sultan's treasury. Now he stood before the huge doors, flanked on either side by towering columns. He wouldn't have volunteered to spend even a day on the far side.

There was no sign of the treasurer. Hector made himself comfortable at the foot of a cherry tree, peeling a thin strip of bark to use as a toothpick. Longstaff sat down beside him.

"I'm sorry," he said. "The attack on the clock was an attack on me."

"You don't know that."

Nothing else made sense. Longstaff knew he was a difficult man to attack directly. His companions were well chosen, his food purchased and prepared by his closest friend, his routines established in collaboration with the most far-seeing woman he'd ever met. He could easily imagine the French ambassador growing frustrated by his apparent imperviousness to poison or accident – but an attack on the sultan's dignity within the walls of his palace? Longstaff didn't think the chevalier knew how to be so brazen.

"Whoever they were," said Hector, "we're lucky they had no idea what they were doing. The damage is mostly superficial. I'm not saying it will be easy, but I'll get your chronometer working again."

Longstaff nodded at the treasury doors. "If you're not too distracted."

"You think my head will be turned by all that gold?" Hector grinned. "Musical instruments, armour, furs, carpets heaped to the ceiling, cloths and satins. God knows how many records, scrolls, paintings, all hidden from the common eye." He sounded like a child in a sweet shop. "The spoils of war and the accumulated knowledge of mankind."

The accumulated knowledge of mankind. Longstaff had heard the expression before. He thought of Aurélie. Her quest to find the fabled Devil's Library had ended in death and destruction.

"It doesn't stir your imagination?" asked Hector.

Longstaff shrugged. "I'm a simple man."

"I know. I was there, remember? I saw you offered your heart's desire by the world's most powerful man – and heard you ask him to set two dozen strangers at liberty."

"You think it was a mistake?"

A procession of men approached along the sanded path. The treasurer and four of his junior ministers, all dressed in glittering kaftans. Hector flicked his makeshift toothpick into the grass. "I think most men would have chosen differently."

The treasurer was still furious with Hector. "If you leave so much as a scratch on any item in there," he hissed, "it will mean our heads."

"I'm sorry, your excellency." The mechanic didn't sound remotely contrite. "It wasn't my intention to cause you trouble."

The treasurer spat in disgust, then gestured at his subordinates to begin work. The first removed an embroidered covering from the padlock. All four junior ministers leaned forward to confirm the seal was intact.

"You've made an enemy there," whispered Longstaff, watching the treasurer produce the most ornate key he'd ever seen.

"I've always had issues with authority." Hector grinned, teeth flashing against the dark beard. "You're no different."

"Me? I was a soldier. Following orders is what I do."

"You're not a soldier anymore. Round peg in a square hole, same as me."

Longstaff sighed. Was there really no one in the city who thought he made a convincing diplomat?

"Anyway," added Hector, "it's not as if I have anything better to look forward to. The sultan wants a canal built between the Volga and the Don. Guess who's going to be spending the next five years in a pestilential swamp?"

The treasurer silenced them with a look. The seal was broken, the huge doors opened with grave ceremony. Light tip-toed inside, offering a slow glimpse of rooms extending into the far distance. Piece by piece, the janissaries piled the battered chronometer alongside silver candlesticks and satin banners, beneath carpets and *kilims* hanging from second-storey arcades. Boxes of dried fruit, cured meat and a barrel of drinking water followed. Hector and the treasurer's young aide were the last to enter, standing awkwardly among the wealth of nations as the heavy doors swung shut.

Longstaff felt oddly bereft as he walked home. Market stalls overflowed with rhubarb, currants, and sweet wines from the east. Tailors' dummies displayed rich silks and intricate textiles. The potential for trade was vast and yet the English in this part of the world were little better than pirates. A trade agreement would give them a chance to operate legitimately, but how many would have the wit to seize it? Longstaff did his best to imagine a brotherhood of nations, overlooking their differences, bound by ties of mutual prosperity.

His belly rumbled; he hadn't eaten in hours. Finding a table at a modest restaurant, he lingered over a glass of Albanian *boza* and half a dozen small skewers of grilled lamb. The light was failing when he stood, only partly restored in spirits. The Ottomans didn't enforce a curfew; he was abroad on legitimate business with enough money in his purse to pay for a *caique* across the Golden Horn – despite the exorbitant price for a crossing after dark. Even for a man as well-travelled as Longstaff, Istanbul had been a shock at first. Now, he carried coins from Venice, the low countries, Austria, and Spain without a second thought. The mechanic was a capable man. He would make the chronometer perform its wonders on the agreed day. Transported by its magic, the sultan would grant the *Capitulations* Longstaff sought without reference to his grand vizier. The silk would fetch an astonishing price in London.

Istanbul was a city of hills, each one contributing its own twist to the impossible tangle of lanes. Turning at random, Longstaff passed through streets raised on artificial terraces, slipped beneath aqueducts, followed walls which cut across gardens – knowing he only had to follow the gentle pull of gravity to find his way. He was looking forward to crossing the Golden Horn by night, staring up at the stars from the back of a swift *caique*. He hardly noticed the streets grow narrower, the shutters more securely fastened. The ground beneath his feet levelled out, the smell of the sea overpowering.

A knife appeared from nowhere, struck at his belly. Longstaff twisted like a fish, felt cold steel draw a line of fire across his guts.

Desperately he lunged, hoping to seize an arm, a shoulder, even a handful of clothing. *Where was he?* Movement in the darkness. The long blade flashed. Longstaff rolled, his thoughts in chaos. Lashing out, he struck a glancing blow. The man took a backward step, blade slashing at darkness. Longstaff rolled again, tore the short cloak from his shoulders and wrapped it round his fist. The man was quick, bigger than him but clumsy. He stabbed again. Longstaff caught the blow on his protected hand, reaching for his own short knife.

It was a miracle he was still alive. He took a step forward, the old song of violence rising in his blood. The assassin struck again. Longstaff let the knife pass between torso and bicep. Clamping the assailant's arm, trapping the blade long enough to step close, crunch his forehead into the bastard's nose. A muffled explosion of cartilage, the hot rush of blood. Longstaff's teeth flashed white in the darkness. He set his feet and shoved, forcing his attacker against the wall, knocking the wind from his lungs. Their eyes locked. Longstaff pressed his knife against the man's throat.

"Who sent you?"

The man fought, gambling that Longstaff wouldn't kill him. The impact of his body against the wall had loosened Longstaff's grip. He lost control of the man's right hand. No choice but to spin inside his embrace, catch his wrist, stop the dagger just a hair's breadth from his own chest.

Longstaff grunted with the effort. Holding the man wedged between his back and the wall, deflecting the knife's course past his own torso, hearing it slice through flesh.

He let the body fall.

"Who sent you?" he demanded. "Tell me and I'll find you a doctor."

The man replied with a blood-stained grin. He died without a word. Longstaff let the head fall back with a curse. The scuffle had taken place in near silence; it couldn't have lasted more than a few seconds. The assassin had picked his moment with care, attacking from shadow. Longstaff peered up at the shuttered windows.

Stop! He was thinking too fast. He took deep breaths, waiting for outraged householders to light the lamps in their windows. *Nothing but the beating of his own heart in a sea of silence.* Longstaff stared at his bloody hands. The wound across his belly was little more than a scratch. The back of his tunic was wet, sticky, growing clammy. He could hide the stains beneath his cloak, pray the long tear would disappear in darkness.

Longstaff remained rooted to the spot. He hadn't done anything wrong. No reason he couldn't start shouting for the watch. Methodically, he searched the body. Nothing, not a purse, nor a coin nor a key. Would a simple footpad take so much trouble to hide his identity? Longstaff bent low over the face. The man was young, powerfully built, with the shoulders of a stevedore or an oarsman. Or a soldier, but the attack had been too clumsy. His hands were rough. Longstaff pulled down the cloth shorts. He was intact – a Christian. What did that prove?

Laughter sounded in the distance. Longstaff rolled the corpse flush against the wall, where he hoped it would lie unseen until morning. There was a fountain at the next crossroads; he washed his hands and face, inspecting himself as best he could by the light of the moon. His boots were spotted with blood, the cloak only partly covered his stained tunic. Nothing he could do but hope for the best. The streets were dark, the wharf mercifully empty of people. God, but he wanted a drink. A Genoese merchant, just then negotiating a price to cross the Horn, hailed him hopefully.

"Shall we share a boat? If you're crossing to Galata..."

"Of course," said Longstaff, "I'd be delighted."

Having supped too well, the merchant fell asleep as the oarsmen pushed off. Longstaff sat facing them, beneath a vast field of stars reflected in the milky soft waters. It felt like a dream, a parallel universe in which the attack had never taken place – in which a healthy young man hadn't just died.

Longstaff might have spent the last few months attempting to acquire the polish of a courtier, but he was under no illusion that he made a likely mark for street thieves. Someone had painted a target on his back – but who?

Chapter 16

Longstaff raised a hand to knock at the door of Aurélie's workroom, then hesitated. Five days had passed since the attempt on his life and he still hadn't told her. She'd been asleep when he returned home. The following morning, after he'd woken from restless dreams filled with the smell of blood – as soon as the house had grown still – he'd taken his stained clothes from their hiding place and burned them in the courtyard.

He took a breath and knocked. It was still early. Aurélie did not generally welcome interruptions. Soon, Hector would emerge from his period of isolation in the Imperial Treasury. The chronometer would either work or it wouldn't and there was nothing more he could do to influence the outcome. His desk was clear. No more meetings to arrange, letters to answer, or documents to prepare for the negotiations he hoped would begin in a few days. He was restless, desperate to get away from the city for a few hours. He hadn't killed a man since France, more than two years ago.

"Come in."

He found her bent over one of her clay tablets. She barely looked up when he greeted her from the doorway. "I'm sorry, I know you're busy."

He feared she might not understand what he wanted from her. "It's beautiful outside," he started again. "When was the last time we dropped everything and went into the countryside?"

She carried on working for a moment. Longstaff was on the point of apologising; there would be other opportunities. She looked up, a broad smile on her beautiful face.

"That's a wonderful idea."

"It is?"

"I'll get my things."

Things? Ready to set off at once, Longstaff paced impatiently in the courtyard. Aurélie handed him a heavy wicker basket when she joined him, her hair neatly hidden beneath a silk scarf.

"What in God's name have you got in here?"

"You'll see."

They engaged a *caique* at the docks, the oarsmen charting a swift course to the Bosphorus, past myriad skiffs and sailboats, heading north away from the city. The warehouses gave way to a succession of large houses, gardens sloping gently to the water. Aurélie leaned back with a sigh of pleasure, one hand on Longstaff's thigh.

"You're worried about the demonstration."

It wasn't a question. She knew him too well for that. Longstaff still hadn't received any word from Hector or the palace. He wasn't worried – he was terrified. "Enough that I'd rather hear about your work."

"I'm getting closer." She spoke English for the extra degree of privacy it gave them. "When we arrived in Suffolk, do you remember how we found your old home?"

"A bloody mess," replied Longstaff with a smile. The windows had been boarded up, the great hall filled with broken furniture, owls and bats living in the rafters.

"I suggested we knock the place down and start again. The Christian Church tried to do the same when they grew powerful enough in Europe, determined to bury the past rather than face it. But then the night-birds can never be released – the same corruptions and abuses creep back in. History provides the only true window through which we can release them."

Longstaff knew she was looking for proof that the stories told in Genesis had their origin in earlier tales. "That's why this is so important to you?"

"You sound surprised?"

"I can't imagine that more than a handful of people will listen."

"Even if I'm right?"

"Especially if you're right."

She nestled closer in the crook of his arm. "Then a handful will have to do."

The river grew narrower here. Looking back the way they'd come, Longstaff saw two janissary soldiers in a following *caique*.

"Friends of yours?" asked Aurélie, following his gaze.

"Nothing to worry about."

"We're being followed?"

"Just me. Ever since the chronometer was attacked."

The janissaries fell back, disappearing from view as Longstaff and Aurélie passed beneath a bridge spanning two bays. Longstaff told the oarsmen to land at the next village, where Francesco had told him he could borrow horses from one of the Ottoman hostels. Aurélie was a superb horsewoman. The picnic basket balanced awkwardly in front of him, Longstaff struggled to keep up as they passed through meadows still littered with debris from the recent *Hizir* celebrations. He pointed at a series of large stones.

"You've seen me practising with the Turkish bow," he said. "This is one of the places where people come to compete."

Aurélie shaded her eyes. "Some of those stones must be two hundred yards away."

"No one in living memory has reached the furthest of them." Longstaff shrugged. "It seems men used to be stronger."

"Or someone would like us to think they were."

They passed over the brow of a hill, descending through thick forest before finally emerging at the edge of a hidden bay. Aurélie gasped.

"Francesco recommended it," said Longstaff.

"It's beautiful!"

Standing at the water's edge, they saw mackerel, tunnies, bream – so many that Longstaff might have scooped them from the water with his bare hands. Aurélie produced a blanket from the basket, spreading it in the shade of an unfamiliar tree, then covering it with a series of treats – fresh fruit, bread, cuts of cold lamb and a lump of goat's cheese the size of a fist. Longstaff's mouth watered. He had no idea how she'd managed to prepare it all in such a short space of time. There was even a bottle of *boza*, which he left to cool between two rocks in the river. His back cracked as he settled on the blanket.

"Come here," she said, beginning to knead the muscles in his shoulders. "You're tense."

Longstaff released a low groan of pleasure. "It's not easy, trying to play Raimondi and the chevalier at their own game. You wouldn't believe how hard I find it not to give them both a smack."

She dug her fingers into his flesh. Longstaff knew immediately that he'd said something foolish.

"Do you have any idea how often I have to bite my lip to keep from offending some man's pride?"

"You manage it with such grace."

"A lifetime's practice."

He looked at her. "What if it's too late for me to learn the same trick? What if violence is all I know?"

"Rubbish," she snorted. "Could you have freed the pilgrims by storming the Fortress of Seven Towers? Or secured an audience with the sultan by challenging him to a duel? Persistence is what you know, Matthew – not violence. Aren't you enjoying it at all?"

"What?"

"The plotting and planning – matching your wits against Raimondi and the others."

Longstaff didn't look round. "As soon as the *Capitulations* are signed, I intend to resign in favour of whoever Walsingham wants to send as my replacement."

He heard a catch in her voice. "And then what?"

"Don't worry," he said. "I won't be dragging you to England, if that's what you mean."

Aurélie shook her head. "We were told to stay away for two years. There's nothing to stop us going back. Not anymore."

"I know how unhappy you were there, Aurélie. I know how happy you are here."

"But what will you do?" she asked again.

"Walsingham's new man will need help." Longstaff rolled onto his back, grinning up at her. "Maybe we'll start that family we're always talking about. I'd be happy raising our child, teaching him swordplay while you continue your investigations in the desert."

"And if we have a girl?"

He pulled her close. "She'll become the finest swordswoman in the Ottoman Empire. Even better than her mother."

He felt her hands grow still on his shoulders. "Our escort have decided to make an appearance."

The two janissaries walked down to the water's edge, carefully unwinding their turbans before wading into the river. They swam for several minutes, laughing and splashing one another, then returned to dry land and settled on their knees to pray. Longstaff retrieved the bottle of *boza* from the cool water. "You see," he said. "Not such bad fellows after all."

They drank in silence while the janissaries retreated into the trees. Eager to follow their example and swim, Longstaff knew it would mean revealing the long scratch on his stomach. "Can I ask you a hypothetical question?"

She frowned. "If you must."

Longstaff finished his beer. "You know the people I have to deal with here. Who do you think would profit most from my death?"

Aurélie raised a hand to her open mouth.

"We agreed," Longstaff reminded her. "It's a hypothetical question."

"Is that why you've started carrying your knives again?"

"You noticed?" He produced one from his boot, throwing it into the exposed roots of the nearby tree. A single bead of dark juice ran slowly down the blade. "Liquorish," he said, delighted by the discovery.

"What aren't you telling me?"

"A man attacked me. He may have been a common footpad."

"He got away?"

"In a manner of speaking."

"The same man who tried to sabotage the chronometer?"

Longstaff couldn't look her in the eye. "The attack happened on the same day. Hypothetically."

"Five days ago? Why didn't you tell me?" Longstaff could see the effort she was making to control her temper. "Two unrelated attacks?" She shook her head. "Have you been going out of your way to offend people?"

"No more than usual. Raimondi and I had a falling out."

"The chevalier strikes me as a likelier candidate."

"He barely acknowledges the fact I exist."

"A long-standing ally of the Guise family? Trust me, he knows you exist."

"I'm hardly a threat to him."

"Not yet. There is one other possibility – you've borrowed a huge sum of money from Joseph Nasi."

"He has no reason to want me dead." Restlessly, Longstaff knelt at the foot of the tree, gathering a dozen drops of the dark juice. Aurélie drank from his cupped hands.

"Delicious.

"Will you swim with me?"

"Not today."

"You don't mind if I do?"

"Matthew, promise me you'll be careful."

"I won't go far."

"Not in the water. Idiot." She punched him on the arm.

Longstaff stripped to his linen shorts, yelling as he raced into the water, windmilling his powerful arms with more enthusiasm than grace. He was fifty yards from shore before he turned to look at her. So beautiful it made his heart break.

More courageous than a company of soldiers. He wanted to stay with her here, sleep for hours in the shade of the liquorish tree. They would come again, he promised himself. Once the chronometer had worked its magic. As soon as the *Capitulations* between England and the Ottoman Empire had been signed – as soon as the threat of violent death had been relegated to a distant memory.

Chapter 17

From her workroom in the courtyard, Aurélie watched Elif and Hamid leave for the day. She hadn't realised it was so late – and had precious little to show for the hours she'd spent at her desk. Too distracted. Longstaff had told her about the attempt on his life. She had repaid his honesty with silence, choosing to conceal her meeting with Hubbi Hatun.

One step at a time, she told herself. They were due at the palace tomorrow, when Longstaff would reveal his chronometer to the sultan and an audience of invited guests. She wanted him to succeed, of course, but if the demonstration were a failure – would the poet's offer still stand? She saw no reason to torture her husband until she knew for sure.

Longstaff served a nation which had sent him into exile twice. He did so – at least partly – so that she and Durant could live as they wanted in Istanbul. Perhaps the Frenchman could help? She found him in the kitchen, enveloped in a symphony of glorious aromas. Aurélie took a seat at the rough-hewn table, watching Durant move around the kitchen like a dancer on the stage.

"If you're going to sit there," he said, throwing her an aubergine, "at least make yourself useful."

He sliced, diced and chopped with the precision of a surgeon. She tried to emulate him, marvelling at the deep purple, the firm skin parting neatly beneath the sharp blade. She nearly cut herself when he started whistling.

"You're in a good mood today."

"Shouldn't I be?" He looked oddly defensive. "I spend my days performing worthwhile tasks."

"I wasn't criticising."

"The people I care about are safe and happy," he added. "I know Longstaff is frustrated at the moment, but tomorrow will be a triumph. I'm sure of it."

"And?" prompted Aurélie.

"What?"

"You've had a letter from France."

"From Laure," nodded Durant. He looked relieved. "She's her mother's daughter; the old family estate is beginning to thrive."

"You're not thinking of going home?"

Durant looked at her in apparent amazement. "What does home have to do with the likes of us, Aurélie? I know you're not missing that pile of bricks in Suffolk." He collected the slices of aubergine. "I love my daughter, but we rub along better by letter than we ever did when we lived together."

They heard footsteps strike the floorboards above their heads. Longstaff pacing in his study. Durant rolled his eyes. "He's driving himself crazy up there. Go and tell him dinner's ready."

Aurélie knocked on the study door – three imperious raps – then went to the dining room and poured as many glasses of wine. Longstaff and Durant appeared a moment later, the latter bearing a platter of cheese and jellied quince.

"The wine is from Crete," said Durant. "I've been saving it for a special occasion." He raised his glass. "To you, Longstaff. You'll be the toast of all Istanbul tomorrow."

Longstaff grimaced before drinking. "Your faith in the future is truly irritating."

"Not in the future," said Aurélie. "In you."

"That's worse."

Longstaff listened to them talk, unwinding after the long day. Durant told them about a patient whose condition had been repeatedly misdiagnosed. "And all because he hadn't told us how much coffee he drinks. Some people would rather die than admit a guilty secret. That reminds me." He snapped his fingers. "Francesco was here when I got home."

"Why should the subject of guilt remind you of Francesco?" asked Aurélie.

"What did he want?" said Longstaff.

"To test you on the ranks and rituals of the Ottoman court."

"Don't mock. This is as much his triumph as it is mine." The Englishman clapped a hand over his mouth.

"What is it?"

"You've made him tempt fate," laughed Aurélie.

"I'm just nervous." Longstaff took a deep breath. Tomorrow, if all went well, he'd show this city that England was more than a fog-shrouded island clinging to the edge of the world. "You should have invited Francesco to eat with us."

"I did. He said he had too much to do. He'll be back in the morning to help you dress."

Longstaff sat back. The chair took his weight with a weary sigh. Better this way, he reflected – just a quiet meal with the two people he loved most in the world. It had been months since he'd spent any time with Durant. Longstaff remembered the first time they'd worked together – the first time they'd placed their lives in one another's hands, assuming the roles of a merchant and a soldier with a consignment of wheel-lock muskets for sale. Nerve-wracking days at a villa in the Italian countryside, frantically hunting for a prisoner held somewhere in the grounds. He was on the point of reminding Durant when someone interrupted his reverie. A cool breeze still lifted from the Golden Horn each evening and the noise of knocking reached them easily through the open window.

"I'll go," said the Frenchman. "I have to check on the fish anyway."

Longstaff crossed to stand at the window, muttering a short curse when he saw who waited in the street outside. On any other occasion, he would have been delighted to see Fitch.

The young priest bounded across the courtyard; the weeks in custody did not appear to have injured his health.

"Aurélie," he said, when his visitor appeared in the doorway. "This is Thomas Fitch."

She extended her hand. "Matthew has told us all about you."

The priest addressed Longstaff directly. "You saved our lives. The least you could have done was accept our thanks!"

Longstaff shook his head. "You should be at sea. I arranged passage for you on a ship bound for Portsmouth."

"Eighteen of our number accepted your offer. Having come so far, four remained, determined to continue their pilgrimage to the Holy Land."

"When do you leave?"

"Yesterday." Fitch smiled. "They were eager to set off before the sultan changed his mind."

Durant entered with the main course. "You didn't tell me we were expecting guests."

"Excuse me," said Fitch. "I've taken up too much of your time already."

Longstaff fought a short, hopeless battle against the demands of hospitality. "We'd be delighted if you stayed."

"It would be an honour."

"Mackerel," said Durant, serving them each in turn. "Filled with rice, currants, pine nuts and onions."

"Without breaking the skin?" said Fitch.

"There's an art to it."

"You said your companions went on ahead," prompted Longstaff.

"I wanted to thank you personally – and give you this." He held out a small leather purse. "From the eighteen who returned home; everything they could spare. We've taken an oath to send you our share of the difference as soon as we're able." He shrugged, a good-natured smile on his face. "Some of them might even remember."

The priest was bright and talkative. Longstaff could see the positive impression he made on Aurélie and Durant, who competed to tell him about the great unveiling due to take place on the following day.

"Extraordinary," said Fitch. "So much happening in your own life and you still found time to secure our freedom."

"More than that," added Aurélie. "He could have asked the sultan to recognise his position as England's ambassador to the Empire. Instead, he thought of you and your fellow pilgrims."

They all looked at him so admiringly. Longstaff scowled. *No good deed goes unpunished.* "It wouldn't have been appropriate to ask for trade concessions. If anything, I imagine my apparent selflessness worked to my advantage."

"You're too modest." The priest raised his glass. Longstaff interrupted his toast.

"You still haven't told us your own plans. Your flock have either returned home or gone to the Holy Land…"

"And here I am." A light blush rose on the young man's cheeks. His smile was infectious. "I do have an ulterior motive for coming. It sounds presumptuous, I know." He cleared his throat. "I believe that God must have interrupted our pilgrimage for a reason. Istanbul will have its first English ambassador soon. Why not its first minister as well?"

"Ministering to whom?" asked Durant. "The Christians of Galata are all Catholics. If you begin casting religion among the Mohammedans, they'll string you up by the balls."

To Longstaff's ears, Aurélie sounded even more dismissive.

"You believe God caused women and children to be stolen from their homes in Tripoli as a means of bringing you to Istanbul?"

"If I preach in an empty house," said Fitch, "God still hears. If I bring His peace to just one soul, my labours will not have been in vain. Think of the risks if I fail to heed his call." He gestured at the food. "Without someone ministering to their spiritual needs, isn't there a danger that our co-religionists will turn Turk."

Durant burst out laughing. "You think we have something to fear from their cooking?"

Longstaff saw the priest's knuckles whiten around his knife. "He's teasing you."

"Am I?" Durant lifted his glass. "Though I wouldn't want to live without wine. God knows what they have against it."

"Mohammed is said to have walked past a wedding once," explained Aurélie. "Everyone was having fun; the bride's father said it was because they'd been drinking. When the prophet returned the following morning, the ground was stained with gore and strewn with human limbs." She shrugged.

Durant laughed, apparently delighted with the story.

"I'm sorry if we appear flippant," said Longstaff, glaring at the Frenchman. "You were held in captivity for several weeks. I know the kind of thoughts that go through a man's mind in those circumstances…"

"We heard them torture people," interrupted Fitch. "You can't imagine what it was like, thinking one of us would be next, thinking we might be crushed in a vice or fed to hungry dogs."

"I wager you kept your fears to yourself."

"I had to. For the sake of my congregation. I had so much time to think in there – and pray."

"I know what the London preachers say," continued Longstaff. "I heard them call Mohammed a drunk. A deceiver who trained doves to eat from his ear so people would think he talked with angels." He paused for a moment. "They know nothing about this place."

There was a long silence. Durant left the room, returning moments later with a plate of halva. "A Turkish sweet," he explained, "eaten to make peace between quarrelling friends."

Longstaff smiled at the young priest. "Do you need a place to stay?"

Fitch shook his head. "I leave for Bursa on the midnight tide. There are English merchants in the city. I was hoping to raise money there."

"Go," said Longstaff. "When you return, come and stay with us. Learn how this city works while I establish myself as Elizabeth's ambassador. In a few months – when things have settled down – we can think about making your ministry public."

The priest clasped his hand. "Thank you."

Longstaff rose to his feet with a weary smile. "I have a busy day tomorrow. It's time I went to bed."

He was already beneath the covers when Aurélie joined him a few minutes later. He saw her dress fall to the ground, a brief glimpse of her silhouette as she slipped in beside him.

"Did you mean to invite him to stay?" she asked, putting her arms around his neck.

"He's young. He's been through hell and he's trying to make sense of it. Reality seems dull and sordid to him now – give him time and he'll come to his senses."

"Or decide we're demons in human form." She kissed him. Longstaff felt the smile on her lips.

Chapter 18

Spring did not last long in Istanbul. It was already hot when Longstaff walked through the palace gates, Francesco at his side with Durant and Aurélie in close attendance. The Englishman plucked awkwardly at the neckline of the heavy kaftan the sultan had given him. He would have felt more comfortable in a simple robe. God alone knew how Aurélie was coping beneath the heavy *ferace*. Hundreds of Istanbul's most prominent citizens had been invited to view the latest curiosity from Europe, including women on this occasion – providing that only their eyes and hands were visible. Anticipating food, drink and entertainment, the crowd was in high spirits.

For them, it was a win-win situation. Either they would witness one of the world's mechanical marvels – or the ritual humiliation of an overbearing foreigner.

Longstaff tried not to think about it. He sensed additional currents of excitement as he made his way towards the pavilion; a simmering feud between the sultan and his grand vizier, unconfirmed rumours of an attempt to sabotage the European machine. After so many decades of unbroken glory, the people of Istanbul had apparently forgotten how lucky they were.

Longstaff and his companions pressed close together, a tight knit unit making its way past row after row of neat flower beds. Aurélie's tulips. They were perfect, almond-shaped, the inner petals like a well, the outer ever so slightly open. Longstaff had completely failed to anticipate the sheer variety of colours.

"A week at most," said Francesco, "before they begin to fade."

"Today is all we need." Longstaff led them towards a raised platform, the chronometer's alien silhouette visible beneath a vast sheet of silk. On the far side, the waters of the Golden Horn had disappeared beneath a press of ornate *caiques*.

"Longstaff!"

"Hector, thank God."

The mechanic forced his way through the crowd, intercepting Longstaff beside the ropes. There were dark rings beneath his eyes. A swell of nausea rippled through Longstaff's gut. "You look awful."

"I haven't had a breath of fresh air in over a week. Don't worry, your contraption is in perfect working order."

"Chronometer." Longstaff corrected him with a smile. "You're sure it's going to work?"

"Your triumph is assured."

Longstaff heard the familiar sound of Aurélie's laughter. Turning, he saw a small, hairless pig pursued through the garden by a young lion.

"I assume we're the pig," she said, giving the mechanic her hand. "The lion represents Islam?"

"Naturally." Hector bowed. "The infidel may be clever in the art of clock-making; true glory remains an Ottoman prerogative."

Trumpets blasted. A regiment of janissaries entered the garden, marching in a straight line to the chronometer, peeling off at the last moment so that they stood shoulder to shoulder between the stage and its audience. Longstaff felt Francesco take hold of his elbow. The sultan and his grand vizier emerged, both riding flawless white geldings. Sokollu did not dismount until the last member of the crowd had fallen to his knees. Selim, dressed in a magnificent kaftan embroidered in cloth of gold, remained on his horse. To Longstaff's eyes, the sultan seemed to be enjoying himself – finding a degree of pleasure in this game of pretending to be at ease. The grand vizier looked less comfortable beneath the weight of so much scrutiny. For all his wealth and power, he remained a slave from a small village in

Bosnia. How he must hate having to behave as if his hard-won wealth and power were a matter of indifference.

There was a flourish. Four servants rolled back the enormous silken cloth, revealing the chronometer in all its glory. Longstaff had seen the drawings. He'd seen the individual parts spread chaotically across the floor of the pavilion. Nothing had prepared him for the sight that met his eyes now. The machine stood sixteen feet high, a small statuette of Winged Victory looking down from the summit. Every surface, whether of copper, brass or gold, had been polished to a near impossible shine, so that he had to squint to trace its contours in the bright sunshine. He smiled at the crowd's collective intake of breath, resisting the urge to fold the mechanic in his arms.

A servant signalled that the two of them should approach. Hector didn't hesitate, slipping beneath the rope with a boyish grin – giving no signal he would soon be one of the Empire's most wanted men. Longstaff followed slowly. His chest felt tight. He hadn't anticipated an attack of nerves.

Hector handed him a key, indicating a particular spot on the main body of the machine. Longstaff wound the mechanism. Haltingly at first, the chronometer began its mechanical dance. The sultan's horse shied as inanimate figures broke into an awkward approximation of life. Selim himself looked spellbound. The sheer improbable beauty of it – life-sized statues and ornaments spun in time to clockwork music, moving with apparent purpose, as if fashioned by God rather than his servants. The machine required more than forty minutes to perform its complete repertoire of tricks. It struck the hour, followed by a chime of sixteen bells and a song played in four parts. Two figures at the corners of the clock's second tier raised silver trumpets to sound a fanfare. Mechanical blackbirds rose from a bush of precious metals, shaking their wings. Slowly, they settled back into their original position. There was a long moment of absolute silence in the garden. Eyes closed against an unexpected rush of emotion, Longstaff listened as it gathered then broke in a great swell of acclaim. Hector clapped him on the shoulder.

"Whatever happens next," said the mechanic, "we'll treasure this moment for the rest of our lives."

Whatever happens next?

A servant appeared at Longstaff's elbow. "The sultan will see you now."

Selim had turned his horse, already retreating into the shadows cast by the Gate of Felicity.

"Go on," urged Hector. "He's offering you a private audience. You couldn't have hoped for more."

Francesco began to follow. The servant barred his way. "The Lord of Worlds will speak with the Englishman alone."

The throne room was just as Longstaff remembered, its opulence no less dazzling in the absence of richly dressed courtiers. Attended by a brace of pageboys, the sultan sat on a low divan. Longstaff fell to his knees.

"Get up," commanded Selim in flawless Italian. He drank from a silver goblet, then slipped a lozenge between his lips. "Take a seat. No need to follow protocol when it's just the two of us."

"Forgive me, your majesty. I had no idea you spoke Italian."

"I imagine there's a lot you don't know about me." The plump monarch seemed in high spirits. "That was quite a performance."

"Thank you, your majesty."

"Did you see the grand mufti?"

"No, your majesty."

"Looked like he was shitting cucumbers." The sultan chuckled happily. "Serve the bastard right for calling me a sinner."

"I'm sure he wouldn't dare, your majesty."

Selim leaned forward on the divan. Longstaff caught the scent of musk and stale alcohol. "They tell me you're a man of action."

"I fear they flatter me."

"An expert on military matters, experienced in Frankish warfare. My janissaries claim we must fight for glory today – or we'll be fighting for our lives tomorrow. Are they right?"

Longstaff hesitated. At close quarters, the sultan wore his authority awkwardly. "I don't believe life can be reduced to a choice between glory and oblivion."

"Exactly what I tell them! However much they talk of my father's valour, they don't really want another sultan cut from the same mould." Selim's expression hardened. "For forty-six years, Suleiman did little more than fight one bloody war after another. He ended up executing one son and arranging for another to be cut down like a common criminal in Persia."

It took Longstaff a moment to realise that Selim was talking about his own brothers. He might have been stirred to pity, had the man's lack of discretion not filled him with a sense of foreboding.

"Are you aware of the angst you inspire in your rivals?"

"My rivals, your majesty? I think they're hardly aware of my existence."

"Spare me the false modesty. No place for it here – not if we're going to be of use to one another. I can't be seen to promote your interests too energetically, of course."

He smiled. Something in his expression reminded Longstaff that monarchs were never truly alone.

"They plot against me, you know. As if Suleiman's blood didn't run in my veins! As much as I might desire military glory for my own sake, my first duty is to the Empire. My people need rest, they need to celebrate our achievements and have fun for a season. The world needs to empty its bowels, Longstaff – and so I show them wonders like your clock. I risk the grand mufti's anger by spending time with dwarves, mutes, buffoons. I write poetry. I sleep with the prettiest women I can find, wear precious stones and line my eyes with kohl."

The Lord of Worlds stuck out his chest and threw back his shoulders. The effect was unconvincing, further undermined when he produced a flask from his kaftan. Longstaff thought of Hector, resigned to his fate in the north – the thankless task of attempting to build a canal from the Volga to the Don. Surely, the mechanic was exactly the sort of man this sultan needed near him. "Your majesty," he began. "I haven't thanked you for lending me Hector. While we worked together, I saw his designs for an observatory in the city..."

Selim waved him into silence. "My father turned his back on the chance to invade Europe when he retreated from Vienna. I hope I'm at least as wise as he was – enough to recognise the natural boundaries of our Empire. If I seek to augment our arsenal, it's only with a view to ensuring that people don't mistake my wisdom for weakness – that no nation is tempted to a course of action which might throw the balance of power into jeopardy. You'd be well advised to remember that when you negotiate with my representatives."

The sultan winked. The audience was at an end. Bewildered, Longstaff gathered his wits sufficiently to make a graceful exit. He wanted to slip away and reflect on what Selim had told him. The crowd spotted him as soon as he emerged through the Gate of Felicity. The master of the miraculous clock. The man from a rainswept island in the far north, who'd been granted a private audience with the Lord of Worlds. Courtiers surrounded him immediately. Longstaff could have cried with relief when Francesco appeared at his side, eyeglasses balanced precariously as he helped force a passage through the crowd. They found Aurélie and Durant waiting in a shaded portion of the garden.

Longstaff brushed their congratulations aside. "Have you seen Hector? This is his triumph, too."

"Not since you were summoned. What happened in there?"

Francesco raised a finger to his lips. "Not here."

The crowd parted, revealing the tall, slightly stooped figure of the French ambassador. He returned Longstaff's courteous bow with a look of malevolent fury. "Enjoy it while you can," he spat. "You will regret forcing me to take notice of you."

"Your grace," said Longstaff. "If I've done anything to offend…"

"Your very existence is offensive!" He turned on his heel. Longstaff exhaled a long breath.

"Have I bitten off more than I can chew?"

"What did you expect?" said Francesco, nodding towards the round figure of the Venetian ambassador. "Your troubles are just beginning, my friend."

"Longstaff!" said Raimondi. "That was priceless. Did you see his face?" The Venetian put an arm around his shoulders. "A new star is born in the diplomatic firmament." He twinkled at Aurélie, lost in her shapeless *ferace*. "Have you ever known a man meet so many challenges with such poise? I tested him myself. Just to see what your husband is made of, you understand. Hard as iron, I can assure you."

I tested him myself. For a moment, Longstaff thought Raimondi was talking about the assassin, then remembered their argument at the ambassadors' meeting house.

The Venetian's stream of increasingly elaborate compliments came to a sudden halt. Trumpets sounded from the walls. Longstaff looked round; janissary soldiers were already flooding the lawn. "What in God's name…"

A great wave of panic seemed to rise from the earth itself. The plumes the soldiers wore in their hoods danced wildly as they took up positions around the walls, stepping forward in time, closing in on the milling guests like fishermen working their nets. A detachment of senior men marched onto the stage, ignoring the chronometer, scrutinising the crowd from their elevated position.

A coup? Against Selim? Longstaff's fingers twitched as if seeking a weapon. The soldiers drew their swords. Shouts of alarm turned to cries of fear. The air itself seemed to darken.

Longstaff took Aurélie's hand – a single false move might trigger a massacre.

"What do we do?" demanded Durant.

"Stay calm," said Longstaff. "Stay close."

The crowd fell silent when the grand vizier appeared on stage. "A thief walks among us," he roared, his deep voice taking Longstaff back to the battlefields of his youth. "As you leave the palace, you will be searched by the sultan's soldiers. All of you, regardless of rank or position. Those with nothing to hide have nothing to fear." Mehmed Sokollu folded his arms across his broad chest, using the force of his personality to cow the crowd into obedience. "You *will* wait patiently – for as long as it takes."

"What now?" Raimondi seemed to have become separated from his own entourage.

Longstaff shrugged, unable to forget that this man may have ordered an attempt on his life. "We join the queue. Unless you've been pilfering the sultan's trinkets?"

"I don't find that funny."

They waited for hours. Despite their relative importance to the day's events, they remained infidels. Relations between the different communities in Istanbul were civil, but it was a matter of common sense to maintain a low profile. Even the French ambassador, further ahead of them in the queue, wasn't stupid enough to demand special treatment. Discreetly, Longstaff studied the janissaries. In the space of just a few days, they had permitted acts of vandalism and theft within the palace walls. Little wonder they looked furious.

A thought struck Longstaff with the weight of a punch. He hadn't seen Hector since returning from the throne room. *Hector* – who had spent the last ten days locked in the sultan's treasury.

He leaned close to Francesco. "What does this mean for us?"

The *dragoman* spread his hands. "Impossible to say until we know more. At least our rivals are as much in the dark as we are."

He nodded in Raimondi's direction. The Venetian may have been a consummate actor, but his confusion struck Longstaff as genuine. They were nearly at the front of the queue. The French ambassador's voice drifted back to them, demanding to know the meaning of this outrage. The janissaries searched him with redoubled vigour, their anger palpable even at this distance. "Smile," Longstaff told his friends. "Be gracious."

The guards made no allowances for Aurélie's gender or Raimondi's rank, searching them with equal – and equally fruitless – determination. The great square beyond the gates swarmed with soldiers. Longstaff set a steady pace at the head of his small party, hardly daring to draw breath until they reached the maze of streets on the far side. Francesco left them soon afterwards – he wanted to return and find out what he could about the theft – but Raimondi was more difficult to shake off. The Venetian ambassador had recovered his poise by the time the four of them boarded a *caique* for the journey back to Galata.

"I have to concede," he said, trailing fingertips in the sparkling waters of the Golden Horn. "I never thought you'd pull it off. A pity your triumph was brought to such an abrupt conclusion."

"The chronometer was only ever a means to an end." Longstaff splashed cool water on his face, partly to hide his expression from the Venetian. What he'd said was true and yet part of him was furious that his moment of glory had been stolen after so much hard work. People might still remember his clock in a few days, but the rows of tulips? His audience with the sultan? Hector had betrayed him – that was the worst of it – exploited him for his own inscrutable ends. Longstaff shook his head in exasperation. Whatever motive lay behind the mechanic's actions, he couldn't help but wish him well – the alternative, if he were caught, was too horrible to imagine.

"How far are you prepared to go, Longstaff?" said Raimondi. "Little birds have begun to whisper of additional services you might be willing to provide – in return for a trade agreement between England and the Ottoman Empire."

"What are you talking about?"

"English lead and tin, my friend." Raimondi affected an air of melancholy. "A sad day indeed when fellow Christians show themselves willing to arm the infidel."

Longstaff bridled at the injustice of the accusation. "Careful," he warned. "Some insults are harder to ignore than others."

"Have I offended you?" Raimondi sounded amused. Longstaff let the silence gather. Would life become easier when he was ambassador? Would he become like Raimondi – constantly scheming, plot after plot in a desperate attempt to stay one step ahead of the competition? Longstaff thought of the grand vizier, who lived every day of his life in indescribable luxury, fawned on by countless minions, but still a slave and never more than a wrinkle's distance from the headman's block.

"Was it you?" he asked.

Raimondi raised an eyebrow.

"Two weeks ago, a man attempted to murder me. Was it you who paid him?"

The Venetian looked neither surprised nor insulted. "Why on earth would I seek your death, my friend?"

The *caique* bumped gently against the landing stage. Longstaff took a deep breath. "I have no intention of selling arms to the Ottomans."

"Then you have nothing to fear."

Raimondi stepped onto the quay, more nimbly than Longstaff would have expected for a man of his size. He bowed to Aurélie then set off for his residence at the summit of the hill, leaving Longstaff to pay the cost of his passage.

Aurélie remained in the kitchen when they reached the house, eyes closed, listening to her husband pacing in his study above. Only a few short hours ago, she'd watched his remarkable clock perform its repertoire of tricks. All those months of careful negotiations, constantly balanced on the edge of disaster. She should have told him about her meeting with Hubbi Hatun. She'd delayed and delayed, telling herself it was for the best – half believing it until Raimondi started baiting Longstaff on the crossing from 'Stanboul.

Aurélie knocked at the study door. Once he'd recovered from his anger, would he baulk at the sultan's price? Refuse to play a part in widening the split in Christianity – a split she'd heard him curse on numerous occasions. Or would he seize the opportunity to make a success of his mission and have done with it?

"Come in."

He sat behind his desk in shirtsleeves and loose *shalwar*, the heavy kaftan thrown carelessly across the locked cabinet.

"I thought you might like coffee." She placed a full cup at his elbow. He rewarded her with a weary smile.

"You're an angel."

"I overheard your conversation with Raimondi."

"Yes?"

"There's something I have to tell you, Matthew." She took the seat opposite, elbows up on the polished wood. "Have you heard of Hubbi Hatun?"

"The courtesan?"

"The poet. She asked me to pass on a message from the sultan." Aurélie watched her husband brace himself for more bad news.

"A message for me?"

"Selim will sign your *Capitulations* – everything you need to ensure England's farmers are rescued from penury."

Longstaff stared at her, blue eyes wide in surprise. "What does he want in return?"

"A second, clandestine agreement." What was it Raimondi had said? Aurélie touched her hair, suddenly aware of how she must look after so many hours trapped in the stifling *ferace*. "English lead and tin," she said. "Men to teach the local smiths how to produce modern artillery and military commanders to teach soldiers how to use them."

Usually when Longstaff looked at her, his eyes were filled with trust. She forced herself to watch them darken with suspicion. "In return," she persisted, wrapping her hands around his, "he will recognise you as England's ambassador."

He shook her off. "When?"

"When what?"

"When did you meet this woman?"

She lowered her eyes. "There was no reason to tell you until after the demonstration."

"Who else knows? Durant? Francesco?"

"No one, I promise."

"Raimondi knows. You heard him. And the sultan knows."

"Well, obviously..."

"You sent me in there blind."

"I couldn't know he'd grant you a personal audience."

"All this time, I thought you were so caught up in the past you had no idea what I was doing. Now it turns out you know more about it than I do. Does everyone in this city take me for a fool?"

"Of course not!"

"Why approach you?" continued Longstaff, ignoring her. "You're not even English."

"They've done their homework, Matthew. Hubbi Hatun knows what would happen to me if I returned to Italy." Aurélie lowered her eyes. "She knows how loyal I am to your interests."

"A poet? An unlikely choice as envoy."

"Selim is keen to act without the knowledge of his grand vizier."

Longstaff gave a hollow laugh. "Mehmed Sokollu knows everything that happens in this city."

She watched him take two long, steadying breaths. "I'm sorry," she said.

"I did everything I could to keep you out of this business."

"I know. I'm grateful."

"I wanted you to concentrate on your own investigations."

"We have to work together now. What will Raimondi do?"

"What can he do?" Longstaff sent a gold coin spinning across the desk, flashing in the candlelight until it struck his cup. She looked at the lion of Venice stamped on its surface, along with a promise that it was made of pure 22 carat gold.

"The coin Nasi gave me?"

"One like it. Raimondi has been minting his own from a mine in Bohemia." Longstaff paused. "If he threatens me with tin, he knows I can ruin him with gold."

Aurélie looked at him in admiration. "You're learning fast."

"Not me. Joseph Nasi."

She whistled. She'd had no idea the merchant took such a close interest in their affairs. Longstaff rose to his feet. "Walsingham would bloody love this."

"He'd approve?"

"It would make him. More money for Elizabeth's coffers and one in the eye for the Catholics across the Channel. Within hours, he'd have England's few remaining church bells melted down, the lead shipped here on the next tide." He spat a curse. "Everything I've done – finding the Yorkshireman, charging around in the desert, taking on all that debt – none of it was necessary. I was just too stupid to realise."

"That's not true. Selim would never have proposed this arrangement if you hadn't proved yourself a worthy ally. You can still win, Matthew."

He stopped pacing. "You think I should accept? Sell arms to the Ottomans?"

"Can you see another way out?" She remembered how wistfully he'd spoken of making way for a replacement – of the English smallholders and merchants who would starve without new markets for their wares. Longstaff would never be free of England's demands until he delivered the *Capitulations*. She put her arms round him. "You know how much I love you."

Longstaff groaned. "It's this place. I can't make sense of people's loyalties."

"I used to think I was clever enough to see the consequences of my actions."

"Not anymore?"

She snorted in disbelief. "The more time I spend trying to understand the web of cause and effect, the more tangled it becomes." She looked into his eyes. "What matters is how people react when they reach the limits of their understanding. Some reach for a sword to cut themselves free. Others make themselves masters of a few sticky strands which they use to trap the unwary. Some ignore it altogether, tuck their tails between their legs and crawl into hiding."

"And?" he wondered aloud. "Which am I, do you think?"

Chapter 19

The sultan's janissaries went everywhere, nosing into every nook and cranny, searching the whole damn city on both sides of the Golden Horn. Days later, as Durant walked to the hospital where he worked, it was still the only topic of conversation at every coffee shop and market stall he passed. No doubt the rich and powerful had been spared to some degree, but Longstaff's unofficial status had offered no protection. With a rueful smile, Durant remembered his own panic – shaking as fists pounded at his bedroom door, a swarm of janissary soldiers around his bed, searching his closets, turfing him from the warm mattress to probe between his sheets. He had cowered in a corner, terrified through the fog of sleep that this invasion had something to do with Leila.

It didn't, of course, and the storm had receded as suddenly as it arrived, the soldiers moving to the next address on their list. The search had been frenetic, unprecedented – now a thousand theories circulated about what was missing from the sultan's treasury. Some claimed it was a bauble, that all the fuss was just a sop to the sultan's pride. Others felt true dread as they contemplated the frantic efforts of his soldiers. Everyone agreed on the identity of the culprit. Hector, the mechanic who'd repaired Longstaff's clock. Durant winced, thinking of what would happen to the man when he was caught. He saw Khalid ahead, sitting in a patch of sunlight in the gardens separating the mosque from the hospital. Durant smiled awkwardly; the two of them had been avoiding one another recently, embarrassed by the heated words they'd exchanged at Ben Chabib's home. Khalid sprang to his feet.

"I've been waiting for you. I want to clear the air between us. I shouldn't have spoken as I did."

"You were disappointed in me," said Durant. He missed his friend, but the idea of being judged by someone twenty years his junior was more than he could bear. "I didn't expect to feel this way about a woman again, Khalid. I wasn't looking for it; now it's happened, I can't pretend I regret it. And I'm not going to stop seeing her, however much you disapprove."

"I'm not blind. I can see how much happier you've become." Khalid looked at his feet. "I don't want to lose your friendship. And I don't want to see you get yourself killed. Perhaps I can help."

"You'd do that?" Durant looked at the young man with renewed affection.

"There are certain circumstances which allow for the possibility of divorce, assuming she can persuade her family to support the petition."

"She has no family," said Durant. "She was kidnapped as a child and brought to Istanbul as a slave."

Khalid winced. "How can she leave her husband if she has nowhere to go? The scandal would destroy her – and you."

Durant thought about Longstaff. The Englishman's position in the city was still delicate. His enemies would not hesitate to exploit any weakness.

"Believe it or not, I only want what's best for her."

"I *do* believe you."

"I have a little money," continued Durant. "Leila has a low opinion of her husband. Perhaps he would be willing to accept money in return for her freedom?"

"Give me his name," said Khalid. "I'll try to find out more about him – discreetly. And for the love of God, Durant, do nothing more to compromise her honour until we know if we can help her."

*

Aurélie rested her palm on one of the clay tablets, finding it difficult to resist the lure of translation. For over a thousand years, the *Enuma Elish* had been lost to humankind. She was breathing life back into it now – a tale of genesis, of Gods who created men and women to be their servants.

Aurélie smiled as she read on. According to the *Enuma Elish*, these same Gods had also been subject to the law of unintended consequences:

> *The land had grown wide, the peoples had increased,*
> *The land was bellowing like a bull.*
> *The god was disturbed with their uproar.*

One God had taken exception to the growing numbers of people and the noise they made. Repeatedly, desperate for sleep, he attempted to destroy them all, first with plague, then drought, finally by causing their crops to fail. Each time, his rival Enki helped mankind survive – until finally the old curmudgeon snapped. The waters began to rise, the beginnings of a flood which would have exterminated all mankind if Enki hadn't told one loyal follower to build an Ark, to fill it with his family and breeding pairs of every animal he could find.

Almost a perfect copy of the story Aurélie had grown up with, except that the Babylonian version predated Noah by centuries. The similarities so strong that they constituted proof, as far as Aurélie was concerned, that the Bible could not be taken literally – and yet it was the differences which excited her more. When the floodwaters had finally receded, mankind struck a deal with the ill-tempered God, inviting him to keep their numbers down through a combination of infertility and infant mortality. In return, they made him promise not to wipe them out completely.

Aurélie tried to imagine how this story had been transformed into the one she knew so well. More than two thousand years ago, during the period of their captivity in Babylon, the Israelites must have absorbed elements of the *Enuma Elish*. They prayed to a very different God, however, one who had no need of sleep and was indifferent to the noise of humans – on the contrary, it was his express command that they be fruitful and multiply. Men and women were foolish but essentially innocent in the Babylonian version, reflected Aurélie, but when the story was rewritten to suit a perfect God, blame for the catastrophe was shifted to the victims: *And God saw that the wickedness of man was great in the earth, and that every imagination of the thoughts of his heart was only evil continually.*

Sunlight fell across the page. Aurélie hadn't realised it was so late. She had translated less than two-thirds of the clay tablets and ached to know what further secrets lay hidden in the strange, wedge-shaped script – but another invitation had arrived from Hubbi Hatun, summoning her back to the *hammam*. Aurélie hurried through the streets of Galata, thoughts still on the *Enuma Elish* as she boarded a *caique*. She did not want to replace one religion with another. Her own research had revealed the temples of the ancients to be slaughterhouses, their gods little more than rapists and adulterers. Jesus had urged his followers to love their peers, commanded them to cease their worship of God-like power and wealth. Aurélie did not want to undermine his message, only make it clearer by removing the corrupting pall of divinity.

She knew it had happened before in history – small groups of men and women finding sufficient courage to deny the possibility of a divine plan. Philosophers in ancient Greece had debated the principles of nature, humanists in the last century had prized the testimony of their own senses above the claims of semi-literate priests. Again and again, these small islands of reason had been swamped by revelation, the evidence of lived experience deliberately refashioned as an entranceway to hell.

Aurélie's secret hope was that the *Enuma Elish* could push that tide back once more. Not forever. But perhaps for long enough that a new group might rise from their knees and carry humanity a little nearer to its true potential.

She took a deep breath at the entrance to the *hammam*. Head up, shoulders back, she gave her name and exchanged her shoes for wooden clogs, just as if she'd been coming here for years.

She remembered her previous visit, asking the poet's maid what she should do – and the young woman's confused reply: *Whatever pleases you.*

Aurélie repressed a flutter of nerves as she entered the huge, steam-filled room. She would not go looking for the poet. Stepping out of her clothes, she lowered herself into a pool of hot water. Eyes closed, half listening to the conversations around her, she willed the water to work its magic, release the tension of the last few weeks. A soft voice spoke her name.

"May I join you?"

Aurélie made room for Hubbi Hatun beside her. She felt oddly safe. There were no men here, nowhere anyone could conceal a weapon. She looked sideways at Hubbi Hatun. The poet made it easy for her, closing her eyes and sighing in apparent pleasure. She wore no make-up today, nothing to soften the strong features. Only vaguely aware of how much she hoped the two of them might become friends, Aurélie thought again of the courage and intelligence it must have taken to carve a place at the Ottoman court.

"Is there any word on what Hector stole from the treasury?"

Hubbi Hatun shook her head. "No one knows except the treasurer, the grand vizier, and Selim himself. You'll be pleased to know that no suspicion attaches to your husband. Apparently, he attempted to intercede with the sultan on Hector's behalf. Hardly the behaviour of a guilty man."

Aurélie snorted. "Longstaff liked him. Even now, after all the trouble he's caused, he won't hear a word said against the man." She hesitated. "I'm afraid he still hasn't reached a decision."

Hubbi Hatun looked amused rather than frustrated. "Hasn't reached a decision? Or doesn't yet know whether he can live with his decision?"

"He knows how important a trade agreement is for England." Aurélie did not add how enthusiastically Walsingham would accept the terms of the proposal. "It will mean breaking a sacred agreement among Christian nations."

"Just words." Hubbi Hatun gave an elegant wave of her arm.

"Unfortunately, my husband places a high value on words."

The poet smiled. "The sultan is not prepared to wait indefinitely. Everything has been arranged – a brief ceremony confirming your husband's new rank will take place at the High Gate. We'll do everything we can to ensure his Queen can plausibly deny the trade in munitions."

A group of female musicians began to play. Aurélie watched a single bead of sweat trace a path along the line of Hubbi Hatun's cheek. "It sounds like you've thought of everything."

"Negotiations for the official *Capitulations* will begin immediately afterwards. The sultan's negotiating committee has already been selected and briefed. They will agree to buy as many kerseys as England is able to send, thereby averting the threat of famine and reducing the likelihood of rebellion or invasion."

Aurélie should have felt happier. The poet was offering everything Longstaff wanted, the only sticking point his own sense of honour. Since arriving in Istanbul, she'd seen him compromise his beliefs on numerous occasions. She'd even criticised him for it – for putting his sense of duty to London ahead of his principles.

"Help him make the right decision," said Hubbi Hatun. "It will allow the two of you to concentrate on what's really important."

A wrinkle appeared between Aurélie's eyes. "I'm not sure I understand you?"

"Did you think I wouldn't notice? If you want to know whether it's a boy or a girl, I know a woman who's infallible."

Aurélie felt as though she were falling through space. As soon as the words had left the poet's mouth, she knew they were true. How had she not realised sooner? She thought of Longstaff, struggling to bring his negotiations to a successful conclusion. She knew how happy he would be. Slowly, a broad smile took control of her own fine features. She looked up at her new friend in wonder.

"How did you know?"

"How did you not?" Hubbi Hatun shook her head. "You Franks are a strange people."

"Do you have children?"

"I have poems. And a sultan who needs saving from his empire."

Chapter 20

Thomas Fitch stood in the doorway, a travelling chest at his feet. Longstaff had forgotten all about the young priest. Fitch had gone to spend a few days with the small English community in Bursa. Now, it seemed, he'd returned to stay.

Longstaff resisted the temptation to curse. "And to think," he said, looking at the chest. "Just two weeks ago you were in prison, nothing to your name but the clothes on your back."

"The Lord moves in mysterious ways." The expression on the young man's face was grave. "What the congregation in Bursa lack in numbers, they make up for in generosity."

Fitch looked past him, as if expecting servants to materialise in the courtyard.

"Already gone for the day," said Longstaff.

Between them, they manoeuvred the heavy chest up the narrow staircase and into the guest bedroom on the first floor. Longstaff remembered asking Elif to make it up for the Yorkshireman, Master Gale, whose remarkable clock was no longer the talk of Istanbul. Whose body had found a watery grave in the Mediterranean. The Lord did indeed move in mysterious ways.

"I hope I haven't arrived at an inopportune moment." Fitch ran his hands across the stiff sheets before taking a seat on the edge of the bed. The congregation in Bursa had replaced his threadbare robe with a suit of fine, black cloth.

"Not at all. Aurélie will be home at any moment. Durant is working late tonight, so it's a cold meal, I'm afraid."

"Whatever you have with be more than ample for my needs," replied the priest.

"I'd better see to it."

Longstaff was assembling a selection of bread and cold meats when Aurélie arrived. She looked well, he thought, a bounce to her step that he'd missed in recent weeks.

"Fitch is back."

"Already?" She scowled.

"My sentiments exactly." He picked up the two full platters.

"Wait a moment," said Aurélie.

"Let's just get it over with, shall we?" Longstaff was already on his way to the dining room, setting the platters on the table, finding plates and glasses, making conversation with the priest. Aurélie joined them with a bottle of wine.

Fitch welcomed her with a short dip of the head. "It seems we have mutual friends in Bursa," he said brightly.

"The Tarlowes?" Aurélie took a long drink before sitting. "I stayed with them for several weeks."

"Engaged on a project in the town? They were vague on the details."

"I was trying to learn something of the area's past."

The priest nodded eagerly. "A worthy project. All Christendom mourns for the days when this country was a part of the Holy Roman Empire."

"Before that," she said, shaking her head. "I was excavating the ruins of a Babylonian temple."

"Aurélie is attempting to decipher their language," interjected Longstaff. "No one's been able to read it in centuries."

"That's the task you've set yourself?"

"You sound disappointed."

Inwardly, Longstaff groaned. He recognised the note in Aurélie's voice. "Please," he said, hoping to change the subject. "Won't you help yourself?"

Fitch spread his hands. "I'm sorry. It just seems like such a waste of time."

"To learn about our past?" said Aurélie. Longstaff prayed the priest would be wise enough to hold his peace.

"Their past," said Fitch, freighting the first word with contempt. "Not ours."

Longstaff took a deep breath. "Aren't we all descended from common ancestors?"

"Amateurs," continued Fitch, "particularly of the fairer sex – are always liable to draw false conclusions."

Aurélie reacted as if she'd been slapped. "Forgive me for stating the obvious," she said, "but you're a priest."

"I am."

"You believe in the literal truth of the Bible. In a world created by God in six days and placed at the centre of the Universe, acting as its minstrel, strumming the music of the spheres."

"You put it beautifully."

"They're not my words – and they describe a model of the Universe which has been comprehensively disproven."

"To your satisfaction, perhaps."

"Aurélie…" said Longstaff.

"Let me finish."

"Gently. Mr Fitch is our guest."

"Our world revolves around the sun," she said. "When you look up at night, every star you see is another sun, each at the centre of its own universe, orbited by a potentially infinite number of planets…"

"God made us incapable of conceiving the infinite," replied the priest. "With good reason, it appears."

"God had nothing to do with it," countered Aurélie. "It's Christianity which forbids us from contemplating the mysteries of the universe, which strains every sinew to keep us in darkness. It's only by pushing at the limits of our knowledge that we make it possible to correct our mistakes."

"Mistakes?"

She dismissed his interruption with a flick of her fingers. "Do you know why European mathematicians use the symbol x to describe an unknown quantity? It's a corruption of *shay,*

the Arabic word for *thing*. Without contact with the followers
of Allah we would never have learned how to incorporate the
unknown – the infinite – into our observations of the world.
Do you understand? Columbus would never have set sail. Our
world would still be flat!"

She spoke with such passion. Longstaff wanted to applaud.
The look on the priest's face reminded him that she had
overstepped the bounds of propriety.

"Even if you disagree with the sentiment," he said, "you
have to agree that she expresses herself well." From the corner
of his eye, he saw how she flinched.

Fitch inclined his head. "Naturally, I understand the allure
of new ideas – but curiosity, absent the proper discipline, leaves
us vulnerable to temptation." He addressed Aurélie directly, his
tone heavy with condescension. "You don't really imagine that
an infinite number of Adams committed original sin an infinite
number of times, do you? That Christ becomes incarnate,
preaches his message and suffers crucifixion over and over
again? The notion is ridiculous."

Longstaff rose to his feet. "You're right, of course." He
was tired. He knew Aurélie would be furious with him, but
the conversation was pointless. She would never succeed in
changing the priest's mind. Or he hers. "If you'll both excuse
me, it's been a long day."

"Of course." Fitch also rose. "How discourteous of me. I
didn't even think to ask. Your demonstration at the palace?"

"Went well, thanks be to God."

"Then it won't be long before you begin your negotiations.
You're doing God's work, my friend."

Longstaff nodded. Pausing in the study on his way to
bed, he treated himself to a glass of brandy. The window
was open. Through it, below the red-tiled roofs of Galata,
he saw moonlight sparkling on the Golden Horn. Nothing
like a visitor from home to make him realise how much he'd
come to enjoy living here. Aurélie was going to kill him. The

way she'd looked at him – understandably furious he hadn't supported her arguments more energetically. He could hear her now through the open window, bidding Fitch goodnight in tones which did not bode well for the remainder of his stay. One more small glass for courage. On top of everything else, he needed to tell her whether or not he would accept the sultan's offer. There *were* Christians who believed in a united Christendom. For a majority, however, the true enemy was less the Ottoman Empire than the heretics and schismatics who refused to acknowledge any interpretation of Christ's message but their own. Walsingham – who lived in daily fear of invasion by Catholic Spain – would leap at the chance to supply Philip's enemies with arms.

Which left Longstaff as the only person willing to wrestle with the moral implications of the decision. He entered the bedroom he shared with Aurélie. She was still awake, washing in a small alcove on the far side of the bed. She did not look at him as he flopped full length on the mattress. The ceiling spun lazily on its axis. He'd had more brandy than was good for him. "I'm sorry."

She turned to him, drying her armpits with a scrap of linen. "You bloody should be."

"I am. Only I don't see why he's worth the effort."

"That's not the point."

"With so much happening in our lives already. Another letter came from Walsingham today, telling me to press on with developing informants. He looks forward to presenting her majesty with the signed *Capitulations*."

Aurélie snorted. "Has he any idea what's happening here?"

"How should he?"

"And yet he gives you orders. When he should be on his knees thanking you."

Longstaff closed his eyes, pleased she'd decided to take her anger out on Walsingham rather than him. His shoulders felt stiff. He sat up, stretching his fingertips towards the ceiling.

"I'm doing my best, Aurélie. Raimondi and the chevalier may not be the most honourable men in the world, but at least they believe diplomacy should take precedence over fighting. In their own way, both are striving to achieve balance, a structure of shared interests powerful enough to check the warmongers. It may be hard to understand, but I do take some pride in helping to make peace more profitable than war."

She kissed him on the lips, a spontaneous burst of affection which took him by surprise. "Why on earth do you think I wouldn't understand?"

They heard it at the same time – the sound of someone moving nearby. Longstaff crossed the room in two long strides, pulling open the door. The corridor was empty. It hadn't been anything obvious – nothing he could identify as a creaking floorboard or muffled cough – yet Aurélie had reacted, too.

"Fitch?" she wondered aloud.

Longstaff frowned. The noise had come from the wrong direction.

"Durant?" he called, one hand still on the door handle. The house echoed to the sound of his voice. He took a step further into the corridor, looking quizzically at the next door along.

"I'm right behind you," said Aurélie.

Longstaff drew the knife from his waistband. They entered in a rush. The study was empty, just as he'd left it.

"Better safe than sorry."

"The bastards have us jumping at ghosts."

Something was wrong. An inch of brandy stood in Longstaff's glass. The trace of an evil smell hung in the air. He raised a finger to his lips, staring hard at the cabinet in one corner of the room.

He'd already been attacked once. Had they come to try again?

On silent feet, Longstaff padded across the room. He put his ear against the cabinet door. Not a damned thing. And then he heard it; a sigh that might have been a breath of wind or the murmur of a ghost. Longstaff threw open the door. A man stood folded in the cramped space, features ghoulish in the dim light.

"Thank God it's you," whispered Hector. "I couldn't be sure. Is the door locked? We don't want to wake the house."

Longstaff wrinkled his nose.

"I know. I stink. You wouldn't believe some of the places I've been hiding. The whole Greek community have had their homes ransacked…"

"We've had the sultan's men here ourselves." Longstaff stood aside so that Aurélie could see what they'd caught. She closed the study door behind her, turning the key. Longstaff did not lower his knife.

Hector raised his hands in a gesture of peace, joints cracking as he stepped out of the cupboard and stretched to his full height. He was filthy. He'd lost weight since Longstaff had seen him last and his face was gaunt.

"I hate to do this to you, my friend," he said, "especially when you already have one unwanted house guest."

"You can't be here," said Longstaff. "Half the city is searching for you."

"I can't approach any of my friends without putting then in terrible danger."

"You appear to have overcome your scruples where we're concerned," said Aurélie.

"The sultan's men have been here already; they have no reason to think you'd help me."

"It was you, wasn't it?" she said. "You sabotaged the chronometer."

"There was no other way I could get into the treasury."

Longstaff's eyes widened in shock. "I should march you straight to the nearest janissary!"

"I thought I'd have time to leave the city before anyone realised what I'd done." Hector helped himself to the unfinished glass of brandy, raising it in Longstaff's direction. "To your triumph."

"I don't owe you a thing."

Hector cocked his head to one side, as if weighing the justice of Longstaff's words. "You know where I'm meant to be right now. Marching north to construct a canal between the Volga and Don – an impossible task which will almost certainly get me killed."

"And?"

"*And* says the free man." Hector shook his head. "I belong to someone, Longstaff – to be bought and sold, and sent to my death at another man's whim."

"What are you saying?" asked Aurélie, "That *you're* what you stole? The sultan would never have gone to so much trouble just for you."

"Your wife expresses herself charmingly."

"She's not wrong." Longstaff folded his arms. "What was it?" he demanded. "What did you take?"

"Is it really possible you haven't guessed? All those hours we spent together – what did we talk about?"

Longstaff racked his brains. They had talked about the chronometer, of course. The extraordinary advances the Yorkshireman had made in the art of clockmaking, but also the new technologies that still had to be invented before the art could be perfected. Longstaff had barely understood half of what Hector told him. He thought of the mechanic's own projects, the rods and staffs that were the indispensable tools of the navigator's trade. Understanding dawned in his eyes. "I remember a story you told me," he said. "Of a hundred astronomers spending more than thirty years recording the movements of the stars in the night sky."

Hector nodded. "Their observations were locked in the sultan's treasury. They're the key, Longstaff. I couldn't leave them to rot."

"The key to what?" interrupted Aurélie. "What's he talking about, Matthew?"

"Longitude."

Hector took another sip of Longstaff's best brandy. "For centuries, navigators have used astrolabes and backstaffs to determine latitude by gauging the height of the sun or a given star above the horizon. I've perfected an entirely new instrument – one which uses mirrors to simultaneously measure the elevation between two celestial bodies, even from the deck of a rolling ship."

"You've solved the secret of longitude?"

Longstaff could hear the disbelief in Aurélie's voice. And no wonder – the world would be changed at a stroke if he was right. Longstaff shook his head. Hector had talked about tens of thousands of individual observations. Ottoman archivists were careful – they would have made their notes in minute handwriting on tightly rolled scrolls – but it must still add up to a huge amount of paper.

"How in God's name did you smuggle thirty years of records out of the treasury."

"That was easy. Getting them out of the palace was the real challenge."

"And you're sure it will work?"

"I still have some calculations to do, converting the observations into a chart of angular distances between the moon and various celestial objects. As the name implies, angular distances are expressed in degrees of arc; they describe the size of an angle created by two lines of sight, running from the navigator's eye to a given pair of objects."

He saw the expression on Longstaff's face.

"Yes," he grinned. "Soon, armed with the star charts and my new instrument, a good navigator will be able to stand on the deck of his ship and work out his exact location anywhere in the northern hemisphere."

Longstaff felt suddenly exhausted, as if he'd lived a dozen lives in a single day. "You make it sound so easy," he said.

"Easy? I told the sultan about my work six months ago. He and the grand vizier want nothing to do with it – why do you think they're sending me north to die in a Russian swamp? Mehmed Sokollu fears that any advantage gained by the Ottomans would soon be bested by the Franks. That's when I knew – it wasn't just an act of cowardice, but a deliberate attack on human progress."

Longstaff groaned. "He sounds like you, Aurélie."

Hector smiled. "Your husband told me about your quest to find the Devil's Library, of your efforts to restore the knowledge of the ancients to mankind. Why else do you think I've come to you for help?"

"Because you have nowhere else to go."

"For all their genius, the ancients were never in possession of the secret of longitude. Just imagine it. A world in which no more..."

"Enough," snapped Longstaff. He had no desire to listen to the Greek spin his tales of a better world. In his experience, that was inevitably the point at which things began to go wrong. "The sultan's janissaries have created an iron ring around the city."

"It won't last. I just need a place to hide until they get bored."

Longstaff saw the flicker of excitement in Aurélie's eye. He knew she was thinking of the old Otiosi network, a loose collection of humanist scholars who had bankrolled her search for the Devil's Library. A group of men who would undoubtedly regard longitude as a prize worthy of their support.

"Where are the star charts?" she asked.

"Safe."

"And your invention?"

"I had to abandon the prototype. I can easily make another. It's the observations which are irreplaceable."

Longstaff shook his head. Some of his competitors had ratlines they used to smuggle galley slaves out of the city. Longstaff hadn't had time to set up anything similar and he could hardly ask the chevalier or Raimondi for help. Briefly, he thought of Padron Lettero, but that would mean getting Hector as far as Bursa. Beyond that, the mechanic needed a safe haven – somewhere beyond the sultan's reach where he could complete his work. That meant a decent workshop, a reliable printing press, a place where he could instruct the seafarers who would undoubtedly flock to his door. All of which would require money. Longstaff had exhausted his own meagre fortune on the chronometer.

"You said it yourself," he said. "We already have one house guest too many."

Aurélie looked at him in amazement. "We can't throw him out."

"We can't hide him here."

"What about the warehouse? You spent weeks constructing a smuggler's hole there. It must be possible to get him that far."

Longstaff shook his head. He'd dug a crawl-space beneath the strongbox; Hector might survive a day or two in there, but no longer. He didn't want to argue with Aurélie in front of the mechanic.

"We can't move him tonight," he said, trying to bring the conversation to an end. Beneath the bravado, he could see fear in Hector's eyes – and shame at having come to a near stranger for help. Longstaff had to get out before he started making promises he couldn't keep.

"Hector," he said. "You'll stay locked in here for now. You're above the kitchen; the servants will be back tomorrow. I can't answer for their loyalty, so for the love of God don't let them hear you."

He ushered Aurélie out of the room, locking the door behind him and pocketing the key. The house was quiet; their hushed conversation did not appear to have roused the priest.

Neither Longstaff nor Aurélie spoke until they were back in bed, and then only in whispers. Aurélie began suggesting and rejecting various plots for spiriting Hector out of the city, each one more outlandish than the last. She mentioned Abu Risha and Padron Lettero. Even if they could be reached, would either agree to help? They were businessmen, their decisions based on a simple calculation of risk and reward. Longstaff almost envied them. His fortunes had sunk low at times – never far enough to force him into outright banditry, which was probably for the best; he suspected he lacked the necessary ruthlessness – but at least the two men were masters of their own destiny.

Longstaff looked at Aurélie, waiting until she fell silent. "We have to get rid of him."

Her lips pressed into a thin white line. "Longitude, Matthew. Would you truly bury his work for the sake of your *Capitulations*?"

The breath stopped in Longstaff's chest. "You and Durant are as bad as each other – both behaving as if your work were the most important thing in the world." Her eyes told him nothing. Longstaff ploughed on. "One of you studying to become a healer, the other restoring long-forgotten knowledge to mankind. Admirable, blameless tasks while I'm reduced to bribing, lying, smuggling and stealing. Believe me, I take no pleasure in living like this."

He thought he saw the ghost of a smile on her face. "You think I don't know that?"

"Then why…"

"Haven't I stopped you?" she completed his sentence. "Why haven't you asked for my help."

You never offered. The words died in his mouth. They weren't true. He hadn't noticed he was plucking at the hem of his shirt until he felt her hands on his.

"If they find him here, do you know what they'll do to us?"

She nodded. "A slow and painful death – the same fate which awaits him if we refuse to help."

Longstaff thought of Aurélie's old mentor. "Giacomo never sacrificed his principles to expedience," he said. "I've been asking myself how he managed the trick."

Aurélie sighed. "He was brave and careful. He denied himself the pleasures of a family and lived his true life in the shadows. And he only managed the trick until the moment Spina stabbed him through the heart."

"I'm tired of scheming, Aurélie."

"Hector has knowledge which might add to our understanding of the world. I know what you've done here and why – but I can also see the toll it's taking. This agreement to supply the Ottomans with weapons is just the latest in a series of compromises. I honestly have no idea anymore if it's the right thing to do. But solving the riddle of longitude?"

Unexpected emotions rose in Longstaff as he listened to her, above all a sense of relief which stilled his fear, and a surge of excitement. She punched his chest. "Apart from anything else, I know how much you like him. I won't let you send him to his death because you're worried about my safety."

"We could lose everything we've built in this city."

Aurélie snorted. "Everything *you've* built. You made this happen, Matthew, giving up the prospect of a quiet life in Suffolk for my sake."

"I wasn't sure you'd noticed."

She hit him again. Harder. "If you refuse to help him, you'll betray everything you stand for. I won't let you."

A sheepish grin spread across Longstaff's face. He held her close, wondering yet again what he'd done to deserve her. "I do have one idea," he admitted. "Could you keep Fitch occupied for a few hours tomorrow?"

Her lips twisted in obvious displeasure. At least she didn't hit him again.

Chapter 21

Longstaff disembarked in 'Stanboul, hurrying towards Joseph Nasi's palace overlooking the Golden Horn. Was it just his imagination or were there more janissary soldiers on the streets today? Efforts to find the mechanic were only intensifying as the days passed. If the sultan's soldiers knocked on their door again, Aurélie had no legitimate reason to refuse them entry. She had promised to get the priest out of the house for the day. Durant would be at the hospital. Neither of the two servants had any reason to enter Longstaff's study.

But still, the thought of what would happen if the mechanic were discovered drove him to take this leap of faith – to trust the only ally he had in the city with sufficient influence to make Hector vanish. Longstaff gave his name to the servant at the gate. Nasi had warned him not to draw attention to their relationship. For a horrible moment, he thought he would be turned away.

"Follow me." The servant led Longstaff along marble-cooled corridors to an antechamber, then left him to admire the gardens. Cyprus trees on either side of a jousting field had been cut to resemble bulls, elephants, and camels. The roof of a small synagogue rose above the outlandish shapes. Longstaff paced back and forth, intimidated by these demonstrations of wealth and power. He was sweating by the time the servant returned to lead him to an enormous library on the first floor.

"What can I get you to drink?"

Dressed like a prince in a silk robe lined with sable, Nasi showed no sign of irritation at the unexpected visit. He poured two glasses of wine while Longstaff pretended to study the rows of leather-bound books. A tall vitrine housed a collection of jade carvings, lit by sunlight pouring through floor-length windows.

Longstaff wasn't sure he'd ever come across a man as urbane, not even in London when he'd been a guest of the Lord Chancellor. He accepted the wine with a feeble attempt to match his host's sophistication. "I understand you met my wife not long ago. The coin you gave her has proven more valuable than it appeared at first."

"Don't get complacent," cautioned Nasi, settling back in one of the generously upholstered chairs. "Raimondi isn't the type to forgive and forget – and it won't take him long to wriggle out of your trap. You can be sure new orders have already gone to the goldmine he controls in Bohemia. He'll be looking for any weakness he can exploit."

Like harbouring the Empire's most wanted man, thought Longstaff. Nasi leaned forward. "I'm sure you haven't jeopardised our agreement only in order to thank me."

Longstaff hesitated, aware he was about to place his life in this man's hands. "I've come to beg a favour."

"Another one?" Nasi poured more wine.

"Through no fault of my own, I've acquired an unlooked-for house guest. He needs a discreet way out of the city."

"The English priest?"

Longstaff rose to his feet with a rapid shake of his head. Through the open windows, he could see a hundred boats ferrying goods and passengers back and forth across the Golden Horn. Barring accidents, there was a chance his silk had reached London by now. Nasi, with his network of informants across the length and breadth of the continent, would hear of it first. Longstaff resisted the urge to ask if there had been any news.

"You know who I'm talking about."

The easy atmosphere evaporated at once. "If so, you shouldn't have come. Selim and I are friends."

"A sultan has no friends. If you help me, I will be in your debt."

"You already are." The merchant's face betrayed the first signs of irritation. "We're not talking about an escaped galley slave. The consequences of discovery would be catastrophic."

"The Greek has a secret," replied Longstaff. "A secret which the sultan has ordered him to bury." In a few brief sentences, he explained what the mechanic had stolen from the treasury – and why.

"The secret of longitude," he concluded. "Hector means to make it freely available, but a man with advance knowledge of his discovery could make a fortune…"

"Please don't try and anticipate me." Nasi steepled his fingers, hiding the manicured nails in his neat beard. "Selim rejected the information?"

Longstaff nodded. "Under Mehmed Sokollu's influence. He fears the secret can't be kept."

"God's teeth." Nasi stood, taking long strides back and forth across the fine carpets.

"Will you help?"

"Can he really do what he claims?"

Longstaff hesitated.

"If you hope to make me an accessory," snapped Nasi, "at least be honest."

"I believe *he's* convinced," said Longstaff. "I can barely tell one from star from another."

"God's teeth." The merchant shook his head as if waking from a dream. "Do you have any idea of what Selim has done for me? How much he's done for my family?"

"I'm not asking you to damage his interests. Only let him forego the pleasure of an execution."

"If someone steals from his treasury and escapes his justice, you think that doesn't harm his interests?"

"The sultan made the wrong decision. Hector has acted for the common good."

For a moment, Nasi looked at him in astonishment. Then he threw back his head and laughed. "What a gift it must be, to see the world in such clear terms. You're like a hero from the old stories, undaunted in the face of overwhelming odds, relentless in pursuit of your goals. But with the same problem a hero always faces. You have to win every fight, one after the other, endlessly. Not even you can manage that forever."

He must have read the confusion on Longstaff's face. "It's like that clock of yours. So many moving parts; if just one of them fails, everything fails. A strategist, rather than a soldier, sets a hundred different clocks in motion, each one independent of the others, thereby insulating himself from catastrophe and creating the conditions to effect change on a grand scale."

Longstaff absorbed the merchant's lecture in silence. The course of his life had nothing to do with heroism, as far as he could see. More a case of being in the wrong place at the wrong time – combined with loyalty to a small number of people and principles.

"Who else knows about your house guest?" asked Nasi.

"No one."

"Servants?"

"We only employ two. They don't know anything."

"I'll take care of them."

"They're not to be harmed." Longstaff half rose from his chair.

"Take care of them, I said, not kill them. I'll have someone offer them new positions, at double their present wages."

Longstaff nodded. "I can smuggle Hector as far as the warehouse I rent on the docks." He went on to describe the hiding space he'd built there. Nasi gave a short nod of agreement.

"I'll collect him at noon in two days."

Longstaff released a low sigh of relief. He couldn't wait to have the mechanic out of the house; he was living too much on his nerves as it was. "Thank you," he said. "I won't forget this."

"You'll pay for it handsomely," retorted Nasi. "For a start, you'll stop your ridiculous posturing and accept Selim's proposal without delay."

Longstaff blinked, not certain for a moment whether he'd heard correctly. "You know about that?"

"My dear fellow, who do you think suggested it?" Nasi smiled. "The Venetians have a saying: *Jura, perjura, secretum prodere noli* – swear, foreswear, and don't reveal the secret. Every man in this city initiates a dozen intrigues for every one that reveals his true aims. Every man except you – which is why you've become the fulcrum around which so many of revolve." He leaned forward. "You can't refuse, not while you're harbouring the mechanic in the home you share with your wife."

Longstaff swallowed. However lightly delivered, he could hardly miss the threat hidden in Nasi's words.

"Is Selim planning to make war on Europe?"

Nasi stared at him for several seconds. "Do you know why I've always been so willing to help you?"

"You stand to make a healthy return on the money you've lent."

"I'm already richer than you can imagine." Nasi gave an irritable wave of his hand. "My relationship with Selim makes me a man to be reckoned with in Istanbul, a position I exploit to harm the interests of Spain and Venice. My principal pleasure in life is finding ways to repay these two nations – in however small a degree – for the cruelty both have inflicted on my family and my people. My grandparents – chased from Castille to Portugal and forced to become conversos. My parents – pursued and persecuted from Antwerp to Venice and Ferrara before I finally found safe haven here."

"You're actively trying to foment war between Christendom and the Ottomans?"

Nasi sighed. "There's no such thing as Christendom – and you can rest assured Selim will do everything he can to keep it that way. I'm not saying he won't use munitions from England to add a few smaller territories to the Empire. He has designs on the Moroccan sultanate, for example. If he could recover Tunis from Spain, it would go a long way towards silencing his critics. He's tempted by Cyprus. Who wouldn't be? But you can rest assured he won't go anywhere near mainland Europe." Nasi peered at Longstaff over the top of his glass. "Does that answer your question?"

Longstaff shifted uncomfortably on his seat. "I hadn't realised this was so personal for you."

"Everything is personal. Anyone who says otherwise is a liar."

Was he right? Longstaff only knew he had no choice – England would agree to supply the Ottoman Empire with lead and tin, as well as experts in manufacturing and military tactics. It was the only way he could save the mechanic and his work on longitude. The only way he could deliver a trade agreement that would rescue England from bankruptcy. The only way he could protect Aurélie and Durant.

It left a bitter taste. Longstaff offered the merchant a weary nod, already afraid his name would ring through the ages as a byword for treachery and double-dealing.

How many times in the last two years had Longstaff climbed the hill from the docks at Galata? His thighs had burned in the early days, still weak from injuries he'd sustained in France. He'd come a long way since then, to the point where he almost thought of these streets as home. Why, then, did he study them so closely now, almost as if he were attempting to commit them to memory? The sailors with their rolling gaits, the smells drifting from the Arab restaurants, cheek by jowl with Jewish-owned shops. The two communities were close; in many cases their families had been forced to leave Spain at the same time. Along with the Italians, Greeks and Armenians in Galata, they had adopted the local preference for monochrome robes and tunics. There were still ways to tell them apart, but Longstaff had allowed himself to grow blind since moving here, preferring to embrace the idea of Istanbul as a place of hope. Unlike Nasi, it had never occurred to him to seek revenge on the country which had rejected him. Instead, he'd gone on doing Walsingham's bidding.

Was it hope, as he'd always thought, or naivety which had blinded him to the tangled webs of self-interest powering this extraordinary city?

An angry knot of men blocked the street in front of his house. Longstaff stopped in the shadows. They must have discovered Hector. For a moment, he was tempted to turn and run – but Aurélie was there, and Durant. What use would he be to them in chains? He could see the green turban of an imam up ahead, but where were the janissaries' nodding plumes?

Then Fitch cried out for help. Longstaff pushed through the crowd, past voices raised in anger until he reached a cowering figure. The young priest was deathly pale, shoulders hunched, fists clenched at his side. The crowd wasn't large, no more than twenty men in total, though a bigger group of onlookers was beginning to form at the rear.

"Heathen bastards," spat Fitch. "They followed me from the church."

Longstaff raised his hands, speaking rapidly in the lingua franca, desperately trying to disguise his relief. There was no time to ask questions. He had to get these people away from his home.

"My name is Matthew Longstaff. I have no idea what this man has done to offend you." He pointed a contemptuous finger at Fitch. "If he has committed an offence against your laws or religion, then I beg you to lodge your complaint with the relevant authority." Longstaff produced his purse. "Many of you have come here from 'Stanboul. Allow me to pay the cost of your journey back across the Golden Horn."

He offered far more money than they would need. The imam raised a hand for silence.

"We have witnesses," he said. "We won't be put off with a few coins."

"You know where I live." Longstaff straightened his robe. "I will personally see to it that this man makes amends for any wrong he's done. But not here. Not like this."

The men looked at their leader, waiting for a sign. The imam raised one slender arm. Behind him, Longstaff heard Fitch mutter. "You're giving them money?"

He didn't dare look round. This was Galata. The imam's authority was far from absolute here; he had to know he risked a riot if he tried to drag a priest through these streets.

"He's not going anywhere." Longstaff performed a low bow. "You have my word."

The imam allowed his servant to sweep the coins from Longstaff's palm. "You haven't heard the last of this."

The man's followers drifted in his wake. Longstaff watched them go, his head still bowed in an attitude of humility. He heard the heavy oak door open behind him.

"Matthew?"

"Get him inside, Durant."

Longstaff didn't follow until the last of the mob had disappeared, some of the bolder men still shaking their fists in his direction. He locked the door behind him, splashed his face with water from the pump. For a moment, he was so overcome with fury he could hardly speak.

"What in God's name did you do?"

"Nothing," said Fitch.

Longstaff took a step forward. Aurélie intercepted him with a glass of wine and Elif's three-legged stool. Longstaff drank. Closing his eyes, he relived the moment he'd turned the corner – imagining his wife and best friend led away in chains.

The priest was pale, a slight but marked tremor in his hands. Longstaff was in no mood to offer sympathy. "Start talking"

Fitch stiffened. "These primitives," he said. "I only wanted to see St. Sophia…"

"You sent him to Hagia Sophia?" Longstaff stared at Aurélie.

"What should I have done? Chain him to his bed. He promised he'd behave."

"This was a Christian city long before the Ottomans came," interjected Fitch. "The Church of St. Sophia..."

"It's not a bloody church," interrupted Longstaff. "It's been a mosque for over a century."

Fitch drank quickly. "I heard a story from our countrymen in Bursa. When the Ottomans sacked this city, a priest who'd been saying Mass disappeared into one of the pillars of St. Sophia. Legend has it he's there still, waiting for men of the true faith to return and set him free." The priest's voice rose an octave. "I went to learn about the people I hope to convert; it wasn't my intention to provoke them. I followed their rules, washing at the fountain outside, removing my shoes before entering. I felt so moved when I entered that I may have fallen to my knees."

"You went to pray for their downfall, in one of their holiest buildings, and you're surprised they took offence?"

Fitch refused to look him in the eye. "You behave as if they're the rightful rulers here," he replied through gritted teeth.

"You broke your promise." Longstaff was sweating, despite the open window. They all were.

"That was not my intention."

Durant spoke for the first time. Of them all, reflected Longstaff, he knew the Ottomans best.

"You were lucky to escape so easily. The Ottomans don't cast for God the way we do, but they still enjoy seeing someone turn. Praying in a mosque could be interpreted as conversion. Once you've accepted Islam, you can't renounce it. Apostasy is punished by death in this country."

"Live as a Turk or find yourself on the gallows?" Aurélie cast an amused smile in the priest's direction. "What would you have chosen?"

"You think this is funny?"

"Not at all," she said. "What do you think would happen if a Muslim were found praying in St. Paul's. He'd be torn limb from limb."

"Islam isn't a religion," said Fitch, as if speaking to a slow-witted child. "It was invented by Mohammad for the purpose of acquiring power. You only have to look at the evidence; the prohibition on wine, the commands to wage holy war against the infidel."

"The focus on alms-giving and pilgrimage," countered Aurélie.

"Popish nonsense," spat the priest.

"Fine. Then the fear of idolatry and the emphasis on a simplified liturgy." She shrugged. "I've heard the arguments before – Islam is a tool, cleverly managed to achieve power. I've never understood how the same arguments can't be applied to Christianity."

The priest stared at her in horror.

"Enough," said Longstaff. "Mr. Fitch is still our guest." He turned to the priest. "Within these four walls, we allow ourselves the luxury of speculation. Beyond them, we conduct ourselves with the humility expected of any guest. Do I make myself clear?"

Fitch attempted a smile. "I promised I would do nothing to draw attention to this household. Without meaning to, it appears I failed to keep my word." The young man's eyes were bright. For a horrible moment, Longstaff thought he might cry. "If it weren't for you, I'd still be a prisoner in the Fortress of Seven Towers."

"We're all under pressure," said Longstaff. "We've all said and done things we regret. All I ask is that you curb your impatience for a few more weeks. I'm vulnerable now, Fitch. My enemies – England's enemies – are turning the city upside down searching for any weapon they can use against me."

Chapter 22

Durant rose early the following morning, woken by the aroma of fresh coffee. Elif had already cleared the plates from the dining room by the time Durant joined her in the kitchen. The meal he'd prepared the previous evening had fallen below his usual standard, the seasonings too far out of balance to restore harmony to the household following Fitch's tumultuous return.

Durant nodded at Elif with suppressed affection when she brought him bread and olives. The old servant insisted on treating him like a spoiled child. The study was directly above his head. Durant listened while he ate, lingering over his breakfast, hoping to God that Longstaff knew what he was doing. The mechanic preserved a perfect silence.

Durant wasn't expected at the hospital for another three hours. His route took him past the huge mosque of Hagia Sophia, where the priest had drawn such unwelcome attention. He was briefly tempted to join the crowd of men gathered on the steps outside. Khalid had told him what to expect; the lines of men on their knees, rising and falling like wheat in a breeze, moved by the rhythm of their devotions. He thought of the great cathedrals of Europe, where merchants negotiated contracts beneath the vaulted roofs and whores beckoned their customers into forgotten corners. Not Godly, perhaps, but welcoming. Durant hurried on, away from Khalid's austere faith, slipping down the familiar alleyway and in at the door. Leila was already there. He caught her in the act of brushing her long hair.

"You look pleased," she said, setting the comb aside. Durant knelt to pour her a glass of iced-sherbert, the small routines lending precious dignity to their meetings. He remembered the

first time he'd spoken to her – a few snatched words at the
flower market, then wandering home with a bouquet of wilting
lilies in one hand, to spend half the night standing at the open
window of his bedroom, the great city below him shrouded
in darkness.

"I have good news," he said. "The Ottomans are on the
point of recognising Longstaff's position."

"It's a great honour," she replied. "He'll be given permission
to ride the sultan's horses, to dine alone with the grand vizier
and attend imperial ceremonies as an official guest."

"You're well informed."

She invited him to sit beside her on the divan. "He's your
friend. I've made it my business to know."

"As his advisor, I'll receive a degree of protection..."

She raised a finger to his lips. "Your friend must be excited."

She was so reluctant to imagine how the two of them might
be together. Durant allowed her to change the subject.

"He's tearing his hair out. To cap it all, we have an
unwanted guest at the house." Durant removed his coat and
shoes, hesitating only a moment before unbuttoning his shirt.
They still couldn't meet more than twice a week – on the days
when Leila made her regular visits to the *hammam*. Stripped to
the waist, he wrapped her in his arms, eyes closed, inhaling the
extraordinary warmth of her.

"Who is he?" she murmured, "Your unexpected
house guest."

"A young man who sees demons wherever he looks. An
English priest."

Durant worried about Leila's safety. The more they met,
the more relaxed she seemed to become. Renting this room
cost Durant a small fortune; he didn't baulk at the expense but
worried she was growing complacent. Everyone knew everyone's
business in this city. At least a dozen women must have noticed
the change in her routines. He kissed her softly. "Sometimes,

it seems I need to become two separate people. One to worry about you. And the other to love you."

"No one knows me at these baths. No one will miss me. My husband doesn't visit more than once a fortnight."

Durant ran his fingertips along the length of her arm. Was she underestimating the danger in order to spare him worry? "I lay awake last night," he said. "Thinking of you."

"That's what love does." She lowered her eyes. "We lose sleep. We practise deceit in return for a few stolen moments of happiness."

"Promise me," said Durant. "Whoever else we deceive we'll always be honest with each another."

"Don't..."

"Run away with me," he implored her suddenly. She shook her head. Durant felt a painful rush of guilt.

"The last time we met," she whispered, "you said there were reasons to hope..."

She was referring to Khalid. In his relief at not losing a friend, Durant had allowed a half-hearted offer of help to grow into unreasonable optimism. She seemed to read the truth in his eyes. A shadow crossed her face, as if she were closing a door on the most precious part of herself. He knew he wasn't worthy of her then.

"There's a world beyond Istanbul," he said. "Just waiting for us. A world where we can be free."

"The hunted are never free." She looked up at him. "And your friends? Wouldn't you miss them?"

Longstaff and Aurélie had their own dreams to pursue – playing at diplomacy or unearthing the long-forgotten past. "They have each other."

"Just as we have each other."

"Hidden away for a few hours each week? I love you, Leila." Durant pressed on, unable to stop himself, fearing he would never truly know her. "I have no secrets from you. My heart is yours. Can you say the same?"

Tears appeared in her eyes, writing slow trails on her cheeks. "Of course I can't. I'm a slave. My heart isn't mine to give!"

Durant swallowed, overcome with rage and guilt. That someone as precious as Leila should have been reduced to such a state. She kissed him, holding him with unexpected passion.

Later, they lay side by side, naked beneath the light blanket. Leila rested her hand on his chest, rising and falling.

"I didn't think I'd ever feel this way again."

"Again?"

"A love affair in my youth. The painter I told you about. He spent hours drawing me, conjuring me from lines in the sand, in charcoal scored on bark. He'd been apprenticed as an icon painter just a few days before the raiders came. We were going to marry..."

Durant framed her beautiful face in his hands. "It won't always be like this. One day we'll live together openly. I'll cook for you. My skill as a doctor will bring us an income." Durant's voice took on a dreamy quality. With a note of melancholy – as if he did not quite believe it himself. "My friends are among the most resourceful people on earth."

"You promised not to tell them about me."

"I'd rather die than betray your trust, but I hope you'll release me from my promise one day. You'd like Longstaff. He performs miracles the way other men prepare a meal."

"His name is starting to become known in the city. Ever since the sultan honoured him with a private audience."

"You wouldn't believe the number of hurdles he's overcome already. Even now, beneath all the official talk of English kerseys, there are parallel negotiations taking place."

"You're talking in riddles," she teased him.

He laughed. "The sultan wants to keep pace with the Franks. He's asked Longstaff to provide him with the raw materials he needs to make modern artillery – it's the kind of information an enterprising mind might put to good use."

Durant had vague ideas about investing in foundries or iron casts. If he were wealthy, he would no doubt find it easier to secure Leila's freedom. He changed the subject, aware he didn't quite know what he was talking about. Certainly, he didn't think he was betraying Longstaff's trust when he added that the secret of longitude might also yield to human ingenuity – after all, no one knew what had been stolen from the sultan's treasury, still less why. The excitement in Leila's eyes took him by surprise. He'd forgotten that she grew up on an island; the blood of generations of seafarers coursed through her veins.

"A man could reach new worlds on such a secret."

"Perhaps we will." Durant lay back on the wide divan, staring up at her. "I'll find a way we can be together. Even if I have to kidnap you and spirit you out of this city myself."

"Flee the Refuge of the World?" There was a hint of sadness in her answering smile. "Your countrymen would see me as a heathen and a foreigner. The Cretans would regard me as tainted by my years as a slave. This is the only place a person can outgrow their history."

For all the strength of his passion, Durant suspected she was right. They were held together by threads of gossamer. It should have been easy and yet he felt certain that if he severed their connection to this city, he would sever the bonds which bound them. He rose to his feet, aware that time was growing short. He had to move – to act; they would not find a solution in words.

She looked startled. He did not let her draw him back onto the divan, only kissed her on the lips and left, returning discreetly to the sun-baked streets of Istanbul.

*

When they wanted to, the wheels of Ottoman bureaucracy turned fast. Francesco strode into the house at midday exactly, insisting that Longstaff accompany him to the palace. Functionaries were waiting to explain what would happen on the following day – when Longstaff would be formally invested as England's ambassador to the Ottoman Empire.

Longstaff hesitated. He didn't want to leave the house again with Hector still hidden upstairs. He hadn't expected the summons to arrive so soon. It seemed that Nasi and the sultan were determined to act before their enemies could launch countermeasures.

Francesco removed his tiny eyeglasses, cleaning them furiously on his robe, clearly startled that Longstaff wasn't already pulling on his shoes. "This is what we've been working for," he said.

Aurélie urged him to go. She would find something to occupy the priest during the day, she said – something that didn't involve another trip to Hagia Sophia. The *dragoman* was a bundle of nervous energy. His excitement seemed to lift Longstaff bodily across the waters of the Golden Horn, transporting him to a small room in the outer walls of the Imperial Palace. Half a dozen kaftan-clad bureaucrats spoke in rapid, court Turkish. Longstaff couldn't make out more than one word in ten. The speakers sat in shadow, lit by a series of narrow windows high above their heads.

"The ceremony will take place in this room," they explained. Longstaff did his best to follow the *dragoman's* translation. They'd been sitting here for hours already. "Neither the sultan nor the grand vizier will be present. It's unusual, but not unheard of; the sultan has indicated he wants negotiations with England to begin immediately – hence the urgency surrounding your elevation to the appropriate rank."

Longstaff resisted an urge to play with the papers in front of him. He tried to emulate the *dragoman*, fingers steepled, elbows propped on the table-top, a carefully neutral expression on his young face. The door opened, another functionary entered, adding to the piles of papers. Francesco took the opportunity to tread on Longstaff's foot. A smile on his face, he murmured a few words in pure Italian.

"Can't you at least pretend to be interested?"

The newcomer offered his superior a satin bag fastened with a silver capsule. Slowly, the senior functionary removed a roll of parchment, dusted with gold and stamped with an elaborate monogram.

"Your papers," said Francesco, his eyes shining with excitement. "You'll be presented with this scroll at the climax of tomorrow's ceremony. It comes directly from the sultan himself. Accept it from his representatives with your eyes lowered and let it rest across the palms of both hands."

The functionary unrolled the parchment, inviting his guests to step forward and inspect the text. Longstaff clasped his hands behind his back, looking down at the highly stylised – and completely incomprehensible – Arabic script. With a polite nod, he stepped aside to give Francesco a better view.

"Everything seems to be in order," said the young *dragoman*, a note of genuine reverence in his voice. Longstaff did not begrudge him this moment. Everyone, from his father down, had counselled him against accepting Longstaff as a client. No one had believed he would be able to achieve so much in just two years. It certainly didn't occur to Longstaff to explain that this was theatre – a performance on which the curtain had only opened when he agreed to supply the Ottomans with lead and tin.

The door opened again. This time, merely to signal that the day's proceedings were finally at an end. Longstaff attempted to hide his relief in a bow, a sheepish smile, shifting from foot to foot like a restless child. Francesco took him to task for a second time in the street outside. "For two years," he began, "you've been a model of patience..."

Two years, thought Longstaff. It felt like a lifetime. "Did they say anything of importance?"

"That's not the point." The young man made a visible effort to control his temper. "Your task is to impress them. The sultan is showing you favour now, but those men know how fickle he can be. At least half will have been offered money to sabotage these negotiations."

Longstaff smiled. He would happily forgo any number of official ceremonies. Soon, the *Capitulations* would be signed and on their way to England for ratification. It wouldn't be long before Walsingham selected someone better qualified to replace him in Istanbul.

He must have looked smug. Certainly, something in his expression provoked Francesco to persevere. "Half the purpose of today's meeting was to give the sultan's negotiators a look at you," he said. "They'll go home this evening thinking they can get anything they want simply by testing your patience. Your carelessness might have extended our task by weeks."

They reached the quay. Francesco let Longstaff step into a waiting *caique* ahead of him.

"You're not coming?"

The *dragoman* shook his head. The oarsman pushed off. Longstaff raised his voice to carry over the water. "Thank you," he called. "I know how hard you've worked to help me reach this point."

Francesco shouted from the quay. "We've both worked hard, Longstaff. Don't sabotage our efforts now that we're so close."

Chapter 23

There was a new spring in Longstaff's step when he stepped onto the docks at Galata. So much had gone wrong in recent weeks – from the attempt on his life to the attack on the clock and Hector's unexpected arrival. Tomorrow, the mechanic would disappear from their lives forever. Tomorrow, Longstaff would be Elizabeth's ambassador to the Ottoman Empire. With a new, guaranteed market for their wool, England's famers would be saved from ruin. And – though it pained him to admit it – the clandestine trade in munitions would provide much needed funds for the royal coffers, reduced to nothing by the present Queen's father. Not bad for a former soldier and thief.

He stood in the sunshine for a moment, eyes closed as he listened to the city, so quiet compared with its European equivalents. A woman, heavily veiled, swept past. Too close. He felt a soft tug at his elbow. "Follow me," she murmured.

Longstaff started with surprise. She slowed, not resuming her former pace until he began to follow. Surely, no one would be foolish enough to attack him in broad daylight. It wasn't long before she turned off the main thoroughfare.

Longstaff hesitated. He didn't have to follow her. It would be the easiest thing in the world to continue home as if she'd never spoken.

Curiosity got the better of him. Muttering a curse, he slipped into her wake, shadowing her as she led him deeper into the warren of streets. The people who lived in these low houses were experts at seeing and hearing nothing. Longstaff slowed, sensing a trap. The woman seemed to hesitate before each turn. She looked back, gesturing for him to keep up. Longstaff wanted to turn on his heel and leave. He was already living with such uncertainty. His heart beat faster as he followed her into an overgrown garden. The gate hung from a single hinge. The woman stood with her back to the wall.

"Don't look at me." Her voice was soft. She spoke the lingua franca with an accent. "I need to get a message to your friend."

His friend? Did she mean Durant?

"I was told to get close to him," she continued. "They studied him for months – the kind of women he likes, a story which would hold his interest. I was promised a reward. Nothing he told me ever seemed important." She hesitated. "Until this morning."

Longstaff felt sick. What had Durant done? How many times had Longstaff warned him? "What did he say?"

"Just more of his talk. But there are people who hide in the walls where we meet. After he left this morning, they were different." She looked directly at Longstaff for the first time. "They said he'd signed his death warrant."

"What did Durant say?" repeated Longstaff.

She held up her hands. Longstaff saw fear in her eyes. It acted as a break on his unfurling fury. "He talked about you," she said. "He said you'd been asked to supply the sultan with weapons."

Longstaff breathed a sigh of relief.

"He talked about taking me away from here to start a new life," she added. "He talked above solving the riddle of longitude."

Longstaff stared at her in horror. "Who do you work for?" He forced the words past rising panic.

"I belong to Mehmed Sokollu."

Longstaff remained frozen in place. The grand vizier would draw the obvious conclusion – that he and his friends were colluding with the mechanic. Why else would Durant be talking about longitude?

Head spinning, he steadied himself against the crumbling wall, felt his plans turn to smoke, eddy from his grip and drift away on the breeze. There was no time and still he couldn't move. When he thought of the obstacles he'd overcome, so many months of work, so many near misses, to have the prize snatched from his hands. When he was so close. From such an unexpected quarter.

"He tells me everything," said the woman, as if apologising. "Otherwise I wouldn't have known how to find you."

Longstaff attempted to shake his head clear. He'd imagined himself enjoying a happy retirement in this city, resting on his diplomatic laurels. He was going to kill Durant. He thought of the severed heads Raimondi had shown him at the palace. The penalty for failure in Istanbul.

"The grand vizier," he said, finding his voice. "How's he planning to use this information?"

Helplessly, she shook her head. "I only know he wants to bring the sultan to heel. He despises Selim."

Longstaff sought for a glimmer of hope in what she said. How would Mehmed Sokollu behave if he wanted to cause the sultan maximum humiliation? What would he have done in the same position? Wait for the very moment when the sultan's favourite was elevated to the rank of ambassador, then reveal him as a co-conspirator in the attack on Selim's treasury. Longstaff knew he was grasping at straws but what else did he have? News of Durant's indiscretion had only reached the grand vizier this morning. Even Mehmed Sokollu would need time to assess the options and lay his plans. The woman might have bought Longstaff a day, time enough to flee. The three of them on the run again, but alive.

Suspicion followed hard on the heels of hope. "Why are you here?"

She lowered her eyes. "Don't tell him," she said. "It's better he think the worst of me. Just save him if you can."

She pushed past him. Longstaff let her go. How could it profit Sokollu to send her like this? Longstaff didn't have time to think through all the possibilities. He gave her a minute to get clear then followed through the broken gate, desperately trying to form a coherent plan of action. He forced himself to saunter – a man with no reason to hurry, with time to greet the guard in front of his small warehouse on the docks. There was nothing of value inside – Longstaff hadn't been here in days. No time to rail against the fates, to beat his fists against the walls or cry for all that would now be lost. Closing the door behind him, he sought inspiration in half a dozen packing cases, bales of straw, the strongbox, his desk in a far corner, a few of the bigger stones and statues which Aurélie had collected. There were two hiding spaces in the warehouse, one he'd inherited and one he'd made himself. He shifted packing cases around the warehouse, creating chaotic tracks in the sawdust.

Longstaff stepped back into the sunlight, aware he was improvising at speed. "What time does your shift end?" he asked the guard.

"I'll be here until midnight."

Longstaff produced his purse. "Stay until dawn. I'll make it worth your while."

The man grinned at the prospect of a few extra coins.

"I'm having some boxes brought down later." Longstaff removed a key from around his neck. "Lock up after the stevedores and keep the key for me."

"Where do you want them?" asked the guard, pocketing both his windfall and the key with the speed of a conjuror.

"Anywhere there's space. It's just a few odds and ends from up at the house." Longstaff was already moving away. "See that no one tampers with them."

He walked nearly to the end of the docks before approaching a group of stevedores, lounging in the shade of the customs house.

"I need two crates brought down from my house."

He began describing where he lived, but it seemed they already knew.

"The crates will be waiting for you after the evening prayer," he said, counting coins into the foreman's hand. "I'll leave the door unlocked."

The foreman raised an eyebrow. "You're not going to be there?"

"I'm entertaining tonight," replied Longstaff, attempting a lewd wink. "I've given the servants the night off and I don't want to be disturbed. Just pick up the crates and close the door on your way out. The guard at the warehouse knows you're coming." Longstaff counted another coin into the man's palm. "Cross me," he added softly, "and I will find you."

The stevedore touched a knuckle to his forehead.

"After evening prayers," repeated Longstaff. Did that give him enough time? He hurried up the hill, whistling to disguise his haste. Should he be running already – to find Aurélie and Durant and convince them they needed to leave before nightfall?

He was so close – less than twenty hours from the moment he'd been working towards for so long. What did the grand vizier really know, anyway? For a moment, Longstaff felt tempted to turn Hector into the street. He didn't want to go home. He wore two knives beneath his clothes, a pair of thick leather wrist-guards beneath the sleeves of his robe. What good would they do him in a battle against rumour and insinuation. The house felt strangely empty when he arrived. Aurélie was in her workroom – not working, just staring into space, fine hands draped across the clay tablets she'd dragged back from Bursa.

"Where's Fitch?"

"I told him about the church of Our Lady of the Fish at Balikli."

Another story from the fall of Constantinople. A monk had been frying fish when news arrived that the city had been overrun. The half-fried fish came back to life and jumped into a well – where it was rumoured to remain, miraculously preserved, waiting until Istanbul returned to the Christian faith. "He couldn't resist the temptation to go and have a look," said Aurélie. "He won't be back for hours."

"Elif and Hamid?"

"Handed in their notice an hour ago. They said to say goodbye." She appeared to notice the expression on his face for the first time.

"You have to find Durant," he said. "He should be at the hospital; I hope to God he is."

"What's happened?"

"It's over." Durant had fallen in love – every word he'd said recorded in a bureaucrat's file. Already, sympathy for his friend's plight was bleeding into Longstaff's fury.

"He fell in love – with a woman working for the grand vizier. Mehmed Sokollu knows about Hector."

She stood.

"You have twenty minutes," added Longstaff. "Make a pile of everything you can't leave. I'll do what I can to keep it safe. Find Durant. Take a boat to the hostel we visited. Buy horses there and head for Bursa. Contact Padron Lettero. If anyone can get us out, it's him."

"What about you?"

"I'll meet you there. It's safer if we travel separately."

For the first time, he saw doubt in her eyes. "Come with me."

"One of us has to get Hector to safety." He did not allow her to question him further. "We still have time but only if we hurry. Mehmed Sokollu will set men to watch the house. If they think I'm here, you'll have a better chance of escaping the city."

He marvelled at the way Aurélie responded to his demands. Without delay – without even a hint of accusation – she began to make a pile of her most prized possessions, then packed a shoulder bag with a change of clothes and sufficient money that she and Durant could pay their way. Longstaff took her in his arms.

"I will find you."

"I know." She looked up at him. "There's something I have to tell you."

They were interrupted, a shadow hissing at them from the kitchen doorway. Hector, trying to get their attention.

"Get back upstairs," growled Longstaff. Something in Aurélie's expression had changed when he looked back at her. "What?" he asked.

"Nothing." She stood on tiptoe to kiss him goodbye. "It can wait."

Longstaff did not see her to the door. There was no time. He followed Hector up the stairs, then stood in the study window with his hands clasped behind his back. He'd been a soldier long enough that he always knew exactly when and where he was under observation. He knew when he was visible to the neighbours and where to step in order to disappear from view. It was the same in the courtyard. From the roofs and windows of his neighbours' homes he knew that fully two thirds of the open space could be seen. The flat roofs of the stables created a thin corridor along one side of the courtyard where he could move without fear of prying eyes.

"They know I'm here, don't they?" There was no trace of surprise in the mechanic's voice. He'd been in hiding for weeks, living permanently with the threat of discovery.

"The grand vizier knows I'm helping you, which isn't quite the same thing. If you were him, what would you do now?"

"If I were him, or if I were you?"

Longstaff looked at him. At least Hector had the grace to look appalled at what he'd done. "Will you turn me out?" he asked in a flat voice.

"I might," said Longstaff, "if you don't answer my question."

"If I were the grand vizier? He doesn't know you know he knows?"

Longstaff shook his head, grimacing at the sentence, at how impossibly tangled his life had become. Durant's lover might have been spotted in Galata. She might even have confessed at the vizier's bidding. Longstaff refused to countenance either notion. There were already too many possibilities too consider.

"I would raid this house while you're receiving your accreditation as ambassador," said Hector. "He knows you'll be away from home. If he were lucky enough to find me, he'd have complete control over you and the sultan both."

"My thoughts exactly," nodded Longstaff.

Chapter 24

It was only after she'd left the house that Aurélie allowed herself to think of what she'd been forced to abandon. She was so close, just a few short weeks away from completing her translation of the *Enuma Elish*. She thought of the small pile of possessions she'd left for Longstaff – a stack of paper covered in her neat handwriting and the few dozen clay tablets she hadn't yet had time to study. Would he manage to spirit them out of the city – or had the months of hard work been in vain?

At least she'd resisted the temptation to tell him about the baby. She told herself it was the right decision; he'd need his wits about him in the coming days.

Aurélie smiled at passers-by, forgetting they couldn't see her face behind the veil. She placed a protective palm on her belly. It felt unreal to be walking these streets as a fugitive, to cross the Golden Horn for what might be the last time. One more game in a city of move and counter-move, a place she'd mistaken for the Refuge of the World. Longstaff had been playing since they'd arrived. A preferable alternative to war, he claimed, but that was still the ultimate destination – at least until people found a new way of playing, one in which every player could share the spoils of victory.

Had he ever had a chance? When it had looked as if he might succeed, someone had attempted to kill him, his clock had been sabotaged. They wouldn't give up until even his extraordinary reserves of strength were exhausted. The time and energy he'd spent on the priest, his generosity towards the mechanic, the lack of support from London. She should have worked harder on his behalf. If Hubbi Hatun hadn't involved her, he'd still be carrying the burden alone, losing pieces of himself each day.

Aurélie had never visited Durant at work before. She walked past the mosque, slowing as she approached the hospital building with its honour guard of cedar trees. By a lucky chance, she found him already on the steps, deep in conversation with a younger man. Aurélie slowed. She was about to break his heart. It would become real as soon as she spoke. No longer a game but a fact; their lives in Istanbul were over.

Durant looked shocked to see her. Aurélie tried to keep her expression neutral. "Is there somewhere we can talk?"

"Of course." He attempted to smile. "On the way back to Galata. I'm nearly finished for the day."

Not trusting herself to speak, Aurélie simply shook her head.

"My home is close by," said his friend. He was a beautiful young man, his dark eyes huge beneath the clean, white turban. She had the impression he was someone for whom the bonds of friendship were sacred.

"How rude of me." Durant made the introductions.

"A pleasure to meet you," said Aurélie, masking her impatience. "Durant talks about you with great affection."

Khalid smiled. "It's not far," he repeated. "You'll have all the privacy you require."

Aurélie knew it would be safer to refuse his offer, but where else could they go? Khalid appeared to have understood the gravity of the situation even before Durant.

"We couldn't possibly impose," interjected the Frenchman.

"Your friend is upset," said Khalid. "Something has happened and she needs to talk to you urgently."

"I'm sure it can't be that..."

"It is," said Aurélie, warming to the young man even more as she followed him through the narrow streets. He looked so pleased to help – an enlightened man, silently congratulating himself on his freedom from religious prejudice.

Her smile disappeared when she looked at Durant. For once, his heavy-lidded eyes were wide open. He was beginning to panic. Mentally, Aurélie steeled herself for the task ahead.

*

Longstaff and Hector made their plans. They had taken the opportunity to eat and drink while Longstaff pointed out the sections of the courtyard from which they couldn't be seen. Now, as the sun's edge touched the great dome of Hagia Sophia, it was time to act. Hector had nothing but the clothes he wore. Longstaff put on his old jerkin beneath a loose robe, hiding one knife in his waistband, strapping another to his forearm. For a moment, he thought longingly of the Turkish bow. There wasn't space for it; there was barely space for his *katzbalger* sword.

He helped Hector through the kitchen window, showing him where to step on his way to Aurélie's workroom. They had less than an hour before the stevedores arrived. Longstaff left the kitchen via the door, ostentatiously pulling two crates from one of the stables and leaving them so that the first third of each would be visible to anyone stationed in the neighbouring houses. He moved casually, filling the visible sections with Aurélie's tablets – as if the time had come to find somewhere else to store them. He felt a swell of shame as he looked at the stack of writing paper on her desk, neatly tied with string. *Keep moving,* he told himself, slipping the papers beneath more of the tablets and taking them out to the crates. There would be time for sentiment later. He added the few books and papers he'd collected from Durant's room, moving back and forth even after his work was done – it was vital that an observer believe that both crates were filled completely.

The remaining, empty spaces were hidden from view by the overhanging stable roof. Hector stared in horror.

"You expect me to get in there?"

It was a gamble, but Longstaff couldn't see any other way. "We've been over this."

"We'll be at their mercy."

"The grand vizier won't want to reveal his hand. We'll be gone by the time he realises I have no intention of attending my investiture." There was no time to argue. The call to evening prayer would sound at any moment. Longstaff began wrapping the blade of his *katzbalger* sword in a scrap of cloth. He would have to hold it against his chest.

A fist rapped against the street door.

The sword nearly fell from Longstaff's fingers. The stevedores? Had he missed the call to prayer? The door was unlocked in anticipation of their arrival. He looked up, expecting to see them march inside.

"Hide," he hissed at Hector.

Another knock at the door. Why didn't they just enter? Longstaff ran across the courtyard. He could ask them to wait. But then the mechanic would have to travel down to the warehouse alone. Longstaff would be trapped in the house. Hector wouldn't be able to find the smuggler's hole.

What then? Flee the city? With Aurélie and Durant already on their way to safety, he would have to stay – remain where his enemies could see him, buy sufficient time for Nasi to spirit the mechanic away.

He opened the door. Thomas Fitch stood waiting in the street.

Weak with relief, Longstaff moved aside to let him enter. At least the bloody priest hadn't led a mob of furious Turks to his door on this occasion. The street appeared to be deserted.

"Packing?" asked the priest, staring at the half-filled cases.

"We need more space," replied Longstaff, still off balance. "Just having a few things moved down to the warehouse."

"Of course," said Fitch. "How did it go today? Has the date of your investiture been confirmed?"

"It's tomorrow." Longstaff forced a smile.

The priest seemed distracted. "England's farmers saved from ruin, eh?" he said, parroting a phrase he'd heard Longstaff use. "No one here?"

"Just me."

"I wonder if we might talk?"

"Now's not the best time."

"It won't take long." Something had changed in the way Fitch stood, head and chest thrust forward like a dog scenting prey. A moment later he was striding into the kitchen. Longstaff hurried after him. Without waiting to be asked, Fitch poured two glasses of wine.

"Kind of you," said Longstaff.

The priest did not appear to notice his tone. "You mentioned you were in danger. That this would be an ideal time for your enemies to attack..."

"You're worried about my safety?" Longstaff resisted the urge to laugh. He went to stand in the window. There was no view of the street, no way of knowing how long he had before the stevedores arrived. "I think it's unlikely anyone will attack me here."

Fitch smiled, an expression empty of warmth. He seemed in pain. "I know how little love you bear for my mission."

Longstaff frowned. "I've nothing against it in principle."

"I can hear it in your voice. After yesterday's misadventure, no doubt you'd prefer it if I simply disappeared. I hate to disappoint, after all you've done for me."

Longstaff's mind was working frantically. He had to get back to Hector. Was there time to rid himself of the priest before the stevedores arrived? "This is a dangerous city," he said. "And I'm a poor protector. I can give you money for an inn..."

Fitch reddened. "Then you won't help me?"

"In so far as I'm able help any young man stranded so far from home. I'm extremely busy."

Fitch replied with a single, decisive dip of the head. "It's what I expected. This place has weakened your faith. Fortunately,

God has given me the means to put you back on the true path."
His voice rose. He looked up at the kitchen ceiling. "I know I'm
not your only house guest."

Longstaff's blood ran cold.

"You said it yourself," continued Fitch. "I have to act now if
I'm to achieve God's purpose. In return for the mechanic, I can
win the sultan's permission to begin my mission here, the funds
to build Istanbul's first reformed church."

"I saved your life." Longstaff spoke through gritted teeth.
Helplessly, he imagined his hands around the young man's neck.

Fitch ignored him. "The Papists have churches," he said.
"God's teeth, man, even the Jews are permitted to worship in
this city."

"Even if Selim agreed, Istanbul's Catholics would ensure
your venture was a failure. No one here will cast so much as a
brick on your behalf."

"You have no faith, my friend. We only need the courage to
take these first painful steps."

The *muezzin's* long, lonely wail reached them from across
the Golden Horn. Fitch sneered at Longstaff. The noise seemed
to infuriate him. He raised his voice in mocking imitation of
the high call to prayer. "Once we set our course, God will guide
us to our destination. Secure your friendship with the sultan
by giving him what he desires. Give him the mechanic and
demand the right to establish a mission in return."

"I took you into my home." Longstaff didn't want to take
the young fool's life. He didn't have time to reason with him.

Excitement and sadness distorted the priest's pale features.
"This is a test, Longstaff – to serve my God, I must break the
bonds of friendship."

"What kind of a God would demand such a sacrifice?"
Longstaff took a single stride forward – away from the window.
He swung his right arm, a perfect punch which felled the priest
as if the bones had been stripped from his body. He couldn't
remember the last time he'd felt such a thrill of satisfaction. He

dropped to his knees, hands around the priest's neck, choking him, determined to still all trace of ingratitude.

Aurélie's face appeared behind his closed eyes. Longstaff felt his fingers relax. Spitting a savage curse, he took the priest beneath the arms, dragging him upstairs, dumping the body in bed, tying his wrists and ankles to the heavy frame, gagging him. It was all taking too long.

Longstaff raced back to the study, lit a candle and set it on his desk. It would burn itself out in three hours – about the time he might be expected to retire.

Was it his imagination or could he already hear the tramp of feet in the street outside? Longstaff tore downstairs and into the courtyard. There was no time to say goodbye to Khamseen, pawing happily at the straw in her stall. He hoped the horse would find a good home.

"Get in," he snapped at Hector. "Stay silent if you value your life. If the stevedores hear us..."

There was no need to complete the sentence. Aware of what would happen if they were discovered, Hector was already climbing into his crate. Longstaff sealed it, then made a show of sealing the other, ears pricked for any sound from outside. He lined the crates up next to one another in the courtyard – one of them now wholly hidden from view – and re-entered the house. He vaulted through the kitchen window, crept along the courtyard wall and slipped inside the second crate. Paper crackled at the touch of his boot. Money would have been more useful. He'd been living on credit for weeks already. Praying no one would see, Longstaff edged the lid into place, securing it as best he could with wooden pegs.

He became aware of the absolute quality of the darkness, the smell of clay and paper. This was the sum of their valuables. Half a dozen languages captured in parchment and paper. Stories from a lost world, recipes, sketches of the human body. Longstaff had nothing but his weapons. The familiar weight of the sword on his chest the final proof he'd always been an impostor here. Where in God's name could the three of them go now?

Almost with relief, he heard the courtyard door swing open.

*

Despite her years in the city, this was the first time Aurélie had ever set foot in an ordinary Turkish home. Trying to show respect, she entered with her right foot first, the way Elif and Hamid always did. Khalid didn't pay any attention. Aurélie reminded herself that he was a physician, not yet wealthy – that much she knew from Durant – yet his home was far more spacious than anything he could have afforded in Florence or London, a four-roomed house with wooden walls and a projecting upper storey. It wasn't unusual. Despite the ongoing efforts of the Ottomans to repopulate Istanbul, there were still empty buildings in many parts of the city.

Offering his warmest smile, Khalid led them to a room on the first floor. Aurélie looked around; a blue *kilim* covered the floor, a copper pail and coffee cups stood on a low table beside the stand for Khalid's turban.

"Make yourselves comfortable." He indicated the cushions spread around the table. Aurélie thought she heard movement elsewhere in the house. "I'll leave the two of you alone," added Khalid. "Call if there's anything you require."

He exited backwards, sliding the door closed behind him.

"Well?" demanded Durant. He didn't wait for an answer. "This is a real imposition. The poor man's wife will have to hide herself in the women's quarters until we're gone."

"We can't go home," interrupted Aurélie. She kept talking. There was no accusation in her voice. Sympathy, if anything, but most of all a weary resignation. She saw the blood drain from Durant's face. He raised his hands as if to defend himself. Anger stiffened his posture.

"Don't blame yourself." She raised a hand to her mouth. It hadn't been her intention to provoke him.

Durant turned his back to her, arms wrapped around his narrow frame. "How did Longstaff find out?"

"He didn't say."

"Could he be wrong?"

Aurélie shook her head. Durant nodded, almost as if some secret part of him had always known. "People watched us while we were together?"

"I don't know the details. I should have asked Matthew but there wasn't time." She reached forward, hand hovering above his shoulder. "I'm sorry."

"Everything he's worked so hard to achieve."

"He's not cut out for this life. If it hadn't been you, it would have been something else."

She felt a tremor run the length of his spine. "Please," he whispered, "your charity is the last thing I need."

"Blaming yourself won't help." She felt herself become brisk in the face of his despair. "We have to find a way out of this mess."

Chapter 25

The stevedores worked in silence. Longstaff bit his lip as they swung him onto their shoulders. It would be fatal to cry out now. Would Nasi keep his word? The merchant had agreed to collect one crate from the warehouse, not two. The stevedores made their way down the hill, forcing Longstaff's head against the rough wood. He braced with his knees, wincing with every jolt across the cobbled stones. Nearing the docks, away from the better sort in their fine houses, the stevedores began talking among themselves again. They sounded bored, unsuspecting. The two words ran through Longstaff's head in time to the rolling gait – bored, unsuspecting – a mantra to protect against the discomfort until he heard the watchman, a key turning in the warehouse door. He held his breath – dockworkers weren't known for their gentleness. They didn't disappointment, dropping the crate with a crash heavy enough to shake his teeth loose. Nor did they linger, thank God.

Silence reigned in the warehouse. Still, Longstaff remained motionless, counting slowly to a hundred, ignoring his aching joints and burning muscles. He removed the wooden pegs and lifted the lid. The high windows cast a gloomy light across the empty warehouse. Longstaff hesitated before releasing Hector, reminding himself what a benefit the discovery of longitude would be for the world. There was a reason his life had been overtaken by chaos.

He did not dwell on the fact that it hadn't been by choice. For months, Longstaff had tried to convince himself he could have his cake and eat it. Now it was time to resign himself to the fact that only crumbs were left.

The whites of Hector's eyes looked enormous in the moonlight. The mechanic wiped a single bubble of blood from his lower lip. "I came within seconds of screaming blue bloody murder."

"Go and listen at the door," said Longstaff. "Warn me if anyone comes."

Silence was more important than speed now. With luck, the grand vizier wouldn't search the warehouse until after Longstaff failed to appear for his investiture. Nasi should have spirited them away by then. The merchant was due at noon tomorrow – at exactly the moment Longstaff was scheduled to accept his papers of accreditation.

The perfect plan, Nasi had called it. Already, Longstaff felt as if it had been made a lifetime ago.

There were two hiding places in the warehouse, one which had been constructed before Longstaff leased the place and one which he'd made himself. He lifted the straw mats from a section of floor, using his hands to brush the earth away, probing with his fingertips until he found the hidden catch. Silently, he transferred Aurélie and Durant's papers into the original smuggler's hole.

Longstaff looked at Hector, seeking reassurance from his friend before approaching the strongbox. He removed a key from his jerkin, muttering a fervent prayer of thanks that he'd thought to oil the hinges earlier that day. The lid rose without a sound. There wasn't much inside – a brace of duelling pistols, one or two encrypted letters from Walsingham, the title-deeds to the warehouse itself. Together with his *katzbalger* sword, Longstaff added them to the papers in the smuggler's hole. He lowered the trapdoor, disguising its outline beneath a fresh layer of earth and straw.

"Where do we go?" whispered Hector, moving away from the door.

Longstaff was already filling the two crates with a selection of bric-a-brac from around the warehouse. If anyone did search here, he didn't want them finding two empty boxes and no explanation of where the contents had gone. He paused long enough to nod in the direction of the strongbox.

"I don't understand," said Hector. "It's the first place they'll look."

Longstaff brushed past him. He leant into the strongbox, removing a hidden pin and gently letting the false bottom fall to one side. Gouged directly from the hardpacked earth, the space below was barely a foot deep, only a little longer than the box itself.

"We'll suffocate," said Hector, eyes widening in panic.

"We'll be fine as long as we remain calm," said Longstaff. "There's a breathing tube running into the wall."

"We'll be trapped."

"We'll leave the strongbox unlocked."

"What if someone fills it? We'll never get out again."

"Not something I suggest you dwell on," replied Longstaff with a grim smile. He stepped aside, indicating that Hector should precede him into the hole.

The mechanic shook his head. "First we have to retrieve the star charts."

"First," corrected Longstaff, "we have to escape the city alive. There'll be plenty of time to return for the charts when things are calmer."

Hector took a step back. "Without the charts, all of this will have been for nothing."

"There's only one way in or out of this building."

"The guard's asleep. I heard him snoring through the door. Tonight might be our only chance."

Longstaff looked up at the ropes and pulleys hanging from the rafters.

"Wait here." He climbed hand over hand, ascending smoothly until he was parallel with the high window. Alert for the smallest sign of movement in the darkness, he listened to the night, trying to hear the beat of a young man's step, the cough of an old man kept up too late. He breathed in, the sharp tang of saltwater lying awkwardly on the smell of dust and wood. Light flared only a few yards from where he hung in space. A man raised a hooded lamp – fair-haired, the cast of his features vaguely familiar. A second man approached. The two of them exchanged places and the lamp floated swiftly away. The newcomer vanished into the darkness, though Longstaff knew he was still there – watching. He thought of creeping out, wrapping one strong arm around the man's windpipe, choking him into silent submission.

And then what? Kill to no purpose or take a prisoner in the faint hope of information? What more did he need to know? The first watcher had been European. The woman set to entrap Durant belonged to the grand vizier. It seemed that Longstaff's enemies had joined in common cause against him.

Lowering himself silently to the warehouse floor, he nodded at the strongbox. "Trust me," he said. "We're not going anywhere tonight."

*

Durant called his friend back into the room. Khalid appeared a moment later, carrying a tray of food.

"My wife had to remind me of my manners." He set the tray on the low table, only faltering slightly when he saw the expression on Durant's face. Aurélie saw the effort the Frenchman made to pull himself together. She looked at the food – cheese, dried prunes, cornel berries. Simple fare but no doubt delicious. Normally, Durant would have gone into raptures. Now he looked nauseous, as if certain that even the choicest morsels would taste like ashes in his mouth.

"I'm sorry," he said. "I wouldn't have come had I realised we were in danger."

Khalid smiled. "It appears you have forgotten our master's lessons on the importance of observation. From the expression on your companion's face, I could tell the situation was serious when I chose to invite you."

Aurélie interrupted. "The grand vizier is plotting our destruction," she said. "But there's no way you could be expected to know that. You're not harbouring criminals – only showing hospitality to friends."

"Tell me what you need."

"A place to stay for a few hours. We'll slip away at dawn."

Khalid nodded. "I'll ask my wife to prepare food for your journey tomorrow." He cleared his throat, looking at Durant. "If there's anyone you want me to contact on your behalf…"

"No!"

Aurélie half rose. Surely, Durant had not intended to speak so vehemently. "That won't be necessary," the Frenchman added weakly, before sinking back on the cushions. Aurélie exchanged glances with Khalid, begging the young man with her eyes not to ask any more questions.

Durant saw the two of them look at each other. He knew what they were thinking. Their pity – and their generosity – burned in his stomach like acid. He didn't look up when Khalid left the room. Aurélie remained silent. Durant could almost pretend he was alone – with the pain and humiliation of Leila's betrayal.

Khalid returned only once, an hour later, carrying two sleeping mats which he unrolled on the floor. Durant forced himself to stand and embrace his young friend. There was nothing more to say. Still dressed, he lay down on the mat and closed his eyes.

Aurélie fell asleep with insulting ease. As Durant stared at the ceiling, every image he'd retained of Leila paraded through his mind, every word of every sentence he'd ever heard her speak. All of it recast in the accents of betrayal. He felt sick. Mercilessly, he forced himself to admire the skill with which she'd reeled him in; that's all he'd been – the fish on the end of a line. To have mistaken a hook for love and then to find himself still caught.

Durant needed to look her in the eye. He needed to hear her say that he meant nothing to her. Silently, he rose to his feet, appalled at his own weakness. Like a sleepwalker, he slipped from the house, helping himself to a selection of flowers from the display in Khalid's hallway, constructing a story as he went – one with sufficient power to encompass death. The story of a man bent on revenge, determined to end the life of the person who'd used him so cruelly.

He drifted through the dark city streets, moving from shadow to shadow as if he were already a ghost. It was dawn when he reached Leila's street, standing beneath the familiar window for the first time in weeks, arranging the flowers where she was sure to see them. To a casual observer, they would look discarded, thrown out to mingle with the rubbish in the streets. But she would know – he had grown eloquent in the language of love since meeting her. Rhododendron petals for danger. And lilac – flower of innocence and memory. He still believed in her, wanted her, yearned to take her back to where their love had blossomed. She would understand, but would she come? There hadn't been any roses in Khalid's house. Durant had no means of demanding that she keep the rendezvous a secret. It made no difference. Her handlers had always kept their distance in the past.

He did not go directly to the flower market. She was unlikely to wake for another hour. It would take her time to see the flowers beneath her window and unravel their meaning. Durant found an itinerant knife-grinder at the edge of a food market, already setting out his wares. Aurélie had told him that Longstaff would salvage what he could from the house, but Durant didn't expect his friend to think of ransacking the kitchen for his cooking knives. There was one beautiful blade before him now, centrepiece of the grinder's collection. Set in a hardwood handle, ten inches long to the tip and two inches wide at the base. Other knives had their specialities – paring, carving, boning, cleaving. This one seemed to have mastered all the culinary arts. Durant imagined himself measuring an ounce of salt with the point. The blade was fine enough to quarter a grape, sharp enough to skin a rabbit, heavy enough at its base to crush garlic.

Durant did not haggle. He paid what the man asked and continued on his way. Like a lodestone, hidden in his shirt, the knife itself seemed to draw him onwards, back to where it all began.

*

Durant was gone. Aurélie knew it even before she knew where she was. She woke with the word 'bastard' on her lips. Despite the stakes, her first emotion was embarrassment. She should have seen it coming. Khalid's cheeks coloured in sympathy when she found him a few minutes later. Aurélie could see how uncomfortable she made him – now that Durant had abandoned his role as chaperone. He sent his wife to her a few minutes later. Tülin arrived with breakfast, offering to stay and keep Aurélie company while she ate. Despite her kindness, Aurélie could see the fear in Tülin's dark eyes. She forced herself to eat, determined to keep up her strength. She couldn't outstay her welcome – that much was clear – but where could she go? Durant's disappearance had thrown her plans into chaos.

Longstaff had told her to head overland towards Bursa. The last time Aurélie had been there, she'd had the protection of the local *Sanjak Bey*. Now, she didn't even have Durant. How could she hope to get that far, travelling as a single woman?

She smiled at her hostess, letting her brain work while she complimented the food. Tülin had a few words of the *lingua franca*, Aurélie had picked up a few phrases of Turkish. The mistakes they made created a welcome illusion of intimacy.

"My husband is sorry to lose his friend from France."

"Durant will miss Khalid," replied Aurélie. "And the city of Istanbul. We all will."

But perhaps it was for the best after all, she thought. Longstaff had never been happy playing the diplomat. But did that mean they had to flee?

Without first striking back at their enemies?

According to Hubbi Hatun, Longstaff was collateral damage, his destruction a ploy to check the sultan's ambitions. Selim was the victim of these machinations just as much as her husband. Slowly, the germ of an idea began to form in Aurélie's mind, patterns emerging from the chaos that might preserve both the sultan's dignity and her husband's good name.

"You've been so kind," she smiled. "I have one last favour to ask before I leave."

Tülin dipped her head.

"May I borrow one of your dresses?" asked Aurélie. "And a veil. I'm sorry, I can't promise that you'll get them back."

Chapter 26

Raimondi Maltrapillo reclined, eyes closed, fat fingers clasped across his ample chest as he anticipated the day's pleasures. He sat alone in a concealed cabinet overlooking one of the grand wood-panelled receiving rooms which occupied the lowest storey of the palace wall. Decades ago, the first sultans to conquer Istanbul had spoken to their people from the High Gate. The tradition had fallen into disuse, but the monumental arch retained symbolic importance for the foreign community in Istanbul, ever since French diplomats had sealed an alliance with Suleiman the Magnificent in its shadow.

In an hour's time, Longstaff would come marching through the doors below. Instead of enjoying his triumph, the Englishman would be clapped in chains and marched directly to the Fortress of Seven Towers. Raimondi rubbed his hands; he could imagine his rival now, dressing for the occasion, admiring his reflection in the mirror, growing excited as the moment of truth drew near.

"I gave him a chance," he told himself, remembering the contempt he'd seen in Longstaff's eyes when the Englishman flicked that forged coin at him – as if the whole business of international diplomacy were beneath him.

More than anything, it was this performance of virtue he found so provoking – the apparently guileless way that Longstaff set about making a place for himself in the city. The Englishman had played his hand reasonably well, for someone so untutored, delaying Raimondi's ultimate victory with a degree of skill in the matter of the forged coins. The Venetian scowled. He still had no idea how Longstaff had found out about them. The whole business had ended up being far less profitable than he'd hoped. Even without the Englishman's intervention it was almost more trouble than it was worth, but a diplomat – if he wanted to succeed – needed a supply of ready money. Longstaff had had none when he arrived and for as long as sufficient Spanish money flowed through London, diverting English merchants from investing in the Eastern trade, Raimondi hadn't needed to take him seriously. The turning point had come when he found out about Longstaff's silk – via an urgent dispatch from his masters in Venice.

The letter had acted on Raimondi as a goad. Initially, he'd thought of using the information to destroy Longstaff publicly, but that would mean destroying the Englishman's network of smugglers and pirates into the bargain.

Instead, he'd paid a dockhand to put a knife between Longstaff's shoulder blades, intending to insert himself between Abu Risha and Padron Lettero once the Englishman was out of the way.

The assassin had been incompetent – at least he'd had the good grace to die before Longstaff could question him. When word had reached Raimondi of Longstaff's plans to supply the sultan with munitions, the dockhand's failure had revealed itself as a blessing in disguise. A quiet death was too good for the English bastard. It was time to make an example of him – and remind Selim that Christendom couldn't be divided as easily as he appeared to think. Below him in the grand receiving room, the sun struck the pearl-coloured marble with sufficient power that he was forced to squint. Bordered by a series of slim, fluted columns, the chamber seemed to float in the morning light.

The door behind him opened. The grand vizier filled the entrance to the hidden chamber. "They told me you were here. Your Englishman isn't due for over an hour."

"I thought it better to arrive discreetly." Raimondi hadn't expected to see Mehmed Sokollu, assuming he'd believe it was beneath his dignity to lurk in hidden rooms. The grand vizier spent several seconds staring down at the empty audience chamber.

"You should have killed him when you had the chance."

"This is better," said Raimondi. "Two birds with one stone." It was time to swallow his pride and give credit where it was due. Longstaff was a man of violence; Raimondi had been a fool to attack him directly. Once again, Mehmed Sokollu had shown himself the subtler strategist, aiming at the point where their enemy was weakest – at his friendships and misplaced faith in human nature.

"If I'd known you had a woman in the Frenchman's bed, I'd never have taken matters into my own hands."

Sokollu smiled complacently. "As it happens, I may have over-estimated my own cunning."

Raimondi felt a small flutter of foreboding. He leant forward to study Sokollu's profile. "What do you mean?"

The grand vizier sighed, the same half-smile hovering on his lips. "It's a good lesson for me. Problems should be divided into two categories; those which we can turn to our advantage and those which simply breed more problems if they're not dealt with immediately." He shook his head. "It never occurred to me that your Englishman might actually be in league with Hector."

Raimondi wished the man would stop referring to Longstaff as *his* Englishman. He still didn't know what the mechanic had stolen from the treasury – he assumed it was something portable. Jewels most likely. Longstaff must have run up astronomical debts since arriving in Istanbul.

"Fortunately," he said, "we discovered the connection in time."

"The woman who established it has disappeared." Mehmed Sokollu gestured at the empty chamber below. "I fear you're waiting in vain."

Raimondi's first instinct was to laugh. No one would dare cross the grand vizier, least of all one of his slaves. It was unthinkable. "Longstaff won't miss his investiture; it's what he's been working towards since the day he arrived in Istanbul."

"Perhaps you're right," said Sokollu, the same infuriating smile on his face. "Or perhaps he's slipping away as we speak. Laughing at us both as he goes."

The door opened in the empty room below. Raimondi and Sokollu leaned forward. Peering between the columns, they saw a servant enter and calmly start gathering up the papers.

"You've already cancelled the ceremony?"

Sokollu shook his head. "This isn't my doing." He sounded amused, as if pleased that people were still capable of surprising him. "It seems Selim is shrewder than we imagined. Adroit of him to have side-stepped our trap so neatly."

"God's teeth." Raimondi fell back in his chair. "What are we going to do?"

Sokollu shrugged. "A troop of janissary soldiers is already on its way to Longstaff's home."

Raimondi followed the grand vizier down a windowless staircase, emerging from behind a tapestry into a small antechamber. The ambassador realised he'd been holding his breath, half-expecting to find a jeering crowd. Outside in the courtyard, people went about their business as usual, while Mehmed Sokollu's good humour seemed undented by the unfolding catastrophe. "What will your soldiers do if the house is empty?"

The grand vizier spread his hands. "What can they do? They're overstretched as it is, searching the city for Hector."

Raimondi could not have cared less about the mechanic. How had Longstaff learned of their suspicions? Who could have warned the sultan that today's ceremony would not take place as planned?

"We have to find him," insisted the Venetian. "Give me a free hand in Galata. I'll raze the bastard's house. His warehouse, too. Find that woman of his and smash every stone she hauled in from the desert with my own hands."

"Whatever you think is necessary." Mehmed Sokollu took a step closer. "If you do find Longstaff, dispose of him. If you come across the mechanic, bring him to me at once. Do you understand?"

"How long do I have?"

"Who can say." Sokollu was already turning away. "Men like us can only live our lives from one moment to the next. Look at my predecessors; the ones who lost their heads were always the ones who looked too far ahead."

*

Not long ago, the women of 'Stanboul had appeared to Durant as an undifferentiated blur. Now, he seemed to see their hidden hopes and fears in a thousand different details.

He recognised Leila at a hundred paces, despite her veil and heavy shawl. She stood before a stall looking at the last of the season's crocuses – the penitent's rose, said to bloom when a loved one forgives the unforgivable. Durant clasped his hands behind his narrow back, moving steadily closer. She didn't look at him – it was clear she knew he was near. She set off in the opposite direction, leaving the market via a covered alley of abandoned stalls. The perfect place for an ambush.

She turned to face him. He heard the breath catch in her throat when she saw the knife. He didn't look at her, preferring to watch the sunlight play along the blade, her reflection in the tempered steel. She unhooked her veil, rising to her full height, head tilted as if to offer him her throat. Durant was tall, but so was she. So close. Such beautiful skin. He hardly knew whether to kill her or kiss her, his hurt a great swallowing darkness. There was a path to be taken. It led through her body. She waited in stillness. He took a firmer grip of the knife, incensed by her pride.

"One of us has to die."

He handed her the knife. She stared at it in confusion. "I didn't risk everything to see you throw your life away."

"I know what you are."

"A slave? Someone's possession?"

Durant reeled. In her eyes, he saw something that wasn't pride. He saw sorrow for the pain she'd caused him. Even more than that, he saw love. "You have no idea what I am," she whispered sadly.

Durant listened for the rush of footsteps behind him. The seconds seemed to stretch into hours. The alleyway remained as silent as the grave.

"Come with me," he said

Tears appeared in her eyes. "After what I've done?"

"You saved me, Leila. I have to leave the city. Come away with me."

"Mehmed Sokollu's men will find us."

"They're too busy looking for Longstaff and Hector."

"The grand vizier is not a merciful man," she said. "He has a long memory – and an even longer reach."

Durant shook his head. He had been a thief. He had been in Istanbul long enough to learn its rhythms, the times and places where a man and woman might hope to pass unnoticed. "We'll go south," he said, thinking of Longstaff's plan. They could travel along the Bosphorus as far as Iskandar, find horses there and set off overland for Bursa.

He checked his pockets. A few coppers, hardly enough to pay for their passage out of the city, let alone the journey south. He was going to get them both killed – and perhaps Aurélie as well. Durant felt suddenly dizzy with guilt.

"I have money," said Leila.

He looked at her in surprise. Tears were running freely down her cheeks. "When I left the house this morning," she said, "I knew I wouldn't be able to return."

He reached out to touch her face. "You didn't really think I'd hurt you."

She laughed through her tears. "I hoped you'd save me. It's not a fortune, enough to keep us going for a few weeks."

Durant looked away. "We have to reach Bursa," he said. "Longstaff is going to meet us there."

He didn't give her a chance to ask what would happen then. Fixing the veil across her face, he led her through the twisting streets of 'Stanboul, refusing to stop – or even pause – until they passed a tailor's shop. The man inside appeared to be alone. He was ancient, shrunk to half Durant's size. Leila took command of the situation.

"My servant needs new clothes," she said. "Something more appropriate to his status."

Durant shrugged out of his student's robe with less regret than he would have imagined possible a few days earlier. He'd had it made a year ago, from finer cloth than most students could afford. Vanity – and the fact he'd been so much older. Like a snake, sloughing off one skin and adopting another, he accepted a fitted tunic from the tailor and a pair of comfortable trousers.

Leila had been busy in the meantime, rifling through the tailor's selection of finished clothes for a bright chemise and ankle-length kaftan of embroidered cloth. She must have been terrified, thought Durant, and yet he thought he also detected some part of her enjoying this sudden reversal in their roles. Emerging from the shop's small fitting room, she seemed transformed into a lady of rank. Even the tailor treated her with more deference, handing her a new *ferace* which she buttoned to her throat before covering her hair and face with a veil.

She handed Durant her purse. "Pay the man."

Durant bowed. "My lady."

The tailor named his price. He was smiling, happy to have played a part in their game – whatever it was. Durant winked as he added a healthy tip, then led his mistress into the street. The nearest quay was less than five minutes' walk away. Durant had no idea if the oarsmen were taken in by their disguise. It was as much as he could do to sit with his eyes appropriately lowered. He felt excitement rise in his chest whenever he glanced at Leila, perched in her finery on the boat's most comfortable seat. She had chosen to bind her fate to his. He couldn't risk speaking as they travelled to Iskandar. Words burst from his mouth as soon as they were alone on dry land.

"I want you to know – we might be fleeing for our lives, but I can't remember when I last felt so happy."

She made a show of drawing herself up to her full height. "Is that any way for a servant to talk to his mistress?"

Durant heard the smile in her voice, following happily as she strode ahead of him towards the hostel.

Chapter 27

Raimondi was well-known in Galata. It didn't take him long to assemble a dozen men from the taverns along the docks, brutal men, who lived by the strength of their arms and an uncomplicated loyalty to *La Serenissima*. The Venetian ambassador sent half up the hill to Longstaff's home with instructions to observe Sokollu's janissaries – whether the soldiers ran their quarry to ground or not, his men were to take possession of the house as soon as they left.

With the remainder of the dockhands, Raimondi marched on the Englishman's warehouse. He was intercepted by one of the men he'd set to watch the place.

"Anything?"

"No one in or out since the stevedores last night."

Raimondi halted in mid-stride. "Stevedores?"

"A small gang. They brought two crates from the house."

"At night? Did Longstaff let them in himself?"

"It was the watchman." The man scratched his head. "There was something a bit strange."

Raimondi stared at him. Fury had reduced his pupils to sharp points. "Yes?"

"There was no one at the house to meet the stevedores. The door was left open for them."

"What?" Raimondi ordered his men to break into the warehouse. The door gave way within seconds, still long enough for Raimondi's impatience to reach fever pitch. The packing cases were in the centre of the room, filled with all manner of junk.

"Turn this place upside down!"

"What are we looking for?"

"Two men."

The dockhands looked doubtful but set to willingly enough. The sound of splintering wood helped calm Raimondi. He took a seat at Longstaff's desk while his men examined the enormous strongbox. It wasn't locked; they threw back the iron lid with a groan of disappointment. Empty.

Raimondi began leafing through the papers in front of him, mostly relating to Longstaff's clock. Another gift gathering dust in the sultan's treasury. A gift or a Trojan horse? The Venetian thought of Sokollu's parting words – *If you find the mechanic, bring him to me.* Longstaff and Hector. The two of them had risked everything to gain access to the treasury. Like everyone in the city, Raimondi had heard a hundred different theories about what had been stolen, each more outlandish than the last. He heard a clay tablet shatter on the warehouse floor.

"We've got something."

Raimondi's head snapped up. His men had stripped the floor of its straw and sackcloth covering. He could see nothing out of the ordinary beneath – just the usual chaos of footprints and scuffmarks.

One of the men dropped to his knees, digging at the hard-packed earth with a piece of wood, revealing the outline of a trapdoor. He worked urgently, scraping the dirt away on all four sides. Raimondi hurried over, rubbing his hands in anticipation, picturing Longstaff and the mechanic lying with their noses pressed against the door's underside, cheek by jowl in their hiding place. "Open it," he hissed.

It took his men an age to find the hidden catch. Two of them produced knives, others grabbed lengths of wood to use as clubs. Raimondi nodded. The trapdoor opened on silent hinges. No one came out fighting.

"Let me see." Raimondi's voice was shrill with excitement as he pushed the dockhands aside, fading as he peered down at a stack of papers and two duelling pistols. He found a recipe for pilaf. Pages and pages of gibberish in the woman's hand. Why even hide this rubbish? Raimondi answered his own question. "To taunt me. The bastard knew I'd find his smuggling hole."

His eyes fell on the iron strongbox on the far side of the room, the bric-a-brac which had been piled against the walls and now lay strewn across the floor. One of the men he'd sent to the house arrived in the doorway, breathing hard.

"They've found someone."

"Who?"

"An Englishman. Bound and gagged. Claims he's a priest though he was cursing like the very devil when they led him away." The man steadied himself against the wall. "He claims it was Longstaff who tied him up. The Englishman and his friends have disappeared. No one's seen them since yesterday."

Raimondi turned the rings on his fat fingers. "We're missing something." Crossing to the strongbox, he had his men throw back the lid once more.

The breathing tube carried every word into the shallow pit where Longstaff and Hector lay squeezed together in the darkness. Longstaff still possessed the soldier's knack of judging the passage of time. It wasn't yet noon, his investiture shouldn't even have started. What in God's name was Raimondi doing here so soon?

He closed his eyes. It made no difference in the inky darkness. He concentrated on breathing – in and out – listening as the mechanic matched him breath for breath. The crawl space was stifling, stale air and the stench of fear. Footsteps came to a halt above their heads. Longstaff pressed his palm against the warm metal. Someone kicked the walls of the strongbox; the vibrations travelled the length of his arm. Another kick. And another.

Did Raimondi suspect a second hiding place or was he just venting his fury? When he spoke, his voice sounded impossibly close. "Tip this fucking thing over."

Swamped in the mechanic's terror, teeth bared, ready to sell his life dearly, Longstaff heard a new voice, a second volley of instructions among the thundering boots. Joseph Nasi had arrived.

"We've come to make an inventory," said the merchant in his clear, confident voice.

"On whose authority?"

"Mine. This warehouse and its contents belong to me now. I'm afraid that means you're trespassing."

Was it a bluff? How many men Nasi did have with him?

"I am here," replied Raimondi, enunciating each word separately, "on the orders of the grand vizier himself."

"I wasn't aware his jurisdiction extended as far as Galata."

"Matthew Longstaff is suspected of treason. He's not at his home."

"So you've come here," interrupted Nasi. "Understandable but pointless. Do you see any sign of him? Look at the mess you've made. For your sake, I hope it doesn't leave me out of pocket."

"You're not making any sense, Nasi." There was ill-concealed loathing in the Venetian's voice. "Stop waving those papers in my face and tell me what you want."

"These papers are a record of the various sums of money I've lent our English friend over the last two years. If I might direct your attention to paragraph six, clause three. Longstaff's property automatically becomes mine if he leaves the city without informing me first, defaults on his repayments, or engages in criminal activity. It appears he's guilty of breaking all three conditions."

Longstaff waited for fighting to break out over his head. How were the rival forces matched? Who would back down first? His hands curled into fists.

"Tip it over," repeated Raimondi.

"That box is my property. Touch it and I'll order my men to attack."

Longstaff heard the beating of his own heart, of Hector's heart beside him in their cocoon. Boots hit the floor with the sound of infantry marching into battle – and then silence.

A minute passed. Then two.

Someone knocked on the false floor above his head. "Are you in there, Hector? The Venetian and his friends have gone."

Longstaff released the catch and sat up, eyes level with the lip of the box. Hector appeared beside him, two corpses rising from the grave. Nasi made himself comfortable on a packing case nearby. "Two for the price of one," he said, lighting his pipe. "I suspected that might be the case."

Three men guarded the door. Another had climbed the hanging ropes to watch at the window.

Long heard joints pop as he turned his head from side to side. "You chased him off with four men?"

Nasi chuckled through a cloud of smoke. "I chased him off with ten. The others are outside. It's best they know as little as possible."

"Are you going to get us out of here?" asked Hector.

"We may be lurching from one crisis to the next, but I hope we haven't lost our balance yet." Nasi indicated two new packing cases, standing in the middle of chaos. "Back in your boxes, gentlemen."

Longstaff groaned. "Where to?"

"Across the Golden Horn." Nasi blew smoke rings in the still air.

"We're not leaving the city?"

"How? With Raimondi's men out there, I have no choice but to take you home."

"That's insane." Longstaff wanted to tell the merchant he was risking too much, but Nasi was right. Ostensibly, he'd come to collect Longstaff's possessions; where else would he take them but home? Where else could he take them that was free from prying eyes?

"I suggest we get a move on," said Nasi. "The longer my men remain outside, the more suspicious our mutual friend will become."

Longstaff pointed at Aurélie's clay tablets and Durant's papers. "There's nothing else of value here."

"And yet we'll take it all, for the look of the thing." He smiled. "And because it will drive Raimondi mad."

Nasi himself nailed the wooden crates shut. Nose flush against the rough planks, Longstaff listened as his men trooped back inside to begin crating up the remainder of their possessions. Then he was lifted onto four shoulders again and carried the length of the docks to a waiting *caique*. He imagined Raimondi and his men lining their path, eyes attempting to burn holes in each crate that passed. Remembering the anger he'd heard in the Venetian's voice, he found it hard to breathe until they were out on the Horn, swaying men replaced by the smoother rhythms of water – plagued by the eerie sensation that this was his funeral procession. He was soaked with sweat by the time they reached Nasi's palace, irrationally furious with the man who'd saved his life. The crate opened, releasing him into darkness, into cool, still air. Nasi held a torch above his head, lighting stone walls – an empty, windowless chamber in the cellars beneath his home.

"Raimondi's men dogged our heels as far as the gates," said the merchant. "Two of them are out there now."

Hector sat with his back against the cold wall, arms around his knees, breathing carefully.

"It seems you backed the wrong horse," said Longstaff.

"Oh, I don't know about that."

"No?" Longstaff had always assumed Nasi would profit handsomely from any trade agreement between England and the Ottoman Empire. There was no prospect of that now. "You encouraged Selim to show me favour. He's unlikely to forgive you for this humiliation."

"On the contrary, no official charges have been brought against you. Nor are they likely to be – it seems the grand vizier's key witness has disappeared. What's more, the sultan's representatives never reached the audience chamber – almost as if no investiture had been planned for today."

Longstaff looked at him in confusion. "That's impossible. How did Selim know I wouldn't come?"

Nasi grinned. "An unexpected visitor arrived on my doorstep this morning, sufficiently early that I was able to bring proceedings to a halt."

The door opened as he spoke. Aurélie stood in the opening, fair hair alive in the torchlight as she ran to Longstaff's side.

"What in God's name are you doing here?" He didn't want to lose his temper in front of Nasi. "You should be miles away by now."

"Durant disappeared."

"You let him out of your sight?" Even as he spoke, Longstaff felt the bitter taste of hypocrisy. The Frenchman had given him the slip before – in equally desperate circumstances.

"It would have been foolish of your wife to travel alone," put in Nasi. "By coming here, she made it possible for us to keep control of the situation."

"You call this control?"

"Why did Durant leave you?" said Hector. "What does he intend to do?"

Longstaff ground his teeth. "He's trying to reach the woman."

"Or the people controlling her?" suggested Nasi.

Longstaff shook his head. "He's a romantic beneath that cynical exterior, not a killer. He's gone to her. You did the right thing, Aurélie. You had no choice once he'd deserted you."

"He didn't desert me. Durant knows I can take care of myself."

The rebuke was pointed. Longstaff stared at her in amazement. They were trapped. Worse, their enemies must suspect they were here; Raimondi was many things, but never a fool. And Aurélie wanted to waste their time defending Durant?

Longstaff opened his mouth to object. Then closed it again in defeat. "Is there anything to eat?"

Chapter 28

That night, Joseph Nasi and two hand-picked men brought a selection of furnishings down to the cellar. A woman he introduced as Sarah brought a selection of delicacies. Neither the food nor the furniture would have disgraced a king, and neither did anything to relieve Aurélie's claustrophobia. She understood why they had to stay below ground; Nasi possessed an army of servants, not all of whom were trustworthy. The cellars were extensive, one cavernous hall and a dozen smaller rooms connected by narrow corridors, but only one way in or out. Two of the smaller rooms became makeshift bedrooms, one for Hector and one for the married couple. Aurélie stared at the black walls, remembering the view from her bedroom window before she fell asleep. The red roofs of Galata sloping down to the sparkling waters of the Golden Horn.

Nasi did not come in the morning. The cellar door was locked from the inside. Longstaff had the key, but no one suggested he use it. Instead, Aurélie questioned the mechanic about the secrets of longitude, listening closely to his explanations, insisting he draw sketches of the various instruments he'd designed – which he claimed would allow seamen to discover the exact location of their floating vessels.

Hector had no suggestions for how they might escape this cellar, this city, and the grand vizier's long reach. Aurélie did not press him on whether the secret of longitude was worth the sacrifices it had demanded of them. She breathed a sigh of relief when Nasi finally arrived. All three of them stood, searching the merchant's face for clues about what was happening in the city. He didn't smile. His gestures were short and business-like.

"I'm sorry I couldn't come sooner. I was summoned to the palace this morning. The grand vizier has asked the sultan for permission to search this house." Nasi stopped pacing for long enough to point in Hector's direction. "Mehmed Sokollu suggested I may be harbouring you. Selim wanted to ask me whether there was any substance to the accusation. It's the first time I've ever lied to him."

"How long do we have?" asked Longstaff.

"Selim will give in eventually. He hates the grand vizier and loves me like a brother, but I'm the one he'll sacrifice."

"How long?" repeated Aurélie.

"Three days, if we're lucky." He sighed. "I'll have to waste half of them being loudly offended that anyone could doubt my loyalty."

"Does Raimondi still have men watching the house?"

"Dozens of them, posted throughout the neighbourhood."

"How were you going to get Hector out of the city?"

"A ship's captain I trust has an aversion to paying the sultan his due. He has a small pink fitted with a smuggler's hold. The original plan was to rendezvous with him in the middle of the Horn. It only takes a moment to pass up a single crate, but even that would have been too long with Raimondi watching."

"Could he take the three of us?" asked Hector.

"Four," interrupted Aurélie. "There are four of us. With Durant."

Nasi stared at her. "Three or four. It's academic as long as you're trapped here. Raimondi's men are intimidating my visitors and inspecting every delivery. They're following my men, searching them if they're carrying anything bigger than a hat box."

Longstaff surprised her then, rising to his feet, knuckles pressed against the tabletop. "We have three of the best brains in Istanbul in this room," he said, looking at each of them in turn. "My right arm, if we need it, and no shortage of motivation."

"More than you realise," said Nasi. "Assuming we can get you out of the city, it won't be difficult to resurrect your agreement with the sultan."

"Even after we release the secret of longitude?"

"Selim has no proof you're helping Hector. Assuming we keep it that way, I'm certain we can salvage something from the situation. In a year's time, after the first shipments of lead and tin have landed successfully, Walsingham will be able to send another man in your place."

He left them soon afterwards, perhaps buoyed by Longstaff's determination, but with worry lines still clearly etched on his forehead. Longstaff and Hector sat at the table. Aurélie listened as they swapped ideas on how to escape from the city. Crates were a common feature – unsurprisingly, given the events of the past two days. Unsurprisingly, too, both sounded reluctant to repeat the trick. They weren't well-matched as conspirators, reflected Aurélie. Hector had a tendency to overcomplicate and Longstaff an inclination to oversimplify – most of his suggestions involved feats of great physical daring. When Hector drew attention to the inevitable flaws in each plan, she saw her husband's hand twitch at the hilt of the sword he'd started wearing again.

"How long did you wait for your chance to enter the treasury?" she interrupted Hector, hoping to approach the problem from a different angle.

He blinked in surprise. "Months. I hardly dared believe it would happen until I was asked to work on the chronometer."

"And once you were inside?"

"There was an official from the treasury watching me." He shrugged. "But no one can keep that up forever, not when they're surrounded by treasures from a score of kingdoms and half a dozen empires. Books, crowns, carpets, musical instruments. A feast for the senses; little wonder he never suspected my true purpose."

"How did you get the charts out?"

"I had a trolley made for the chronometer with a triple layer of wooden planks – ostensibly to carry its weight, but actually in order to create a hidden compartment. After I transferred the clock to the platform in the courtyard, I took the trolley to the kitchens. Hundreds of tradesmen were coming and going, bringing food and drink for the sultan's guests. No one paid any attention when I joined a train of empty carts returning to the city."

Aurélie picked up her wine glass, turning it to catch the candlelight, studying the smooth surface for imperfections. "People tell so many stories about the sultan's treasury. You've been inside; you could tell any story you liked about the contents – we'd almost certainly believe it."

Hector cocked his head to one side, thinking. "Do you know the story of the Turkish traveller who went to meet the King of Cathay?" he asked.

Aurélie shook her head.

"It took him months just to reach the border. He crossed Persia, saw the cities of Samarkand, Bokhara, and Tashkent, passed through countries inhabited by savage clans, where the land was so poor he nearly starved. Still, he pressed on, until at last he reached the passes guarding the kingdom of Cathay. Soldiers asked him where he'd come from and what he'd brought for their king. The traveller, who had lost everything by then, replied that he would give their king whatever he most desired in return for a single meeting. The soldiers relayed his answer by smoke in the daytime and by fire at night until it reached the capital. In the same manner, the king was gracious enough to grant the traveller an audience and his journey began again. Everywhere he went, he learned what he could about the people of Cathay. Most particularly, he was struck by their mastery of the art of printing, on paper made from the cocoons of silkworms..."

"What did the king desire?" interrupted Longstaff.

"A lion," said Hector. "An animal which can't be found anywhere in that country. The traveller called for paper and ink. In all his travels, he'd seen a lion only once, and then fleetingly. He drew an animal that more closely resembled a jackal, with a great head of hair modelled on the tresses of a Circassian woman whom he'd once loved. The king sent him home a rich man."

Aurélie nudged Longstaff. "Do you remember when Makarios arranged for a pig to come to Istanbul? Most people in the city had never seen one; they came in their hundreds for a glimpse, but none of them would touch it."

"There's another story," said Hector, "about a man who wanted to send a package to Bursa without anyone looking inside. He put the package in a sack together with a piglet. When a janissary patrol stopped his messenger, the piglet began to squeal. The soldiers drew back at once, shouting that he could take the filthy animal and be damned."

Aurélie began laughing in excitement. Longstaff was looking at her as if she'd lost her mind. She put her hand on his forearm. "We've been looking at the problem backwards, don't you see? We can't sneak past our enemies. Everyone always sees the slightest movement of a shadow, but no one can look at the sun without being blinded."

An hour later, they had the outline of a plan – one which would cost Nasi a small fortune if it were to stand any chance of success. Longstaff and Hector had both contributed important details, but Aurélie was the architect. She would present it when Nasi finally came to see them in the cellar.

"Do you think he'll agree?" asked Hector.

"No way of knowing until we ask."

"No way of asking until he comes."

"Look around," said Aurélie. She could feel how the waiting was getting to them. "He can certainly afford it."

The hours ticked by. Cut off from any view of the sky, unable to judge the passage of time, she looked towards Longstaff.

"Late evening," he said. "He can't leave us waiting much longer."

"I've been thinking about Durant," said Aurélie. "About how we can get a message to him..."

"He made his decision when he abandoned you," Longstaff attempted to cut her off.

Aurélie took his hand. "Don't do that," she said. "Don't give up on him. The three of us have been through too much."

Someone struck the heavy door. Aurélie leapt to her feet. Two knocks, then one, then two more. She turned the key in the lock. "We need to talk..."

A woman stood in the doorway. Nasi's servant. It took Aurélie a moment to think of her name. *Sarah.*

"The master is waiting for you in his study."

The woman was about her own age. Her expression gave nothing away. Aurélie hesitated. "Is that safe?"

"For one of you. I will return with food for the two who stay."

Longstaff and Hector both motioned for her to go. How long was it since any of them had seen the sky? Not much more than a day, not enough to explain how she yearned for it – so much that she almost forgot her fear. Aurélie followed Sarah up the deserted staircase, trying desperately to gather her thoughts. Nasi was the final arbiter of what was possible, what was foolhardy, what might stand a chance of success. Their only shield and their only hope. Aurélie grew suddenly frightened. He'd been bankrolling Longstaff from the start, providing him with introductions to smugglers and pirates. And she had no idea why.

Longstaff had described the room to her. While Nasi let a silk drape fall across the terrace door – hiding her from prying eyes – Aurélie looked around, matching her husband's description to the reality; the rows of leather-bound books, the tall vitrine with its collection of jade carvings.

Sit," said Nasi, gesturing to a chair. "Make yourself comfortable. I've given the servants permission to take their evening meal in the garden, well away from here. No doubt they're wondering what's come over me." He smiled. "Can I offer you something to drink?"

She shook her head. "We have plenty of food and drink below."

"I've done my share of hiding. I know how the walls begin to close in."

"But that's not why you're helping us." She needed, suddenly, to know the reasons behind his extraordinary generosity. Their lives were at stake.

Producing a long-stemmed pipe, the merchant applied a lit taper with a small sigh of pleasure. "You want to know my price for helping you and I want to know about your work. Have you made any more progress with your translation?"

He smiled, gesturing with his pipe that she should begin. Aurélie remained silent for a moment, weighing the man. He seemed determined to play this game on his own terms. Softly, she began to recite:

> *By the rivers of Babylon, there we sat down, we wept when we remembered Zion.*
>
> *We hanged our harps upon the willows in the midst thereof.*
>
> *For there they that carried us away captive required of us a song.*
>
> *If I forget thee, O Jerusalem, let my right hand be forgot.*
>
> *Let my tongue cleave to the roof of my mouth if I do not remember thee; if*
>
> *I do not elevate Jerusalem above my chief joy.*

She watched him while she spoke, the eyes half-closed, smoke drifting in lazy spirals from his lips.

> *O daughter of Babylon, who art to be destroyed; happy shall he be, that repays thee as thou hast served us.*
>
> *Happy shall he be, that taketh and dasheth thy little ones against the stone.*

Nasi smiled. "You've chosen a bloodthirsty theme for today's lesson." He poured himself more wine.

"You recognise it?"

"It's the story of my people. Of course I recognise it. My ancestors were enslaved, forced to leave their homeland and serve idolators in the city of Babylon."

"The Babylonians invited your people to sing and be happy."

"To forget themselves. My ancestors chose to remember instead." He shrugged. "This was the only song they would sing – a way of reminding themselves to remain true to their faith."

"The tablets I discovered tell a story from Babylon called the *Enuma Elish*. Among other things, it describes the creation of mankind."

Nasi inclined his head in a gesture of polite inquiry.

"When Babylon fell," continued Aurélie, "the Israelites carried their former masters' stories with them when they returned home. Slowly, they were adapted to meet the needs of their own, very different God. It's the only plausible explanation for the parallels I keep discovering."

Nasi remained silent for several seconds. This was the first time Aurélie had shared her conclusions. Despite the circumstances, she waited anxiously for his verdict.

"I'm not a particularly religious man," he said quietly. "Still, it strikes me that you're treading on dangerous ground."

"If I'm right, then isn't that irrelevant? We've made the past into something it never was. A paradise – which we destroyed when we disobeyed our creator. Wouldn't all humanity benefit from the truth?"

He leaned forward. "I'm curious – what do you think will happen if you publish your tale?"

Aurélie thought for a moment. She knew what she believed – that nothing could be crueller than telling people their suffering had been brought about by a single mistake, made by a single man and woman thousands of years ago – but what did she want to achieve? To show people that perfection wasn't something which lay in the past, but something which might lie in the future if they were willing to work for it. Wouldn't faith in a better future bring out the best in mankind? Wouldn't people be slower to embrace depravity then, more inclined to help their neighbours as a way to help themselves?

"It would give people hope," she said. She didn't like the expression on Nasi's face. "You don't agree?"

"If you're right, then isn't that irrelevant?"

He settled back in his chair. "Before you can change the world, we have to spirit you and your companions out of the city. I assume that's what you really want to talk about?"

"We have a plan," said Aurélie, doubting it now, unsettled by the sudden change of subject.

"One that stands a chance of success?"

"That depends on how much money you're willing to spend." Gathering her wits, Aurélie explained what they had in mind. Nasi blanched at the cost – for which she could hardly blame him – but did not baulk.

"I approve," he said. "A plan after my own heart."

"You still haven't told me what you want in return."

"Nor will I. The price for my assistance will be settled by your husband. Not you."

Aurélie thought of the baby growing in her womb. "Does he know what you want?"

"Not the details," replied Nasi. "But I imagine he has an idea of the overall scheme." Putting his pipe aside, he showed her to the door. "Anyway," he added. "It's not as if he's in a position to bargain."

Chapter 29

The preparations began early the following morning. A troop of messengers were sent to visit caterers and carpenters. Nasi himself unlocked the doors of his printing house. The machine was his pride and joy – one of only two in the whole city and far superior to the model owned by the Greek patriarch. The invitations were ready by noon, sealed in beautifully embroidered envelopes and on their way to the great and the good of Istanbul before the call to evening prayer. An hour after sunset, Nasi led a team of craftsmen and servants onto the roof of his palace to inspect a series of extraordinary balsa wood constructions. Made to Hector's specifications, the first was a perfect replica of a Venetian galley – as long from bow to stern as a man was tall. The sails were made of rice paper. At Nasi's signal, the craftsmen lit the oil lamps positioned at intervals along the length of the ship's deck. The sails inflated with a low rustle. The ship quivered on the rooftop for a moment before lifting slowly into the air, carried gracefully seawards on the night breeze.

Nasi watched it fly, a gorgeous sight against the coal black sky until an arrow pierced the fragile hull, passing clean through both ship and sails to send it plummeting. *Bastards.* He smiled grimly. "Light the next one. Let's see how long their courage holds."

If Mehmed Sokollu and Raimondi Maltrapillo wanted to search his palace, then he would invite them in – along with every other merchant, landowner and foreign dignitary in Istanbul. That was the essence of Aurélie's plan. A summer party, in honour of the sultan himself. The flying lanterns added a touch of glamour. All Istanbul would be talking about them tomorrow. Whether the archer belonged to the grand

vizier or the Venetian ambassador, Nasi could not believe he
would dare go on shooting – the people of Istanbul were not
forgiving when people interfered with their entertainments.
The next three lanterns were ready, in the shape of two crowns
and one enormous moon. Nasi gave the order, then watched
the sails slowly inflate. The bowman waited longer this time,
until the lanterns were already over the Golden Horn. From
his position on the rooftop, Nasi heard a murmur of collective
disappointment. Crowds had begun to gather in the streets
around the palace, drawn by whispers of the ghostly apparitions.

Nasi called for the last three to be lit: another crown, one
more moon, and a cage with its door hanging open – homage
to the sultan's majesty, power, and mercy.

Aurélie could not see the balsa wood lanterns. It would
have been too dangerous for her to appear on the roof. Instead,
she lay in her makeshift bed underground, Longstaff tossing
and turning beside her, trying and failing to fall asleep.

"What did you tell me once?" she whispered in the
darkness. "Lie on your back with your arms at your sides. Wait
for sleep, don't chase it."

He rolled onto one elbow. "Does the plan have to be so
elaborate? In my experience, the simplest schemes are the ones
which work."

"Your experience as a soldier? What do you suggest; strap
on your sword, go out there and challenge them to a fight? First
Raimondi's men, then the grand vizier's?"

He grunted. "Honestly, there are moments it doesn't strike
me as such a bad idea. At least we could stop hiding then. We
have unfinished business in this city."

"Which will have to remain unfinished. Welcome to the
real world."

"I know," he sighed. "I just hate all this skulking."

"You prefer sulking?"

"I want someone to fight."

It was dark in the room, not a glimmer of light anywhere. She found him by touch, felt the warmth of him for a moment before replying. "You've always known when to cut your losses in the past. Why is it so much harder now?"

"Who said it was easy then?" They were both thinking of Italy, when he'd fled from his position as lieutenant to the mercenary warlord Il Medeghino.

"It was just you then," said Aurélie. "On your own, I have no doubt you could cut your way out of this city. But you feel a duty towards me…"

"I love you."

"And the mechanic," she added. "And Durant. Which means you can't do it alone. You need help; that's what infuriates you, but there's no escaping it. If you want to do more than survive, you always have to rely on other people eventually."

"I came within a day of becoming England's first ambassador to the Ottoman Empire," he said quietly. "Now I'm a wanted man."

Was that it? Did he think he'd failed? Softly, Aurélie reminded him of how much they still stood to gain – the secret of longitude, a lifeline for English farmers, the small contribution to learning which her translation of the *Enuma Elish* would make.

She did not mention the baby growing inside her. She wanted to tell him when he could revel in the news, not when it would plunge him into terror on the child's behalf. For the same reason, she held back from demanding to know the price of Nasi's help.

Instead, she snuggled close.

"Will it work?" he asked.

"The city will help," she told him. "There are places in Istanbul where Turks rarely venture and places you don't often see Christians. If we stick to the grey areas in between…"

"Life would be so much easier," muttered Longstaff, "if I hadn't managed to unite our enemies against us."

*

The thought of being taken for a slave made Durant's skin crawl. In the past, he'd been imprisoned and tortured. He'd been forced by poverty to do the bidding of other men. Somehow – even though it was only a disguise he'd assumed – this felt worse.

He thought of how Leila had manipulated him. Hector had enjoyed a privileged life in Istanbul. With each step Durant took along the road – eyes lowered from a sense of shame as much as decorum – the insane risks the mechanic had run in pursuit of freedom began to make more sense.

Durant and Leila had only spent one night at the hostel – the mistress in a private room, the slave curled up in the corridor with only the hard, wooden floorboards for a mattress. They did not make good time the following morning. The most direct route to Bursa would have taken them inland. By unspoken agreement, they preferred to travel by the coast road, casting searching looks towards Istanbul across the width of the Bosphorus. In the brief moments when she judged it safe, Leila schooled Durant in how a woman of her rank expected a slave to conduct himself. They were both exhausted by the time they reached an inn on the outskirts of Üsküdar. Durant handed his mistress's horse to a waiting groom. Leila handled the arrangements with the landlord, dismissing Durant as if he were mute as well as servile. She did allow him to precede her into the well-appointed chamber, however, on the pretext of wanting him to open the shutters and ensure her peace of mind wasn't disturbed by spiders. She closed the door behind her, shoulders sinking in weariness. Durant forgot his complaints immediately, taking her in his arms. She stepped swiftly away, raising a finger to her lips and pointing at the open window.

Their room offered a fine view of the Maiden's Tower, a small rock off the coast where a Byzantine emperor had once locked his daughter away – an unsuccessful attempt to protect her from a prophecy of early death.

Durant ached to take Leila in his arms again. She shooed him out of the room. If he hadn't seen the worry in her eyes, he might have thought she was enjoying her new role. He stepped outside to breathe the fresh air before assuming his position in the corridor. It was a clear night. A mile away across the Bosphorus, torches burned fiercely on the walls of the Fortress of Seven Towers. Candles in a thousand windows cut tiny holes in the fabric of night. An hour after the sun disappeared into the Sea of Marmara, but before the stars were revealed in their full majesty, Durant thought he saw a shooting star that rose instead of falling, so slowly it might have been a dream – a burning ship in miniature hovering above the city rooftops.

It disappeared soon afterwards. More followed. Other shapes, too indistinct for him to make them out at this distance.

Durant slept badly that night – the hard, wooden floorboards and a sense of excitement he couldn't quite account for. He was awake before Leila, loitering near the stables, fishing for news from the latest arrivals. It wasn't slow in coming. The apparitions had risen from a palace owned by the merchant Joseph Nasi. He was throwing a party in honour of the sultan – the whole city was talking about it. The apparitions had been carefully chosen; a ship for Selim's mastery of the seas, three crowns for his mastery of the world, the moon for his generosity, and an open cage for his mercy.

Durant would have danced a jig if he'd been alone. He was a slave, however, and kept his eyes lowered accordingly, climbing the stairs to the room of his mistress with a sober step. She was already dressed, sitting before a sheet of polished copper to arrange her hair.

Durant struggled to suppress a smile. "There's been a change of plan," he announced.

*

Raimondi Maltrapillo resisted the urge to tear the gold embossed invitation into a thousand pieces. He was damned if he'd accept Nasi's hospitality – yet feared he would find it impossible to stay away.

A party! A stroke of genius, in its way. Raimondi had personally started the rumours that the merchant was suspected of treason; he had never expected Nasi to respond so brazenly.

Scattering the pieces of paper across his desk, the Venetian ambassador returned to the task at hand – an Englishman, in a filthy tunic, who seemed incapable of uttering a word in any tongue but his own. At Raimondi's signal, the men who'd been holding him became a blur of motion, delivering half a dozen measured jabs to the gut. A stray elbow caught the Englishman's nose, drawing a gout of blood. He looked terrified, still babbling in his incomprehensible language. The translator arrived a moment later.

"He begs you to stop hitting him. It's not necessary. He'll tell you everything he knows."

"Why was he left bound and gagged in the house?"

The story dribbled out. The man identified himself as Thomas Fitch, a priest in what passed for England's Church.

"Longstaff was harbouring a fugitive from the sultan's justice. Naturally, I urged him to turn the man in. He knocked me down – a brutal, unprovoked attack. When I came to, I was already trussed and bound, just as your men found me. I could have died. I might have choked on the gag at any moment."

Raimondi looked at Fitch with disgust. "What's he crying about now?"

"He's thanking you," said the translator. "For rescuing him from the clutches of the Turks."

"Tell him I've done no such thing." He approached Fitch directly. "The grand vizier is allowing me to question you as a courtesy. The Turks have already identified you to their satisfaction. They have a dozen witnesses who'll swear they saw you praying to their God." He smiled. "It seems you'll be given a choice, my friend. Live the rest of your life as a good Muslim or suffer execution for the crime of apostasy."

Raimondi had the satisfaction of seeing blood rush from the Englishman's face. Fitch attempted to throw himself forward – a last ditch plea for mercy.

"Please," he begged. "You have to save me."

"I don't *have* to do a damned thing – until you start telling me the truth."

"The truth?" sobbed the false priest. "I attempted to blackmail Longstaff. I wanted the sultan's permission to build a reformed church in Galata."

Raimondi gestured for his men to take the priest away. Fitch looked round in confusion as hands gripped his shoulders.

"I couldn't care less why you betrayed your host," said the Venetian ambassador. "Give me something I can use."

"I heard them talking," said Fitch. "The mechanic claims he's solved the riddle of longitude."

Raimondi hesitated. *It wasn't possible.* A moment later he sat down heavily in his chair. It would certainly explain why the sultan's men were searching so desperately, why Longstaff himself had been prepared to risk so much. The thought of England with such a secret in its power...

Raimondi's fat fingers curled into fists. He imagined them around Mehmed Sokollu's neck – they were meant to be allies; the bastard hadn't said a word.

Raimondi would have done the same in his place. The secret of longitude was worth a thousand Bohemian gold mines – it could change everything, raise Venice back to its position as the world's pre-eminent maritime power.

"You'll let me go?" interrupted Fitch. There was new hope in the young man's eyes. Clearly, he'd seen the effect of his words. Raimondi looked him up and down. There was no longer any question of setting him at liberty – the information he possessed was far too valuable.

The Venetian ambassador smiled. "Rest assured," he said, "you won't spend a single day of your life as a Muslim. You have my word on that." He nodded at his aides, confident they would understand his meaning. They took the Englishman away. Raimondi dismissed the man from his thoughts a moment later. He had more important matters to attend to now – like ordering his spies to stop co-operating with Mehmed Sokollu's representatives.

Chapter 30

Longstaff scrutinised Nasi when he came to visit them that evening, his appearance as well as his words, his scent as well as his tone, parsing every gesture for signs of optimism or despair. The merchant was their only contact to the outside world, their only window on a reality filled with carpenters and caterers, gardeners and embroiderers, wholesalers coming and going, a perfect hive of activity which Longstaff imagined must be working with the same precision as his magnificent clock.

It needed to be, if it was going to push the city into temporary new shapes, overwhelm people sufficiently to provide the three of them with an opportunity to escape.

Nasi looked worried. Longstaff felt the walls close in on them a little more.

"What now?"

"I have good news and bad news," said the merchant. "Which do you want first?"

"The good news."

"Your silk has reached London in perfect condition. In a few days, I should find out what price it fetched."

"And the bad news?" asked Aurélie.

"Still no sign of our enemies growing complacent. Their archers shot down the flying lanterns. Their men continue to examine every item which leaves this house. You can't imagine what this is doing to my reputation…"

"The sultan…"

"Won't lift a finger. Their persistence already has him half convinced." He looked at Longstaff. "Why on earth didn't you tell me about the priest?"

"Fitch? What's he done now?"

"Disappeared, apparently. But not before confirming that you and Hector are working together."

"If he's disappeared, then he can't testify against us..."

"No one would listen to an English priest anyway..."

Nasi ignored their protests. He could afford to, thought Longstaff – trapped here below ground, what could they possibly tell him that he didn't already know. Instead, it was they who clamoured for information, Aurélie and Hector desperate for every last detail of how their plans were being realised. Longstaff listened without hearing, as if separated from them by a rising wind. How could he put his faith in a scheme which relied so heavily on sleight of hand? Aurélie and Hector were two of the most intelligent people he'd ever met. Longstaff had never felt so restless. Try as he might, he couldn't free himself from the suspicion that Aurélie was keeping something from him. All of them were. Nasi kept hinting at the price of his help.

"What of the star charts?" asked Hector. "We won't have another chance to retrieve them after tonight."

"I'll get them," said Longstaff without thinking. It was just what he needed. An opportunity to actually do something. The three of them stared as if he'd taken leave of his senses.

"I think it would be better if you left that to me," said Nasi gently. "Tell me where they are – I'll get them to the boat via a different route, along with Aurélie's translation of the *Enuma Elish*."

Longstaff didn't argue. He fell silent again while Hector gave up the location of his precious charts – concealed in the crypt of a Greek Orthodox church.

They grew listless once Nasi had left them. No one even thought to remark on Longstaff's earlier foolishness. They had prepared as best they could; nothing to do now but gather their strength for the following day. Longstaff was the first to turn in, forcing his body into sleep, waking himself through sheer force of will in the small hours of the night.

Aurélie lay beside him. Longstaff listened to her breathe for several minutes before rolling onto the floor. The cellar was silent. He gathered his boots in the darkness, his sword and a length of rope, then let himself out through the only door. The merchant was a prudent man. He would have servants patrolling the corridors of his palace. Longstaff reached the upper storey without incident. He paused outside the library, slipping a note beneath the door for his host, leaving one corner visible in case he failed to discover a way to leave the building unseen.

The flame of a torch appeared at the far end of the corridor. Longstaff inched forward, keeping to the shadows. A servant guarded the short flight of stairs up to the roof. Longstaff waited, wracking his brains for any way past – he didn't want to hurt any of Nasi's people. Twenty minutes passed before the servant set his torch in a wall-sconce, turning to relieve himself in a chamber pot beneath the stairs. Longstaff knew he wouldn't get a better chance, the faint sounds of his passage covered by a steady stream of piss against the ceramic pot. He took a lungful of precious fresh air before easing the door closed. There was a full moon above, obscured behind thick cloud – not a good omen for tomorrow's festivities. Longstaff lifted one eye to the low parapet, peering down at the street below.

It had occurred to him that Nasi might be exaggerating the number of watchers, increasing their dependence on his help. The grand vizier and Raimondi were fearsome adversaries, but they couldn't know for sure that Longstaff and Hector were imprisoned here. Surely, some portion of their resources must have been diverted to investigating other possibilities.

The street appeared to be deserted. Longstaff cursed himself, painfully aware of how stupidly he was behaving. It was a warm night. He had to assume there was at least one watcher lurking in the street, another in the building opposite. How alert would they be? How would they react when they saw him descend from the roof? Sound the alarm, attack at once, attempt to follow him without his knowledge?

Longstaff sat with his back to the low wall; he felt a bead of sweat slide inside his collar. Even if he did manage to get past them, he still had no idea of where to look for Durant. Did he truly want to slip into the streets unnoticed or was he hoping to be seen? Longstaff suppressed a sudden surge of giddy anticipation. He felt as if he'd been hiding for months, not days. Slowly unwinding the rope from around his waist, he made one end fast to an iron rail, heard the rasp of a tinderbox in the darkness.

A small shower of sparks, the glow of tobacco nestled in a pipe. "Going somewhere?" asked Nasi.

"My God, don't sneak up on a man like that." Longstaff raised a hand to his hammering heart.

Nasi drew the smoke into his lungs. "They'll have seen the sparks," he said. "Half a dozen pairs of eyes will be trained on this section of wall for at least the next hour."

Longstaff tried to make out the merchant's expression in the darkness. "I promised Aurélie I wouldn't give up on Durant."

"You think she'd want you to do this?" Nasi shook his head in disappointment. "You've already sent him a message, remember?"

"He may not have seen it. He's probably on the road to Bursa already. I can overtake him."

"You're planning to abandon us."

"It's me they're looking for. Aurélie stands a better chance if it's just the two of them."

"You're not thinking, Longstaff. They're looking for Hector." Nasi took another long draw on his pipe, tobacco glowing in the still night. "If they find him with Aurélie – and you're not there to protect her – what do you think will happen to her?"

"You wouldn't understand."

"You sound like a child." Nasi sighed. "Come and have a drink. If I can't persuade you to stay, I promise I won't prevent you from leaving."

Dressed for violence, Longstaff felt ridiculous in Nasi's well-appointed library. He refused the offer of a glass of wine. "Say your piece, then, if you must."

"You're a man to be reckoned with, Longstaff. Aurélie, for one, has unlimited faith in your ability to perform miracles, but if you go out there tonight, you will die." He paused. "Durant made his decision. There's no sense in you throwing your life away when you could still be of so much use."

Longstaff narrowed his eyes. When was the last time anyone had suggested he could be of use? "We're in hiding, in case you hadn't noticed."

"You survived in Istanbul longer than anyone expected."

"Not long enough," replied Longstaff bitterly.

"Don't tell me you enjoyed it," said Nasi. "Cosying up to men like Raimondi and the chevalier. Is that any life for a man of your talents?"

Longstaff folded his arms across his chest. Part of him *had* hoped he'd be seen, the part which loathed hiding and waiting – the endless talking – and yearned for the release of combat. The part which would always choose to fight when the alternative meant putting his life in another man's hands.

Nasi knocked the ashes from his pipe. "A diplomat is defined by the ability to wait," he said. "You're a soldier, Longstaff, with a talent for inspiring fear, not confusion. You did what you did in this city from a sense of duty. You wanted to help. That's who you are – and that's why you can be of use."

He spread a map of Europe across the low table, stabbing Holland with one carefully manicured nail. "The Duke of Alba is slaughtering thousands in his attempt to suppress a Calvinist uprising. Philip of Spain faces challenges to his rule on several fronts; from the Moriscos in Granada to the Valois in France, but he's weakest here." He turned to Longstaff. "You know something of my background, chased across Europe by Catholic monarchs. Our interests coincide, Longstaff. You want to prevent Philip from bankrupting your country. I want to win back a degree of dignity for my people. With sufficient money and the right leadership, the rebels in the Low Countries could free their country from Spanish control."

Longstaff looked at Nasi in confusion.

"I've studied your career, my friend," continued the merchant. "I know you foiled the pope's spymaster in Naples. I know you went up against the Guise in France, destroying their plans to force an invasion of England. Who else in Europe has been such a consistent menace to Catholic interests?"

"That was never my intention," said Longstaff. Spain's Catholic fanatics were no worse than the reformists in his own country – as Thomas Fitch had demonstrated so eloquently. "I have no axe to grind."

"They're all as bad as each other – is that it?"

"Neither side gives a damn for right and wrong. Both will bury any sign of progress if they think it goes against their interests. Your sultan is no different. Look at the effort he's making to prevent the secret of longitude from becoming public knowledge."

"Do you know Amsterdam?"

The sudden change of topic took Longstaff by surprise. "I've been there."

"Go again," said Nasi, producing two bundles of paper from beneath his map. Opening the first, he turned directly to the final page. "Your signature goes here."

"A contract?"

"You're giving me possession of the silk. In return, I will give you approximately a tenth of its value in gold."

Longstaff waited for him to continue.

"The second bundle contains letters of introduction to my factor in Amsterdam. Through him, I've been supplying the rebels in Holland with funds to continue their fight against the Spanish. Unfortunately, the poor man understands nothing of war; half the men I'm trying to help are robbing me blind. You were a soldier, Longstaff. Take charge of my money. Ensure it's well spent. Lead the rebels yourself if that's what it takes. In return, my factor will give you the remainder of the profits on the silk in regular instalments over a three-year period."

"And if I refuse?"

Nasi ignored his question. "There are also letters here for Walsingham, explaining our intention to purchase as much tin and lead as England can supply."

Longstaff sat back in his chair, seething. He should have gone over the wall. Whatever dangers had waited in the street below, it would have been preferable to this. Viciously, he pinched the soft flesh on the inside of his forearm. "You seem to have thought of everything."

Nasi spread his hands. "I'm merely trying to make the best of a difficult situation. You're in my debt, Longstaff – a dozen times over. Do you have any idea what your diversion tomorrow is going to cost me? There are limits to my generosity."

"Three years of my life?"

Nasi nodded. "That's all I ask."

Longstaff stared at the ceiling. He could see wraiths of smoke from Nasi's pipe hanging in the still air. "How long have you been plotting this?"

"To help the rebels in Holland? Ever since King Philip sent that murderous bastard Alba. To involve you in my plans? Only since it became clear you can no longer stay in Istanbul."

Longstaff sat in silence. It would be dawn soon. Too late to begin his search for Durant. Nasi had been right when he claimed that was a fool's errand. What else had he said? *Aurélie has unlimited faith in your ability to perform miracles.*

Longstaff felt a sudden swell of nausea. He'd made a mess of his diplomatic mission and now, it seemed, he would have to turn his back on his best friend. He looked up at Nasi, suspecting the image of Durant – terrified, hiding in a hole somewhere – would haunt him for the rest of his life.

"I assume you have a pen I can use."

Chapter 31

Locked below ground, Longstaff, Aurélie and Hector listened to the thunder of carriage wheels, the tramp of feet. Nasi had been as good as his word, the wealthy residents of Istanbul unable to resist the lure of his invitation – especially with so many rumours swirling through the city streets. Servants had been at work in the gardens since before dawn. Nasi had claimed he was throwing this party in order to raise funds for a monument to Selim the Magnanimous. No one believed that for a second.

Neither Mehmed Sokollu nor Raimondi were stupid. It stood to reason both would conclude that that this event – thrown together at such short notice – was intended to provide cover for an escape attempt. Surely, thought Longstaff, that would only make them redouble their attentions. Nasi had invited them. Neither had deigned to reply. Would they be able to resist the temptation of an open door? How many of the guests arriving now were in their service, here to poke their heads into every nook and cranny?

And the watchers in the street outside? How many had left their posts, tempted by the merchant's largesse, the irresistible urge to see inside the walls?

Longstaff and his companions were unable to judge for themselves. They jumped when Nasi knocked at the door, waiting for the completion of the code before allowing him to enter.

"I can't stay long," he told them, dressed in a layered kaftan of coloured silks. "The guests are already arriving. I just wanted to make sure..." he didn't seem to know how to finish the sentence.

"We're ready," said Aurélie.

Nasi raised a hand to his jaw, as if preparing to defend himself. "Your translation of the *Enuma Elish* and the starcharts are already on their way to the pink."

The three of them spoke at once.

"The remainder of the clay tablets?" asked Hector.

"Longstaff's sword?" said Aurélie.

"Durant's possessions?" asked Longstaff.

Nasi dealt with them one by one. "The sword is on its way to the ship, but we don't have time to transfer the tablets, not without risking unwanted attention. I'll keep them here, Aurélie. Along with Durant's papers." He looked at them each in turn. "You know what to do? The timing has to be perfect."

Longstaff urged him to rejoin his guests before turning to Aurélie. She looked suddenly bereft, no doubt contemplating the chapters of the story she hadn't yet translated. The precious tablets would remain here, stacked and forgotten in a corner of Nasi's vast palace, their contents hidden in a script only she could understand. He watched as she lifted her shoulders – head back, chest out – consciously erasing every trace of despair by an act of will.

"I know it's awful," said Longstaff. "We'll retrieve them in a few months, when the grand vizier relaxes his watch on this house."

She did not quite look him in the eye. "We have work to do."

Longstaff sat while she darkened his complexion with walnut juice. She shaped his nascent beard to a fashionable point before shaving his head. They swapped positions a moment later. Suspecting he must look ridiculous, Longstaff barely glanced at himself in the mirror. On another occasion, he thought, Aurélie would have teased him. Once they reached the street, her face and hair would be hidden behind a veil, but it was part of their plan that she should show her face in the garden. Of Nasi's guests, they had to look like the people with the least to hide. Aurélie changed the shape of her cheeks and lips with a few extra strokes of make-up. She was a gifted actress; she knew enough to change her gait, rearrange the set of her jaw and the shape of her eyes. After admiring her work for a moment, Longstaff set to work with the scissors, removing her golden hair, his heart aching as the young woman he'd met years earlier reappeared before his eyes. She'd been shorn then, too, by a priest determined to cast the demons from her soul.

"What?" she asked, seeing the look in his eye.

"As beautiful as the day I met you."

"Bruised and bloody," she replied. "Hardly able to stand?"

"In Florence," nodded Longstaff. "Not an hour after Durant nearly got me killed. God, but he was drunk. Wine-skin beneath one arm, offering me as payment for his gambling debts."

"He was there when you needed him."

Longstaff remembered that night, the two of them watching as a mob of religious fanatics marched Aurélie into the small church. "You were unconscious by the time we reached you. It took us hours to get you back to the inn, stopping every few paces to avoid the watch." He took a deep breath before gently touching her cheek. "We'll get through this."

"I know." She took his hand in hers.

He made a terrible mess of settling the dark wig. Time had dragged all day; now it seemed to accelerate beyond their control. Longstaff hid a selection of knives about his person – calf, chest, small of the back – his fingers opening and closing as if seeking the reassurance of his sword. He hadn't drawn the weapon since meeting Abu Risha – hadn't even worn it since returning to Istanbul.

A knock sounded at the door. It was time.

The three of them looked each other up and down. With their new hair, changed skin tones and borrowed clothes, they were almost unrecognisable. Spontaneously, they held each other in a fierce embrace.

"Deep breath," muttered Longstaff, nodding at Hector to open the door. Sarah waited on the far side, dressed in robes as fine as Aurélie's. Longstaff took her arm as they climbed the stairs. He could hear the beating of his own heart. The waiting was finally over. He should have been happy. He couldn't think of anything beyond what he stood to lose. *Aurélie.* Why hadn't he taken a moment to look at her – fix the clear blue eyes and the determined set of her jaw in his mind's eye? He couldn't stop now, couldn't tell her what she meant to him – the end of bloodshed and the birth of hope. A true home for the first time in his life, which he found whenever he took her in his arms.

After the cool cellar, the heat hit them like a hammer. No one appeared to notice their arrival in the garden. Longstaff tried to keep his expression neutral; Nasi had overseen an extraordinary transformation – the beds new-planted with flowers for the occasion, peacocks strutting on the grass, parrots commenting from the trees. Cooled by temporary pools and protected by arbours, the guests stood in delighted knots around wrestlers and strong men, musicians and buffoons. One group had gathered to watch the pyromancers prepare their fireworks display, due to begin at sunset.

Longstaff's route had been planned in detail. Steered discreetly by Sarah, fighting an unexpected wave of fear, he led his small party past two of the city's most famous swordsmen, feinting at one another with scimitars. He saw no sign of Raimondi or Mehmed Sokollu, though there were faces he knew in the garden – the chevalier, Makarios the Greek philosopher, Master Ben Chabib who'd agreed to take Durant on as his pupil. Did the doctor's eye flicker with recognition? Longstaff looked past him, emptying his face of expression. Ben Chabib turned away. Longstaff couldn't breathe, could barely respond as Sarah nudged him towards their host to make their farewells – it would arouse suspicion if they simply left – just as Nasi disengaged himself from conversation, the whole performance planned to the nearest second.

Three servants emerged from the house at that moment. Two men and a woman, they walked swiftly towards a waiting coach with their eyes lowered. As they began climbing inside, Longstaff stepped in front of his host.

"I'm afraid we have to leave you already," he said, certain that a hundred eyes were scrutinising him.

"So soon? Surely you'll stay for the fireworks?"

"We intend to watch them from our garden. Thank you again; it really has been a wonderful day."

"No," replied Nasi. "It's I who should be thanking you."

The merchant didn't betray himself by so much as a raised eyebrow. The two women hid their faces behind veils as Longstaff and Hector escorted them into the street. With luck, all eyes were still on the rapidly disappearing coach. Why hadn't the watchers stopped it? Had they seen through the disguise? Or did they intend to follow, overtake the luckless servants somewhere on the road north? Now or later, it hardly mattered. The servants only knew they'd been sent to open Nasi's summerhouse in the hills above Tarabya.

The street was crammed with carriages, grooms stood patiently by their masters' horses. Any or all of them could be spies. Longstaff felt the back of his shirt grow damp with sweat. Only a few of the less distinguished guests had arrived on foot. Those who would expect to be overlooked in the normal course of events.

"The perimeter is just ahead," murmured Sarah.

Swaying slightly, as if rolling on a sea of Nasi's wine, Longstaff patted her hand, smiling as if she'd said something funny. "How many men?"

"Enough." She shrugged lightly. "They try and keep themselves hidden."

Men appeared a moment later, running hard. Two crashed into Longstaff and Hector. Longstaff willed himself to fall, sprawling on the ground. Sarah screamed, a noise she stifled when the third man produced a knife.

"Your purses. Now, if you value your lives."

Longstaff played fear, cringing and cowering, refusing to make eye contact with his assailants as he handed up a fat leather purse. It was snatched from his fingers. The men were already running. Footsteps sounded from the opposite direction. Men with drawn swords, breathing fast.

"Are you all right?" said the first to arrive. "We saw them attack."

"We're fine." Longstaff dusted himself down, trying to make his movements awkward with wounded dignity.

"They took your purse."

"No great loss," he said quickly. "Just a few coppers."

"It might have been so much worse," added Sarah, "if you gentlemen hadn't come to our assistance."

"Common footpads," muttered Hector. "In this quarter? I've never heard of anything like it!"

"It's the party," explained their rescuer. "Events like these always attract a bad element. Lucky we happened to be near."

"A godsend," agreed Hector. He hadn't lost his purse and was naturally more inclined to be generous. "You have to give me your names. I'll see that you and your comrades are rewarded."

The young man reddened. Had he disobeyed orders when he left his hiding place? If so, orders from whom – Raimondi or the grand vizier?

"No need for that," he said. "Anyone would have done the same."

He and his friends took their leave soon afterwards, never once looking closely at the men and women they'd rescued. Frowning – a picture of injured pride – Longstaff took Sarah's arm once more. "Time to get you home, darling. You've had a shock."

Contrary to appearances, it was she who led them through the twisting streets, applying gentle pressure to Longstaff's forearm whenever it was time to turn left or right. A slave greeted them at the door of a fine townhouse. He looked nervous.

"If the master and mistress find out…"

Sarah placed a hand on his forearm as soon as the door was closed, calming him as if he were a restive horse. "They won't," she said. "No one will find out. Keep your peace – and my master will have you freed before the year is out. You understand? Freedom."

The man nodded, swallowed, nodded again. "Everything is ready," he said. "Just as you instructed."

Longstaff, Aurélie and Hector changed again, hurrying into another set of clothes – browns and greys instead of bright colours. Two tradesmen and a wife. A moment later, Longstaff understood why Nasi had sent them through this particular house. Standing at the corner of two streets, it had been repeatedly enlarged and subdivided so that its true contours were impossible to guess. Sarah – a seeming miracle of calm good sense – led them to a second exit, ushering them into a nearby side street without a word of farewell.

Longstaff breathed more easily now, happier walking the streets of Istanbul as a man of business. He let Hector take the lead. The mechanic knew the city better than he did. The slightest delay could ruin their carefully laid plans. He strained his eyes for signs of pursuit as they walked to a little-used quay on the waterfront. It was deserted, in stark contrast to the Golden Horn, still busy with numerous sailing boats and *caiques* in the setting sun. The tide had just turned, a single pinnace carved an elegant line from the Imperial Dockyards towards the Fortress of Seven Towers and the open waters of the Sea of Marmara. Behind it, having paid their dues and been given permission to sail, two larger merchantmen were nosing their way through the sultan's warships.

A sudden splash of oars. Longstaff turned to see a sleek *caique* bear down on their lonely quay. From a distance, the craft was indistinguishable from those used by the sultan's *bostanci*. The oarsmen slowed long enough for the three fugitives to leap aboard, then pointed the prow into the heart of the Horn.

*

Three crowns in the night sky above Istanbul – one each for Longstaff, Aurélie and Hector. Two moons to mark the days before they attempted to escape and a ship to reveal how.

Since receiving Longstaff's message, Durant had transformed Leila into the widowed wife of a moderately successful merchant. Before his death, her husband had invested in a risky trading venture – something which had no doubt played its part in his recent heart attack. His ship should have returned to Istanbul by now. Unwilling to wait any longer – suffering the silent pity of her servants and neighbours – Leila had travelled with one faithful retainer to a fishing village near the entrance to the Bosphorus, resolved to watch for the ship that would restore both her fortune and her good name.

The jannisary soldiers in the village appeared to find the story plausible. As soon as he felt the weight of Leila's purse, the landlord at their inn ceased asking questions and hurried to provide them with his finest rooms. She was certainly not the first widow to come and pass her nights in this village – and her days haunting the bluffs above.

Two moons to mark the days. Had Durant understood Longstaff's message correctly? He woke early on the appointed day, pacing the exposed clifftop for hours before hunger and thirst drove him back to the village. Enveloped by the sharp scent of fish guts and salt water, he drifted to the wooden quays and narrow boats – no more than twelve feet long, a tiny, windowless hold at the bow, painted in the colours of sea and sky. Local men, gathered to exchange gossip through the afternoon, continued talking as Durant swapped a few misshapen coppers for a tall pot of Albanian *boza*. A slave in their eyes, he felt invisible as he hunkered nearby, listening to the talk of fish. The stallholder wore a rudimentary telescope around his neck on a chain of beaten copper. When Durant rose to leave, he offered him a silver coin for the instrument.

"My mistress," he explained, rolling his eyes and raising a finger to his temple. Still, they stared at him. Durant shrugged. The stallholder took his coin, handing him the telescope with the air of a man confident he'd had the better of the deal. There was still an hour of sunlight remaining. Time enough to collect Leila from the inn and return to the bluffs above the village. If nothing else, it would burnish their story a little more – the grieving widow framed in the setting sun, hand raised to shade her eyes as she stared across the waves.

Chapter 32

The pink was on a broad reach, its single sail ghostly in the gloaming. The oarsmen strained to intercept it, great threads of sweat rolling down their necks. Longstaff willed them on as the wind blew up. He heard the rumble of fireworks but didn't look back at the sudden explosion of light and colour above the roofs of Nasi's palace. One final distraction, he thought – hopefully the last they would need. The pink heeled over, creating a tunnel between gunnels and sails. The low *caique* slipped alongside. Hands were extended from the deck, hauling Longstaff, Aurélie and Hector aboard. By the time Longstaff looked back, clear water had opened between the two boats.

"Heads down!" shouted the skipper, a heavy-set man, his forearms covered in tattoos.

Longstaff ducked as the boom swung across deck, bringing the pink onto a new course. White horses pranced in their wake as they made for a point on the coast of Asia, south of the Maiden's Tower.

"I hear you have a bauble," barked the skipper.

"Just an old necklace," Longstaff completed the password.

"Our possessions," shouted Hector, "do you have them on board?"

The captain nodded. His men went about their work in silence. The boat was light and fast, designed for running goods up and down the coast. Not luxurious, but if the crew were as good as Nasi claimed, adequate to get them as far as Crete – a week's journey even with favourable winds. They would land by night, far from prying eyes in a small bay the skipper had used before.

From there, it would be up to Longstaff and his companions to make their way. They would still be in danger – the island was a Venetian possession, after all – but beyond the grand vizier's reach at least.

Another low rumble shook the air. Nasi's fireworks continued to light the sky but this was something different. Thunder. Even now, Longstaff could see dark clouds slowly covering the moon, sitting squat and huge on the horizon.

Then Hector released a howl of pure joy. He'd been quiet during the day, exhausted from so many weeks of living on his nerves and all too aware of the sacrifices his friends had made on his behalf. Longstaff grinned. Even Aurélie closed her eyes, as if to prevent tears of relief from falling down her cheeks. Longstaff reached out to take her in his arms. A torch sparked into life in the gloom. A *caique* sitting quietly, oars shipped apart from one to hold their position. A man standing in the bow, legs spread. The familiar silhouette, rings glinting as he raised a fist in their direction.

It wasn't possible.

The Venetian ambassador roared at his crew, his face a mask of triumphant fury.

They'd been so close.

Longstaff stared in confusion as the *caique* accelerated away from them across the rising waters.

"We've been seen," he shouted, pointing into the darkness. "Why don't they attack?"

The skipper spat. "Too low in the water. Eight spent oarsmen wouldn't stand a chance of boarding us – not with our sails full and a following wind.

"Then we're free?"

"In our dreams." The skipper shook his head. "They're making for the Imperial Dockyards. There are galleys at anchor there swift enough to run us down in a matter of hours."

He looked up as a single drop of rain struck his forehead. "Get to the stern," he told Longstaff. "Keep your eyes on the Dockyard."

"If we can't outrun them?"

The skipper clapped him on the shoulder to send him on his way. "We still have the advantage, my friend. They can't catch what they can't see."

Longstaff peered into the gathering darkness. He could see the light of the Maiden's Tower to his right, a dozen sails to his left, glowing in the moonlight. Raimondi's *caique* had vanished utterly. The pink swept on, close enough to make out individual buildings on the Asian coast before tacking again. Nasi's fireworks display had come to an end. The clouds continued to gather above Longstaff's head. The calm before the storm, he muttered to himself, unaware that Aurélie had joined him at the rail.

"It won't be long before we round the point." She pointed at the distant Fortress of Seven Towers. The two merchantmen Longstaff had seen earlier were there as well, sailing through the shadows of the great towers. Another flurry of raindrops struck the deck, driven ahead of the storm on a gust of wind. Longstaff's fist crashed against the rail. "Look," he pointed.

"It's nothing," said Aurélie. "They're lighting the Dockyard lamps."

Longstaff shook his head. "Not unless they've put the bloody place on wheels."

They rounded the point a moment later, the pink ploughing into the white-flecked emptiness of the Sea of Marmara. Longstaff looked along the coast. North and south, as far as he could see in both directions, an endless line of hollows and silences. "Shouldn't we stay close to land?" he shouted. "If we can't outrun them, maybe we can hide."

"What did you see?" asked the skipper.

"A war galley," said Longstaff. "Lit up and weighing anchor."

The skipper nodded at the bluffs above. "Always a crowd up there. Women pining for their men at sea, merchants pining for their goods of trade. The same for fifty miles in every direction. Too many eyes, my friend."

The first flash of lightning lit the sky. The skipper barked orders at his men in a language Longstaff couldn't identify. They did his bidding in silence, hauling on ropes, shifting the passengers into a small space amidships, above the shallow hold. Longstaff didn't know enough to understand what they were doing, but he felt the increase in speed. The pink flew through the water now, lifting his spirits along with the bow.

"Four miles off the coast," shouted the skipper, "there's a group of islands. Get that far and we may be able to lose them. The less you move about, the better our chances."

Longstaff pressed close to Aurélie as the boat began to pitch. They were sheltered from the rising wind, but not the rain which fell in earnest now. She smiled at him in the darkness. "Originally, the hulls of these boats were constructed from oxhide," she said. "Stretched over a frame of bent wood and wicker. Light, with a shallow draft, they were designed to slip over currents, over waves and over tides."

Was she trying to reassure him? Aurélie might know the history of boatbuilding, but it wasn't the kind of knowledge which could help them now. Longstaff had never felt so useless – while men he barely knew strained every muscle to deliver him from danger. Raising his head into the wind, he looked back at the Fortress of Seven Towers, waiting for a flash of lightning and the looming shadow of an Ottoman warship.

*

Durant and Leila weren't the only people on the bluff that evening. Others had heard rumours of a fireworks display in

Istanbul. Forced to stay in character, Durant presented the telescope to his mistress with a degree of formality.

Leila made a show of scanning the horizon before looking back at the entrance to the Golden Horn.

"Well?" murmured Durant, eyes studying every ship, skiff and sloop.

"How much did you pay for this?" she asked, handing him the instrument.

Durant cursed. No wonder the fisherman had looked so pleased with himself. He lowered the telescope, staring at the wide expanse of water, aware that freedom lay just beyond the horizon. His mood sank with the lowering sky. Had it been a mistake to come here? Perhaps he should have taken Leila directly to Bursa.

A cheer rose from the people on either side. In the distance, a smudge of light over the city might have been fireworks. They disappeared as soon as Durant raised the useless telescope to his eye. The first drops of rain began to fall, chasing most of the crowd down from the clifftop. Leila tugged at Durant's sleeve. The moon would shortly disappear behind the gathering clouds. They should return to the village while there was still sufficient light to see by.

A single-masted pinnace appeared from behind the fortress, heading their way. Durant squinted, cursing the telescope. Most ships leaving Istanbul kept to the central channel under a bare minimum of sail until clear of the Bosphorus. This one sailed as if pursued, haring across the channel under full sail, touching the shadows cast by the high bluff before jibing.

Three silhouettes flowed like liquid from one side of the boat to the other. Three more clambered after them. And Durant knew, without a shadow of doubt, that he was looking at his friends. There may have been other men in Istanbul with shoulders like Longstaff's, but none who moved with the same awkward grace.

Durant filled his lungs and roared into the night, half a greeting and half a cry of happiness. There was no reaction. His friends were too far away, their eyes trained on freedom.

"Godspeed," he thought, turning to Leila with a broad smile on his face.

Her eyes were wide with fear. "Have you lost your mind?"

"I apologise, my lady." He could hear the joy in his own voice. There was no one else left on the clifftop. "It's time we were getting back. Stay close behind me on the path."

They weren't halfway down when they met a group of men hurrying in the opposite direction. It wasn't Durant's cry which had summoned them. They ran past without stopping. The rain began to fall in earnest. Durant looked back in confusion. He wanted to follow them back onto the bluff. More men were streaming up the path. He had to get Leila back to the inn – what self-respecting widow would stand out in the rain like this. There were lights on the Golden Horn, growing in the darkness. Durant stood rooted to the spot, watching with a growing sense of dread. Nothing that size could move on water. Nothing but an Ottoman warship. No wonder people were returning to the clifftop. It wasn't every day that one of the sultan's fighting ships put to sea, glittering with power and purpose. Even above the wind, Durant could hear the drums, beating time for one hundred and fifty-six galley slaves below deck. Fifty-two oars powering the monstrosity towards the Sea of Marmara.

"Gaetan, we have to go."

He looked at her with a prayer in his eyes. She had grown up on Crete. She knew ships and the sea. He read the answer to his unspoken question in her eyes.

"They don't have a big enough start…"

They weren't caught yet. The gathering storm would help, surely. His heart rose with a fluttering sense of optimism. Night would fall…

Leila cleared her throat. "People are watching."

"We have to help them."

"Your friends?" She shook her head. "We can't."

They didn't speak on the way back to the inn. Somehow, despite her wet clothes, Leila still looked regal, summoning the landlord with an imperious flick of her fingers. "I'll take dinner in my rooms. My man will serve me."

Hollow inside, Durant waited impatiently at the kitchen door. He sought distraction in the noise of a busy inn, the creaks and groans, whispered arguments and muffled laughter. When the tray came at last, he accepted it with lowered eyes. The dutiful servant, climbing the stairs with bowed shoulders, opening the door to her room.

He stopped in surprise. Changed from her long widow's robe into *shalwar* trousers and fur-lined jacket, Leila stood packing their small bag of possessions.

"Wrap as much of the food as you can," she told him. "We'll take it with us."

"Where?"

"To find your friends, of course."

His mouth fell open. "We'll never catch them."

She shrugged. "Could you live with yourself if we don't at least try? Anyway, we can't stay here."

She smiled, seeing the confusion on his face. "You," she explained, "shouting like a berserker from the top of the cliffs. Paying silver for a broken telescope. Not everyone in this village is an imbecile."

*

Trapped amidships, under strict instructions not to move, Longstaff felt like a wild animal caught in a snare. The wind whipped spray across the bows. From the crest of each wave he could see the dark islands ahead or look back at the monster gaining on them with every stroke of its oars. With a following wind, the warship had also set its sails. A monster which grew in size with each new flash of lightning.

The pink slipped down the side of another wave. The warship disappeared, replaced by the skipper, rain streaming down his face.

"Well?" shouted Longstaff, louder than he'd expected. It took him a moment to realise why. The wind was dropping. The eye of the storm? The lee of the islands? He had no idea. The sea grew noticeably calmer, the sail began to billow along the length of the mast, the crew hauled on ropes, making it taut again as their captain looked back and forth, measuring distances. The pink heeled over as a fresh gust hit the sail, dying a moment later. For the first time in hours, the night was quiet enough that Longstaff heard water break and run along the bows. The black islands continued to grow.

"Well?" he repeated.

Seconds slipped past like hours. A jagged fork of lightning lit the skipper, jaw set, knuckles white on the boat's wheel. Longstaff counted eight seconds before a distant rumble of thunder shook the night. The storm was moving off, passing to the north, leaving them exposed.

So faintly at first that Longstaff thought it was the coursing of his blood, the steady beat of drums reached them across the water.

The skipper smashed the wheel with the palm of his hand. "We're not going to make it."

Longstaff couldn't believe it. The islands loomed huge ahead of them. They were so close.

"Bring up the box," ordered the skipper.

"Captain," began Longstaff as two crewmen pushed past him into the hold below. The word died on his lips. A string of lamps formed a smudge of light in the darkness. High above them, torchlight flaring in the sky, trailed a tail of sparks back and forth.

"They're signalling us," said the captain. "They want us to heave to."

"They'll kill every man aboard," said Longstaff

"We can still outrun them," said Hector.

"Not when we lose what little wind we have. We'll be trapped. The current's running fast and true tonight. No time to escape it and hide before they're on top of us."

"You're giving up?" said Aurélie.

The skipper spat over the side as his men dragged a heavy packing case from the hold. Longstaff saw his sword, strapped to the lid with a length of rope.

"Your possessions are inside," said the skipper. "Sealed against the elements with wax and leather, alongside two inflated bladders." He managed a smile. "It's a trick we've used before; throw the contraband overboard when the sultan's ships sail too close."

"They know we're here," snapped Longstaff. "Raimondi Maltrapillo looked straight at me. They'll tear this ship apart."

"You go with the box," said the captain, pointing ahead. "We can delay them long enough to give you a start. The current will take you between those two islands. It might take all night, but you'll reach open sea again eventually. We've been boarded before. A little cunning, a few gold coins in the right pocket. We'll come for you in the morning."

The noise of the drums reached them clearly now. Longstaff looked down at the cold, dark waters rushing past on either side. He looked at the slim box. The man was insane. Raimondi had seen them. He would never agree to return home empty handed.

Longstaff freed the old *katzbalger* sword from the ropes which held it fast. He'd had enough. Enough of hiding, enough of trying to still the beating of his own heart while men poked and probed around him. He felt the contours of his fear – with him since he'd arrived in Istanbul. Fear of falling into one of Raimondi's traps, fear of exposure, failure, disgrace.

Fear of losing Aurélie. He lifted the sword, finally able to face the demons which had circled him in darkness for so many months. "We keep sailing," he said. "If we can't outrun them, then we stand and fight."

Chapter 33

Wearing all the clothes he owned, Durant looked through the window. It was dark outside, a cold rain driving in off the sea. Leila pressed the bag into his hand. Even with the food and a full water-skin, there was more than enough room for all their worldly possessions.

They descended the stairs in silence. The ground floor was empty, the back door of the inn unlocked. Once outside, Durant fell into step behind Leila, his life in her hands, the sheer fact of being in motion enough to lighten the worst of his gloom. The two of them were wanted fugitives with no plausible reason for being abroad after dark.

In this weather, it was no surprise to find the streets deserted. Durant stayed close enough that he could see Leila's silhouette in the darkness, far enough that he wouldn't stumble into her if she came to a sudden halt. He concentrated on maintaining this distance, strangely indifferent as to where they were going, half aware of water lapping against stone piles nearby. The night swallowed their shadows as they moved across wet cobblestones. Fishing boats strained against mooring ropes, rain drumming a low tattoo on the wooden decks. Durant had no idea how Leila made her decision. The boats all looked the same to him. She was already stepping aboard when he heard a sound that didn't belong. A muffled cough? Boot leather on cobblestones? He stared hard at the darkness, crouching to retrieve a fishing spear from where it rested on a pile of nets, listening for the beat of a watchman's step, the cough of an old man unable to sleep through the night.

Light flared a few yards away. A man stood at his ease, features ghoulish in the dim light of a hooded lamp, curved sword levelled at Durant's head.

"Dead or alive," he said. "The grand vizier won't mind which."

He wore the uniform of a janissary soldier, which meant he knew how to use the sword. Durant rose slowly to his full height. "You're alone," he said in broken Turkish. "No reason we can't come to some arrangement."

"One that can compete with the praise of my masters and the envy of my peers? I know who you are. I'll receive a commendation for this."

One hand outstretched in a gesture of appeal, Durant took a step closer. He gripped the spear in his other, the shaft slick with rainwater. The soldier moved back, maintaining a safe distance with a smile on his face.

What would Longstaff do? Cut the man down and spit on his corpse. Durant set his feet like the Englishman, squaring his shoulders and raising the spear.

The soldier set his lamp down, then beckoned Durant forward with his free hand.

Durant blinked rainwater out of his eyes. "I'll come quietly if you let the woman go."

The soldier grinned as if he'd already won. "Surrender now and I promise you won't have to watch her suffer."

Lightning flashed in the sky. Hard and fast, Leila threw a belaying pin from the boat. The soldier raised an arm to bat it away. The pin struck his wrist. Durant heard bones crack. "Now," screamed Leila. The fishing spear arrowed forward. Durant hardly knew how. He felt the tip strike bone, a searing pain in his own arm as the two bodies crashed together. The soldier was built like rock. Durant used his legs, knees pumping, teeth sinking into the man's throat, the spear still gripped in his fists, he felt the tip shudder along the edge of a rib, burying itself in the soft organs beneath.

When had he last drawn breath? Durant felt his strength ebb, stars appearing against the lids of his tightly closed eyes.

A crack sounded close beside his ear. He fell forwards, landing full length across the motionless soldier. Leila stood over them, the belaying pin in one hand, its tip splashed with blood and hair. "Is he dead?"

Durant felt for a pulse. "Soon. Fetch me the anchor."

"What are you going to do?"

What I have to. Looping the anchor chain around the limp body, Durant rolled it into the water. He winced at the pain in his shoulder. He was covered in blood – how much of it was his? Leila pulled him into the boat.

"It's hopeless. I don't know how..."

"I do. My father was a fisherman. I knew how to sail a boat before I knew how to walk." She cast off, then sat beside him in the centre of the boat. "Take an oar and row."

She took the other. A few minutes later, Durant felt a powerful current take hold of their small boat, propelling it forward into the night. Leila had chosen well. The boat was slim and swift, the hull free of seaweed and barnacles. They shipped the oars soon afterwards, Leila crawling forward to raise the single sail.

"Is that wise?" said Durant. The moon was hidden behind cloud, but he worried the scrap of canvas would be visible from the coast.

She snorted. "None of this is wise."

The wind blew steadily enough. Leila set their course, roped the tiller in position, then unrolled a striped awning along the length of a wooden pole above their heads. Intended to offer shade from the sun, it gave precious little protection against the driving rain. Soaked to the bone, they huddled together for warmth. Durant shrugged out of his travelling cloak. He needed to check his wound.

A flash lit the darkness, a great spiral of flame which had hardly died before a noise like thunder rolled towards them across the black water. Then a second flash. Durant stared ahead, unwilling to understand.

Two evenly spaced fusillades – not a battle but an execution. He closed his eyes, seeing the faces of his friends in the darkness. Longstaff and Aurélie. Knowing he would never see them again.

*

Lit by a hundred torches, the warship's great bow broke water strewn with splintered planks and torn sails. Raimondi peered down, past two banks of massed oars, searching feverishly for any sign of the pink's crew, passengers or cargo. Further away, he could see the lights of half a dozen longboats, the men aboard combing the debris for signs of life.

Raimondi spat in disgust. When the crew had first primed the huge, deck-mounted cannon, he'd assumed they intended nothing more than a warning shot. With the distance rapidly narrowing between the two boats, he had carried on rehearsing his moment of triumph. Longstaff – trussed, bound and made to answer for his arrogance.

And longitude. Raimondi had been so close, anticipating every move his enemy made. While the rest of Istanbul made small talk in Joseph Nasi's garden, Raimondi had spent the day haunting the docks between Galata and the Imperial Dockyards, looking for anything out of the ordinary. He'd barely noticed the small pinnace at first. The crew of four had made no objection when a customs officer boarded to inspect their cargo. Raimondi would have walked on without a second glance except that one of the sailors wore a straight sword at his side, a *katzbalger*, favoured by German Landsknecht soldiers. Strange choice of weapon for a Levant seaman. Raimondi had taken a *caique* out into the Golden Horn, from where he could keep a careful watch on every move the pinnace made.

His patience had been rewarded. The grand vizier had given him sufficient authority to order a war galley to sea.

No one on board knew the true nature of the prize. Certain he could find a way to sequester the mechanic and whatever cargo the pinnace carried, Raimondi had pictured Venice – the serene republic – restored to the days of its greatest glory by the secret of longitude. Once more unrivalled mistress of the world's oceans.

The warship had overhauled the pinnace with frightening ease. They hadn't resisted for long, turning into wind and bobbing quietly on the waves, the figures onboard sitting quietly as if resigned to their fate. Raimondi had looked up then in idle curiosity, surprised to hear the captain order his cannoneers to fire. The race was done; there was no further need for a warning shot.

He'd screamed when the iron ball struck the pinnace dead amidships. The bodies smashed in an explosion of wood and canvas. Longstaff and his companions hadn't even seen it coming.

Raimondi begged the captain not to fire a second cannonade. Perhaps there was still some slender chance.

"They surrendered, you fool. You gave them no warning."

But the captain had been implacable. "My orders come from the grand vizier," he'd replied, then commanded his men to fire again.

The drums began their infernal music. The deck shivered beneath Raimondi's feet. The great oars dipped, backing water, holding the war galley in position while the last of the debris flowed on, disappearing into a narrow channel between two islands. The fragile pinnace, obliterated by two direct hits.

This was Mehmed Sokollu's work – tidying up loose ends, burying the secret of longitude at the bottom of the sea.

The captain hailed him. A member of the Ottoman elite, so pleased with himself, so proud to serve the Lord of Worlds. "The longboats have returned, ambassador. Empty-handed. Would you like the men to keep looking?"

There was nothing Raimondi could say that would wound the man's dignity. He looked down again before replying. By the light of the torches, he saw part of what might have been a ship's wheel. He shook his head in helpless rage; there was nothing here but death and destruction.

The captain smiled, lingering for a moment before he issued new orders.

*

Durant felt Leila stiffen in his arms. Her ears were sharper than his. A moment later, he heard it too. The low beat of drums. The wind had dropped, the rain reduced to a light drizzle. Leila was already moving, lowering their small sail and stowing it in the hold, furling the striped awning and hiding it beneath Durant's soaked travelling cloak.

"Stay low," she whispered. "Don't say a word."

Her eyes were sharper than his, too. Long seconds passed before Durant saw a faint light in the distance. Lamps, lining the sides of the great warship as it made its way back to port, propelled into wind by two banks of oars, rising and dipping in eerie synchronicity. Durant thought of the poor wretches chained below decks. Even at this distance, he imagined he could smell the baleful sense of triumph. He lowered his eyes, silent tears fell from his cheeks — the dutiful slave reduced to a grieving friend. The bastards had won. The cynics and their chilling determination to trample over everything that was good in this world. Durant looked at Leila. Raimondi and the grand vizier had made a mockery of love, they'd murdered his friends, returned the *Enuma Elish* to its tomb beneath the sands, and shattered the dream of longitude. And for what?

He did not stir until Leila raised their sail again, when the first creeping rays of light grew visible in the east.

"We still have money," he said.

"We'll have to put in somewhere for food and water. Somewhere quiet."

She was right; they were still in Ottoman waters, still wanted by the grand vizier. Leila might be able to sail the boat, but she could hardly pass for a fisherman. Durant had no idea what mix of lies he could string together to explain their present circumstances. She put her hand on his arm, waiting until he looked at her. "Any survivors will be clinging to shreds of wreckage. Following the current. They won't be moving fast. There's a chance we can overhaul what's left of the debris."

She was trying to raise his hopes. "And when we find no trace of them?"

"We'll cross that bridge when we come to it."

"Lost at sea – and the lady expects to find a bridge."

He saw her teeth flash white in the dawn. Durant put his arm around her, the tiller between their two bodies. They were passing into a channel between two islands. Gripped in the current, there was little to do except stare at the inky waters, a mirror for their gloomy thoughts. The world returned with the sun, the sea calm, the sky washed a pale blue by the storm. Durant did not want to face it. In the darkness, he'd been spared from thinking about where they could go. They made a cold breakfast of the previous night's dinner, eating and drinking sparingly, uncertain of when they would be able to replenish their supplies. The sun was a blessing. Within an hour, the day had grown warm enough that they could strip to shirts and *shalwar*, spreading the rest of their clothes across the bow to dry. The scent of rosemary, myrtle and thyme drifted to them from the islands. A mist began to form when they reached the open waters of the Sea of Marmara. A piece of broken wood drifted past. Durant stared blankly for several seconds before he understood what he was seeing. He lurched forward, nearly upsetting the small fishing boat.

"It must be them!"

They stood, scanning the horizon for what seemed an eternity.

Nothing. Leila found a wooden bucket in the forward hold, a net alongside it still damp from the previous day's work. She tore a strip from the awning, folding it loosely into the bucket. "Do you have your tinderbox?"

"You want to light a fire?"

"Quickly."

She lit strip after strip of the sun-dried awning, creating a thin tendril of grey smoke, almost invisible against the pale sky, refusing to give up until she ran out of fuel for her small fire. Durant stood, one hand on the delicate mast, scanning the horizon. They overtook more splintered planks, ropes trailing in the water behind scraps of canvas. The useless telescope still hung around his neck. He clapped it to his eye, then flung it overboard with a cry of frustration. Filling his lungs, he shouted the names of his friends into the empty sky.

Nothing.

Durant slumped to his haunches, exhaustion flooding every muscle. He looked at Leila, still scouring the horizon as if she could not bear to face him.

"Did you hear?"

He did not reply.

"There's something there."

He couldn't look.

"...ant."

"There!" He heard the excitement in Leila's voice – and something else, drifting on the light breeze.

"...rant."

Chapter 34

It wasn't possible; that much he knew. Someone stood on the water, arms waving frantically. The figure disappeared a moment later, then reappeared. Durant and Leila seized hold of the oars, rowing closer, necks craned to see over their shoulders.

Aurélie! It was *Aurélie*, climbing to her feet and falling again. Standing on some kind of box with two more heads bobbing in the water. Tears streamed down Durant's face.

"It's not possible," he roared when they were within hailing distance, steadying himself against the mast.

"Sit down and row," snapped Leila.

They had bound themselves to a floating box. All three were exhausted. One by one, Durant cut them loose, hauling them bodily into the small fishing boat while Leila tied the box alongside. No one spoke for several minutes. There was too much to do. Aurélie was shivering uncontrollably, Hector had fainted, even Longstaff looked more like a ghost than a man. Durant and Leila helped them out of the wet clothes, wrapping them in their own sun-warmed garments. They fed them by hand, small measures of water poured over cracked lips, bread torn into manageable pellets.

"We heard the cannon-fire," said Durant. "We heard the bastards celebrating on their way back to port!"

Longstaff forced himself into a sitting position, head hanging low between his broad shoulders. "The captain sent us overboard then turned into wind, giving us time to drift clear before the warship drew too close. He thought he could reason with Raimondi."

"We never thought they would fire without warning," added Hector in a hollow voice.

Durant saw the expression on his friend's face. "What happened?"

"They never had a chance," whispered Longstaff. He sounded close to tears.

"The three of you have been in the water all night?"

"We'd already drifted between the islands. We tried to paddle across to one of them but the current was too strong." He took another sip of water before wetting Aurélie's lips. "I thought we were going to die."

He looked up, as if realising for the first time that they were alive. "Until you appeared." Now a tear did roll down his cheek. "How in God's name did you manage it?"

Durant nodded at Leila, his voice breaking as he replied. "I had an angel at my side." He held his breath, unsure of how Longstaff would react, confronted by the woman who'd betrayed his plans and dreams. He needn't have worried. The Englishman's honest face creased into a smile. "Thank you," he said to her. "This is the second time you've saved our lives."

Crowded together on the small boat, the five of them dozed in the sun. Leila was the first to move, climbing to her feet and rigging a makeshift awning from their sail.

One by one, they woke, staring over the calm sea, listening to the box bump against the stern as they drifted with the current. Their strength was returning, fuelled by a sense of wonder at their extraordinary good fortune.

"I'm sorry," said Durant. "If it hadn't been for me, you'd be ambassador now."

Longstaff shook his head. "I was out of my depth from the day we arrived."

"They fired without warning," repeated Aurélie, as if she still couldn't believe it. She looked up. "Longstaff wanted to stay and fight. Said he'd had enough of hiding. You should have seen him, desperate to take on a war galley with nothing but his sword. You know the look he gets."

Durant smiled. He knew it exactly. "How did you persuade him over the side?"

"I told him a secret."

Longstaff stared up at the blue sky with an awed expression on his face. "I'm going to be a father."

"What!" exploded Durant. The boat rocked wildly from side to side. Longstaff dipped his head, colour rising in his cheeks.

"A baby?" said Durant.

"Obviously," said Leila.

Hector sat up. "I hate to spoil the moment, but there are five of us adrift in this small boat. We don't know where we want to go; even if we did, we don't know how to get there."

Catching Longstaff's eye, Durant burst out laughing. "Pregnant!"

"I know," said Longstaff.

Hector threw up his hands in exasperation.

"Our enemies think we're dead," said Aurélie.

"Marmara is an inland sea. We're not going to die of exposure," added Durant.

"I won't be happy until we're further from Istanbul," said Longstaff. "We have to make for the Aegean."

"And then where?" asked Hector. "I have work to do."

It was so easy to believe they were safe, together again beneath the blue sky, borne towards freedom – towards a future that seemed to take on the contours of a dream. Longstaff sat in the bow with his eyes half closed, Aurélie's hand on his thigh.

"The Aegean is full of islands," said Durant. "Hundreds of them inhabited by just a few farmers and fishermen."

"The simple life?" asked Aurélie.

"It doesn't have to be forever. Haven't we had enough of being dragged into affairs?"

Longstaff cleared his throat. "I have to go to Amsterdam."

They listened as he explained the agreement he'd struck with Joseph Nasi. "I owe him three years of my life. After everything he's done for us, what else can I do?"

"Where are the papers?" asked Durant, thinking that there must be some loophole, some way to free Longstaff from his promise. He looked at the box, following in their wake like a faithful puppy. His friends were still weak. He and Leila dragged it out of the water and up across the stern. The wood stank of pig grease, even after so many hours submerged. Durant hesitated before throwing open the lid. The wax seals must have given way during the night; a hand's-width of water lapped at two leather-bound parcels nestled on either side of an inflated sheep's bladder.

The five of them exchanged glances. The leather was stained a dark, unforgiving shade of grey. Durant couldn't look at the expressions on the faces of his friends. Which of his possessions had Longstaff smuggled from Istanbul? A few recipes, sketches of the human body – nothing he couldn't live without.

"Where's your sword?" he asked.

Longstaff shook his head. "At the bottom of the sea. Where it belongs."

Gingerly, Aurélie lifted the first parcel from the chest, broke the wax seals and unfolded the broad sheet of leather.

The neat stack of paper had become a congealed, oozing mass. Lumps came away in her hands. Again and again, she attempted to separate the individual pages before finally slumping in defeat. There was a cloth bag at the bottom of the parcel. She tossed it aside, ignoring the jingle of coins when it struck the wooden deck.

Aurélie looked at Hector before turning to the second parcel. The mechanic watched as she unfolded the sheets of soaked leather. A brief flash of optimism lit his tired face. Aurélie withdrew a second, smaller package. The celestial observations were stacked below, recorded on scrolls of parchment tightly wound on wooden rollers. Hector's face fell. Aurélie made way for him. Ink dripped from his fingertips. Clumps of parchment broke apart like rotting wood.

Durant looked away while Hector pawed at the ruins of a dream.

Aurélie managed a brave smile. "There's nothing left. All over again, there's nothing left."

Longstaff picked up the small package which had been enclosed – the only one to have survived. He found a letter addressed to the three of them, alongside the coded letters he'd been given for Walsingham and Nasi's factor in Amsterdam Haltingly, he began to read aloud.

My friends,

If you are reading this letter, then our plan has succeeded and the three of you are safe and free, for which I give thanks to God. I do not exaggerate when I say that our time together has gone some way towards restoring my faith in Him – sorely tested throughout the course of my life.

Hector, I pray that you act wisely and share the secret of longitude without fear or favour. Assisting your departure from Istanbul with the sultan's charts was not a decision I took lightly. The Ottomans have provided a place of refuge for me and my family; allowing you to leave represents a poor return on their generosity. I do so only in the sure knowledge that you are motivated by a desire to follow the path of human progress, rather than the narrow course of profit.

Aurélie, it is many years since I have met anyone – man or woman – whose intelligence and courage have so inspired me. Good luck with your translation – and publication – of the Enuma Elish. *I fear you have set yourself a mighty challenge. Where you see proof of collective error in this ancient tale – and a possible means of repairing those mistakes – I worry that others will find the means to spread yet more division. If anyone can prove me wrong, I have no doubt it is you.*

Longstaff, I pray you remember the part I have played in securing your safe departure from this city and that you serve me well in the Low Countries. Three years is all I ask. You have my word I will do what I can to promote a lasting trade agreement between England and the Ottoman Empire.

Godspeed and good fortune, my friends,

N

Aurélie placed a hand protectively across her belly. "I'll never know how the story ends."

"You've always known," said Durant gently. "The *Enuma Elish* ends like all stories. It ends in forgetting. First death, then destruction, then the willed forgetting of an entire people and their way of life."

He opened the leather bag which Aurélie had tossed aside. It was full of gold coins. Ten percent of the value of Longstaff's silk.

"There's more than enough here to make a fresh start," he said. "How long since any of us knew what it feels like to live as free men and women?"

"I gave my word," said Longstaff.

Durant snorted. "Nasi thinks you're dead – or he will do soon enough."

"And the trade agreement with England?"

"You think they won't find another way?"

"He got us out of Istanbul. We'd be dead if it weren't for him."

Hector's shoulders began to shake. He looked up at them, eyes glittering between his fingers. "I don't know whether to laugh or cry."

"You're free," said Durant. "The observations are gone, but you're alive – and among friends."

Leila was the first to move, rising to her feet and making ready to hoist the sail. Durant suppressed a sudden, giddy urge to smother her with kisses. He could understand his friends' disappointment, but he didn't share it. They were alive. Surely that was more important than either the *Enuma Elish* or longitude. Aurélie could recreate the outline of her story from memory. Hector could publish what he knew and let others continue his work in the decades ahead. Or not. How much did it matter either way? One more ripple, more or less, across the surface of history – another weapon in the callous hands of kings and their advisors.

Durant could see that Longstaff believed he was honour-bound to travel to the Netherlands, but the five of them had to reach a safe harbour first. Then, surely, the Englishman would want to remain for the birth of his first child. And Durant would put that time to good use. Longstaff loved to talk in lists – shepherd, shearer, smith, carpenter, dyer, weaver, ploughman. These were the people he thought he could save with a trade agreement between England and the Ottoman Empire. It was rubbish. Durant should have told him so years ago. It wasn't the closure of European markets which had reduced them to near starvation, but the enclosure of common lands by their own ruling class. There was nothing Longstaff could do – either in Istanbul or Amsterdam – that would change the determination of England's nobility to sell the nation's wealth for profit.

Durant looked at his friends with love. Weren't they worth a thousand stories, a hundred thousand observations? Ancient texts and modern innovations could be put to evil ends as easily as good. If hope lay anywhere, it was in Longstaff and Aurélie themselves – in Hector and Nasi. Each of them a truer model of the principles of freedom and humanity than any number of stars in the night sky.

Men like Raimondi and the grand vizier were nothing by comparison. They would go on destroying and corrupting the fruits of human ingenuity. Scheme as they might, it would never be sufficient to release them from their fear.

Durant began to laugh. Leila rolled her eyes. The others looked at him as if he were mad. It was still too raw, but they would understand in time. He would make it his mission. Adrift in the Sea of Marmara, he suddenly felt as if were the luckiest man alive. The people with him in this boat were his family. They needed him – as well as rest and a safe harbour. A place where they could prepare for the arrival of a perfect new life in this imperfect world.

If you have enjoyed this book, the author would love it if you could leave a review on Amazon, or on the channel through which
you purchased this copy.

Also by Tom Pugh

"A gripping, atmospheric debut. I couldn't put it down."

Eve Harris, Booker longlisted author of
'The Marrying of Chani Kaufman'

*"Pugh's first novel is a magnificent achievement. Let us hope he
returns to enthral us with another very soon."*

David Dickinson,
author of the Powerscourt series

The Otiosi? As far as Mathew Longstaff knows, they're just
a group of harmless scholars with an eccentric interest in the
works of antiquity. When they ask him to travel east, to recover
a lost text from Ivan the Terrible's private library, he can't think
of anything but the reward – home. A return to England and
an end to the long years of exile and warfare.

But the Otiosi are on the trail of a greater prize than
Longstaff realises – the legendary 'Devil's Library'. And they
are not alone. Gregorio Spina, the Pope's spymaster and Chief

Censor, is obsessed with finding the Library. It's not the accumulated wisdom of centuries he's after – a swamp of lies and heresy in his opinion – but among the filth, like a diamond at the centre of the Devil's black heart, Spina believes that God has placed a treasure, a weapon to defeat the Antichrist and pitch his hordes back into hell.

Only Longstaff, together with the unpredictable physician, Gaetan Durant, can stop Spina using the Library to plunge Europe into a second Dark Ages. The two adventurers fight their way south, from the snowfields of Muscovy to the sun-baked plains of Italy, where an ageing scholar and his beautiful, young protégé hold the final piece of the puzzle. But is it already too late? Can the four of them take on the might of the Roman Church and hope to win?

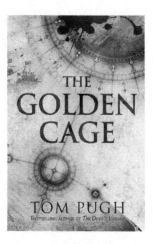

"*Pugh excels at weaving together different historical threads into a single narrative...The book is sure to appeal to fans of the works of Dan Brown and other conspiracy-curious storytellers.*"

Kirkus Reviews

1565. Their last mission on behalf of the Lord Chancellor nearly got them killed. Now back in England, former soldier Matthew Longstaff and his Italian wife, Aurélie, are living quietly in the countryside when news arrives from France; their closest friend has disappeared.

In London, fledgling spy-master Francis Walsingham suspects a traitor on Queen Elizabeth's Privy Council. In France, the physician Gaetan Durant is held at a secret location and forced to produce forgeries which will trigger a war. In Rome, the pope prepares a Bull of Excommunication against Elizabeth. Everything is connected. Trapped in this game of plot and counter-plot, Longstaff must journey to Paris in pursuit of his missing friend – and evidence of the enterprise taking shape against protestant England. Meanwhile in London, Aurélie's attempts to track down the traitor lead to a lethal battle of wits against London's most notorious astrologer.

Even if both succeed, it may already be too late. Wild, apocalyptic rumours race ahead of the separated lovers: of a lost Gospel in Christ's own hand; of heretic queens and caged prophets. Only one thing seems certain – war is coming, an unholy inferno which threatens to consume all Europe…